DRACHENFELS

THREE TIMES BEFORE had the killing frenzy fallen upon her. This time, however, there would be no regrets. This was the righteous killing for which she had been made, the killing that would pay back all those whose lives she had sapped. Her muscles corded, her blood took fire, and the red haze came over her vision. She saw through blood-filled eyes.

Detlef hung from Drachenfels's fist, screaming like a man on the rack. Oswald – smiling, treacherous, thrice-damned Oswald – had his knife in Karl-Franz's throat. These things she would not tolerate.

Her teeth pained her as they grew, and her fingers bled as the nails sprouted like talons. Her mouth gaped as the sharp ivory spears split her gums. Her face became a flesh-mask, the thick skin pulled tight, a mirthless grin exposing her knife-like fangs. The primitive part of her brain – the vampire part of her – took over, and she leaped at her enemy, the killing fury building in her like a passion. There was love in it, and hate, and despair, and joy. And there would be death at the end.

WARHAMMER®

DRACHENFELS

Jack Yeovil

BLACK LIBRARY

A BLACK LIBRARY PUBLICATION

First published in 1989.
This edition published in 2018 by
Black Library,
Games Workshop Ltd.,
Willow Road,
Nottingham, NG7 2WS, UK.

10 9 8 7 6 5 4 3 2 1

Produced by Games Workshop in Nottingham.
Cover illustration by Adrian Smith.

See Black Library on the internet at

blacklibrary.com

Find out more about Games Workshop
and the worlds of Warhammer at

games-workshop.com

Printed and bound by CPI Group (UK) Ltd, Croydon, CR0 4YY

PROLOGUE
TWENTY-FIVE YEARS AGO

I

THE FIRST GENEVIEVE Dieudonné knew of the treachery of Ueli
the dwarf was the prod of a blade-end in her right side, just
above the hip. Cloth and skin dimpled, and she felt a wasp-
like sting. There was something about the knife. It slipped
under the flaps of her padded leather jerkin and into her flesh.

Silver. The knife was edged with silver.

Her body took fire at the touch of the charmed metal. She
felt the weapon withdrawn and half-turned, ready for the
killing thrust, for the heart-strike. She heard herself hissing
and knew that her face – the face she had not seen for six centuries – was twisted, eyes reddening, sharp corner-teeth
bared. The wet hole in her side closed, tingling. Blood trickled down the inside of her britches.

Somewhere, on one of the nearby crags, an unclean bird
was squawking as it devoured the weakest of its young. Rudi
Wegener was on his knees, trying to wrestle Sieur Jehan
down, a hand pressed to the spewing hole in the scholar's
throat.

This pass they had come to, this stony and unfruitful spot
high in the Grey Mountains, was a filthy place. It was late

afternoon and she was still slowed by the sun; otherwise, Ueli would never have dared strike at her.

She brought her ungauntleted hand up, palm out, and placed it beneath her breast, shielding her heart. The knife leaped forward and she saw Ueli's face contorted in a feral snarl. His thumb-size teeth were bloodied from Sieur Jehan's neck and she could see torn fragments of skin caught between them.

She pushed outwards and caught the knifepoint with the centre of her hand. The pain was sharper this time, as the bones were displaced. She saw the point pricking outwards from the back of her hand. Flesh parted and the red metal emerged from between her middle knuckles.

Even through her slow-flowing blood, the silver caught the last of the sunlight. Ueli swore and spat red foam. He put his shoulders into the attack and tried to push her arm back, to staple her hand to her chest. If the silver so much as scraped her heart, there would be no more centuries for poor Genevieve.

She could ignore the pain of the sundering of her flesh – by tomorrow, there wouldn't even be the slightest scar – but the silver burned inside her. She shoved the dwarf back, the blade sliding through her hand by agonizing inches. She felt the hilt against her palm and made a fist, gripping the dwarf's weapon with still-strong fingers.

With his free hand he punched her in the kidneys, twice. She was ready for that; the blows didn't bother her. She kicked him square in the chest and he backed away from her, leaving his knife in her blood-slick grasp. He reached for the curved dagger in his boot and she backhanded him. The blade that stuck out like a spiked extra finger from her fist carved a deep rut across his forehead. Her hand hurt as the knife jarred against Ueli's skull.

The dwarf fell back, blood in his eyes, and three darts appeared in a diagonal line across his chest, sunk to the feathers in his ribs. Anton Veidt had used his trifurcate crossbow well. Genevieve pulled the knife out of her hand and threw it away. She made and unmade her fist as the stinging wound closed. Ueli still staggered as Veidt's venom shocked his body, the little smears of death coursing through his veins, reaching

for his brain. The bounty hunter mixed his poisons with unri-
valled skill. Stiffening, the dwarf fell.

Erzbet, the dancer-assassin, looped her wire noose around
Ueli's neck. She pulled it tight, cinching until she was satisfied of his death. Genevieve held out her bloodied hand.
Oswald von Konigswald was there with a kerchief, which she
took from him. She licked the slit clean, savouring the tang of
her own blood. Then, she wrapped the kerchief tightly about
her hand, pressing shut the already-healing wound.

'Dwarf bastard,' said Veidt, hawking phlegm at Ueli's dead
face. 'You never know when one's going to turn.'

'Less of the dwarfish bastardy, bounty hunter,' said Menesh,
who had joined them with Ueli. Genevieve had always supposed they were related. 'Look.'

The traitor was growing in death. At least, his skeleton and
insides were expanding. His dwarf shell and clothes split, and
showed raw pink and purple through great tears. Human-
sized bones twisted on the ground, their wet contents
pouring through the remaining, ragged strips of Ueli's skin.

Oswald stepped back, leery of getting his fine Tilean leather
boots in the mess. Ueli's still-glaring eyes popped and mag-
gots writhed in their sockets, spilling over stretched-tight
cheeks and into his beard. His tongue slithered out of his
mouth like a strangling snake, twisted down impossibly long
towards his chest and then died. Erzbet voiced her disgust
loudly as she pulled her noose free.

'He was no true dwarf,' said Menesh.

'That's certain,' said Rudi Wegener, who had given up
stanching Sieur Jehan's wounds, leaving the doctoring to his
tame warlock, 'but what was he?'

Menesh shrugged, his harnessed weapons rattling, and
touched the still-spreading body with his boot-toe. 'A daemon, perhaps. Some creature of Drachenfels.'

The dwarf kicked Ueli's swollen helmet off the wide ledge.
It fell, striking the ground long after they had forgotten it.

The stink of the grave wafted away from the remains of the
dwarf-seeming thing who had ridden with them for three
months. Ueli had shared quarters with them and broken
bread with them. He had never spared himself in their fights
and Genevieve knew that without his deftly-thrown knives

she would have been orc-meat several times over. Had Ueli always been a traitor to them? Always in the service of Drachenfels? Or did his treachery begin a few moments ago, when the shadow of the Fortress fell upon him? How little she really knew about any of her companions in this adventure.

An adventure! That is what it had seemed when Oswald von Konigswald, eyes ablaze, had recruited her in the Crescent Moon. She had been working in the tavern at Altdorf, trading one drink for another, for a hundred years or so. Longevity brings a heavy burden of tedium. Genevieve, suspended eternally between life and death since the Dark Kiss, had been willing to do almost anything to relieve her boredom. Just as Anton Veidt was willing to do almost anything for gold crowns, or Sieur Jehan for a chance to increase his learning, Rudi Wegener to expand his glory, or weeks-dead Heinroth to achieve his cherished revenge. And Oswald? What was Oswald – Crown Prince Oswald, Genevieve reminded herself – willing to do almost anything for?

An adventure! A quest! The stuff of ballads and chap-books, of legends and tavern tales. Now, with so many dead behind them and two more dying in her eyesight, Genevieve was less certain. Now, their business here seemed just a nasty, messy job of murder. A nasty, messy life had to be ended, but murder it still was.

'Sieur Jehan?' Oswald asked.

Rudi, the ruddy cheeriness gone from his bluff bandit's face, shook his head. The scholar was still bleeding, but his eyes showed only white. He had stopped kicking. Stellan the Warlock looked up from the corpse.

'He had no chance. The dwarf bit clean through his throat to the bone. He'd have bled to death if he hadn't been strangling for lack of air. Or the other way round. Either would have done for him.'

'Enough,' said Oswald, 'we must go on. It's nearly nightfall. Things will be more difficult after dark.'

Difficult for the others; better for her. The sun dipped below the horizon and Genevieve felt her night-senses come back. She could ignore the echoes of pain in her hand and side. Above them all, the fortress of Drachenfels stood against the crimson sky, its seven turrets thrust skywards like the taloned fingers of a deformed hand. The clifftop gates were, as ever, open, a maw in the side of the stone. Genevieve saw the eyes in the darkness beyond the gates, half-imagined unwelcoming shapes flitting past innumerable windows themselves shaped like eyes.

This was where their adventure would end. In a castle as grey and jagged as the mountains around it. A fortress older than the Empire and darker than death. The lair of the Great Enchanter.

Drachenfels.

II

CONSTANT DRACHENFELS, the Great Enchanter, had been old, had been ancient, long before the first birth of Genevieve Sandrine du Pointe du Lac Dieudonné. And that, she never allowed herself to forget, had been six hundred and thirty-eight years ago.

In true life, Genevieve's home had been the city of Parravon, in the east of Bretonnia, where her father was minister to the First Family and her sisters were counted among the greatest beauties of a court renowned throughout the Known World for its great beauties. Drachenfels had been more often abroad among men in those days and wont to show his metal-masked face in the courts and palaces of Bretonnia and the Empire.

The stories were fresher then. Tales were told in a whisper of his vast debauches, of his inconceivable crimes, of his devastating rages, of his titanic sorceries, of his terrible revenges and of his single defeat. Drachenfels had been one of the powers of the world. She supposed, though half-forgotten, he still was. He had only been bested once, at the hands of Sigmar Heldenhammer. Strange to think that Sigmar had

13

been deemed a man then. A hero, but still a man. Now, the priests called him the patron deity of the Empire. Sigmar was gone, no one knew where, but the monster he had once humbled was still here. The evil of Drachenfels was still very much with the world.

As a girl of twelve, four years before the Dark Kiss, Genevieve had seen Drachenfels in person. He rode through Parravon with his army of the dead, bedecked in gorgeous silks, wearing his mask of gold. The heads of the First Family's militia captains bobbed open-mouthed on pikes. An assassin dashed from the crowds and was torn to pieces by Drachenfels's rotting lieutenants. Daemons danced in the air, bearing away pieces of the martyred daggerman. Genevieve hid behind her sisters' skirts, but got a good look all the same.

Her father's friends had discussed Drachenfels in her presence. His origins were unknown, his weaknesses unknown, his powers unlimited, his evil depthless. Even his face had not been seen by living man. She had tried to conceive of a hideousness under the mask, a hideousness so dreadful that it would make the skull-and-meat faces of Drachenfels's armies seem attractive. Or, as her sister Cirielle suggested, a handsomeness so awesome that all who gazed upon it were struck dead in an instant. Cirielle was always the silly one. She had died of the plague some fifty years – a heart's beat, really – later.

Drachenfels had his tribute from Parravon, but slew the First Family nevertheless. As an example. Genevieve's father also perished, served with other public officials as a meal for one of the Enchanter's attendant daemons. Six hundred years later, Genevieve could summon little thirst for vengeance. Her father would have lived another twenty, thirty years – thirty-five at the most – and would still be lost to her memory. It's hard to think the premature death of a mayfly any great tragedy. She sometimes found the faces of her parents, her sisters, her friends at court, popping into her mind. But mostly those were lost times, a life that had happened to someone else.

A few years later, years that were now minutes to her memory, Chandagnac came to her uncle's house. Chandagnac with his dark eyes and plaited beard, his needle-like teeth and tales of the world's youth. She received the Dark Kiss, and was born a second time, born into this half-life.

Chandagnac was dead, too. He had always been too flamboyant for their kind and made too many important enemies. Finally, the priests of Ulric hunted him down and pinned him to the ground with a length of hawthorn while they sawed off his head with a silver scimitar. That was three hundred years ago. She was the last of his get that she knew of. There were many others older than she, but they lived far to the east, on the borders of Kislev, and kept to themselves. Occasionally, mindless dead things would come to the Crescent Moon, drawn by her presence, and she would turn them out, or put an end to them, depending on how she felt. Sometimes, they could be a nuisance.

Centuries had passed and everything had changed many times. Empires, dynasties, wars, alliances, cities, a few great men, numberless little ones, monsters, arts and sciences, forests; all had come and gone like the seasons of the year.

Genevieve was still walking the earth. And so was Drachenfels.

She wondered if he felt the same suppressed kinship for her that she felt for him. There were songs that they alone of all the world would recognize, once-famous names that they alone knew, extinct animals the taste of whose meat they alone could recall. Probably, he did not feel for her. Probably, he was only dimly aware of her. She was what she was, at best the cousin of humanity, but Drachenfels was beyond even that. He had ceased to be any kind of a man long before he rode into Parravon. The face he kept beneath his bland collection of metalwork masks would not remotely resemble anything else that drew breath.

Tonight, one way or another, she would look upon that face. Perhaps long-dead-and-dust Cirielle was right after all. Perhaps she would not survive the sight. And perhaps, after six and a half centuries, she would not mind dying all that much.

She had followed Drachenfels's career down through the ages, kept a mental note of the kingdoms sacked and bled dry, the plagues unleashed, the tributes exacted, the daemons set free. He had been quiet for a few centuries now, quiet in his impregnable fortress in the Grey Mountains. Some believed Drachenfels dead, but there were too many evidences of his continued handiwork throughout the Old World. The wizards who frequented the Crescent Moon would talk about him sometimes, about the disturbances he was making in that sphere beyond time and space where the greatest of enchanters venture in search of the vast principal beings of the universe. They knew enough not to sign up with Oswald's expedition. Some said he was too old to be the monster he once was, but Genevieve knew that immortals grow rather than diminish in strength as they put years behind them. Some ventured that the Great Enchanter was voyaging within himself, trying to plumb the depths of his own darkness, to summon the worst of his personal daemons. One song, sung only by a strange-visaged Bretonnian minstrel, suggested Drachenfels was meditating his many sins, finding the strength to battle again with Sigmar and that this time he would vanquish the wielder of the warhammer forever, bringing about the end of all things.

She had heard all manner of rumours, but none had touched her more than any other tavern gossip until Prince Oswald von Konigswald, son of the elector of Ostland, walked into the Crescent Moon. He told her that Constant Drachenfels was preparing to return to the world and take over the Empire, and that the Great Enchanter would have to be stopped before he could bring down fiery doom upon an entire continent.

That had been three months ago. Oswald was a year or two older than she had been when Chandagnac had kissed her. She supposed him a handsome youth and could see around him the aura of the great and noble man he would grow into. He would be elector after his father, of course. The elector of Ostland could sometimes sway the others completely and hold the course of the Empire in his hands. Never had a candidate opposed by Ostland succeeded. Never. Oswald's father lived in a comparatively modest palace, but upon occasion Luitpold himself came to his court as if the elector were Emperor and he the supplicant. If Luitpold's son, Karl-Franz, were to succeed him on the throne, he would need the support of Oswald's father. Indeed, since the elector had married late and was now nearing the end of his middle years, the Emperor would soon need the support of Prince Oswald.

Genevieve had heard that the prince was a serious youth, a young man capable of outstripping all his tutors in everything from gastronomy to philosophy, and who was as skilled with the Estalian guitar as with the longbow of Albion. The tavern jesters told jokes about the grave-faced boy who had, it was rumoured, once shamed Luitpold into withdrawing a proposed edict against harlotry by asking if the Emperor intended to set an example by burning at the stake a certain substantial Tilean fortune teller much in evidence at court functions since the demise of the lady empress. And Genevieve had read, with interest, a slender but acclaimed volume of verse in the classical style, published anonymously but later revealed, through a careless boast on the part of the elector's tutor-in-residence Sieur Jehan, to be the work of Oswald von Konigswald. Nevertheless, she had been unprepared for his ice-clear eyes, the strength of his handshake and the directness of his speech.

In the back room of her tavern, Oswald had offered her his wrist. She had declined. Aristocratic blood was too rich for her. She depended upon the friendless, the unmourned. In Altdorf, there were many without whom the Empire, indeed the world, would be much improved. And they had been her meat and drink since she had decided to settle down.

Sieur Jehan was with the prince, a bagful of scrolls and bound books with him. And Anton Veidt, the bounty hunter who cared for his weapons as others care for their women. Oswald knew about her father. Oswald knew things about her that she had herself forgotten. He offered her a chance for revenge and, when that hadn't been a temptation, appealed to her need for variety, for change. The young Sigmar must have been like this, she thought, as she sensed the excitement Oswald was suppressing. All heroes must have been like this. Suddenly, rashly, she longed for a taste of him, a flavour of the pepper in his blood. She didn't mention her rush of lust, but somehow she knew that he had seen the desire in her, and answered her longing with a need of his own, a need that would have to be postponed until after the accomplishment of his current mission. She looked into his eyes, into the eyes

in which her face was not reflected and, for the first time in
centuries, felt alive again.

Sieur Jehan laid out the proofs of Drachenfels's recent
doings. He read aloud the testament, obtained through a
medium, of a wizard who had lately been found flayed and
boneless in his chambers. The dead sorcerer alleged that all
manner of magical and daemoniacal forces were converging
on the fortress of Drachenfels, and that the Great Enchanter
was reaching new levels of power. Then the scholar talked of
a plague of dreams and visions that had been reported by the
priests of all the gods. A masked man was seen striding over
a blasted land, between the fires that had been cities and the
deserts that had been forests. The dead were piled high as
mountains and the rivers were nine-parts blood to one-part
water. The forces of evil were gathering and Drachenfels was
at their heart. Oswald intended to face the monster in his lair
and vanquish him forever. Again, he offered her the chance to
join the party and this time she relented. Only then did he
reveal that his father, and presumably Emperor Luitpold himself, had refused to believe Sieur Jehan's evidence and that he
was pursuing this venture unsupported by any Imperial
forces.

They set out from Altdorf for the Grey Mountains the next
day.

Later, others joined. Rudi Wegener, the bandit king of the
Reikwald Forest, threw in his lot with them and helped fight
off the possessed remnants of his own comrades during one
long, dark night in the thick of the woods. Along with Rudi
came Stellan the Warlock, who had lived with the bandits
and was determined to pit his magics against those of the
Great Enchanter, and Erzbet, the dancer-assassin from the
World's Edge who recited every night like a prayer the names
of those she had killed. Ueli and Menesh had been recruited
at Axe Bite Pass, where an entire community of peaceful peasants had turned out to be daemons in disguise, and where
young Conradin, Oswald's squire, was spitted and eaten by
an altered ogre. The dwarfs had been travelling south, but
were willing to pledge their swords for gold and glory.
Heinroth, whose soul was eaten away by the murder of his
children, joined them soon after. A raiding party of orcs from

the fortress had made sport with his two little sons and killed them afterwards. He had vowed to scar himself with his serrated blade every day he let Drachenfels live, and grimly sliced at himself every morning. One day, they woke up to find Heinroth turned inside out, with words carved into his bones.

GO BACK NOW.

None of them had heard a thing, and the sharp-witted Veidt had been standing guard.

Through it all, Oswald had been at their head, undaunted by each new horror, keeping his followers together – which in the case of Veidt and the dwarfs or the licentious Erzbet and the fanatically ascetic Heinroth hadn't been easy – and forever confident of the eventual outcome. Sieur Jehan told her that he had been like this since childhood. The scholar evidently loved the boy as a son and chose to follow Oswald when the prince's real father had refused to listen. These were the last great days, Genevieve had thought, and their names would live in ballads forever.

Now, Conradin was dead. Sieur Jehan was dead. Heinroth was dead. Ueli was dead. And before the night was over, others – maybe all of the party – would be joining them. She hadn't thought about dying for a long time. Perhaps tonight Drachenfels would finish Chandagnac's Dark Kiss, and push her at last over the border between life and death.

Oswald walked straight up to the open gates of the fortress, looked casually about and signalled to them. He stepped into the dark. Genevieve followed him. And the others came after her.

III

As THEY VENTURED further, Stellan the Warlock began chanting in a language Genevieve didn't recognize. He glowed slightly and she fancied she saw his attendant spirits dancing around him. Sometimes, she could see things the others couldn't. Stellan's voice grew louder as they advanced down the stone corridor and his gestures more extravagant. Firefly entities spiralled around him, clustering to his amulets, stirring his long, womanish hair. Evidently, he was invoking great powers. He had done so before other battles and claimed credit for their victories.

At the end of the passage was an aged wooden door, with inset copper designs. It was too easy to see a face in the abstract curlicues. Genevieve knew the effect was deliberate. Nothing in this place happened unless it was by design. Drachenfels's design. The face she saw was that of the impassive mask the Great Enchanter had worn in Parravon. Maybe there were other faces for the others: a cruel parent, an implacable foe, an unbanished daemon.

Erzbet was badly affected. Genevieve could hear the dancer-assassin's blood quickening. Even Veidt and Rudi were tense. Only Oswald kept his chilly calm, his princely composure.

Oswald went ahead, a torch held high in one hand, sword out like a blind man's cane. Stellan followed close behind, feeling the way with his magics. Genevieve heard rhythms and repetitions in his chanting now, and noticed Rudi praying in unison with the warlock, his thick lips mouthing silently Stellan's words. The warlock's spirits were around him like a protective garment. They all must be praying to their gods now. All who had gods.

In this heart of Drachenfels, Genevieve's night-senses told her things she wished not to know. It was as if a million insects crawled upon her skin, biting with silvered mandibles, shrieking in a cacophony. There was great danger nearby, great evil. But you didn't have to have the heightened perception of vampirekind to know that. Even poor, half-witted Erzbet could tell they were walking into a great and dreadful darkness. Their guttering torches were pitiful against the blackness of the interior of the Fortress.

'The door,' said Stellan in Reikspiel. 'It's guarded by spells.'

Oswald paused and extended his sword. He touched the metal and sparks flew. The inlay grew white hot and foul smoke curled out as the wood burned. The imagined face looked angered now and glared hatred at them.

'Can you open it, warlock?' asked the prince.

Stellan smiled his confident one-sided smile. 'Of course, highness. A mere conjurer could penetrate these petty charms. I'm surprised that an enchanter of Drachenfels's standing would stoop to such things.'

The warlock reached into a pouch and, with a flourish, threw a handful of sweet-smelling dust at the door. The face went dark again and Stellan reached for the doorknob. He twisted it and pushed the door open, standing aside to let the Prince through before him. With a mocking grin, he bowed.

'See,' he said, 'it was simple.'

Then, Stellan the Warlock simply exploded.

They were drenched in gore. The door hung with ribbons of cloth and meat. The stone walls dripped red for ten feet behind them. Stellan's naked skeleton stood for a moment, still grinning, then collapsed.

Rudi, Menesh and Veidt swore loudly, and frantically scraped at themselves, dislodging the chunks of flesh and scraps of clothing that had plastered them. Oswald calmly wiped off his face. Genevieve felt her red thirst rising, but fought it back. This was no banquet for her. She would rather drink pig's swill than feed like this. Stellan's spirits were gone, snuffed out with their summoner.

'The walls,' said Veidt. 'They're changing.'

Genevieve looked up at the ceiling. The stones were molten, reshaping themselves. There were faces in the walls and jutting rock claws reaching out for them. Oswald swung his sword with practiced grace and a dead hand fell to the floor, shattering as it landed. Rudi drew the two-handed sword slung on his back and began to hack away at the emerging creatures.

'Careful, fool outlaw,' shouted Veidt, barely avoiding Rudi's blade. 'That's not a corridor weapon.'

A stone head rolled at Genevieve's feet, its glass eyes milked over, swollen tongue poked out. One of the creatures, a squat gargoyle, had detached itself completely from the ceiling and dropped down on her. It grabbed for her hair. She made a fist and struck it in the chest. It was like punching a mountain; any human hand would have been pulverized. Pain ran up through her arm to her shoulder and she knew her wound was reopening.

The gargoyle was shocked to a halt, a hairline crack across its torso, running from horny shoulder to waist. It lunged for her, stone hands creaking as it made razor-sharp talons. It was too near for her to draw sword against it, so she was pushed back. The wall behind her writhed with life, sprouting claws of its own.

She braced herself against the shifting stones, turning to face the wall, and kicked out with a booted foot, aiming high, aiming for the crack. The gargoyle staggered back, split. The top half of its body slid from the bottom and crashed to the floor. It was a pile of dead stones.

They fought their way through the creatures, smashing them when they could, and found themselves forced through the open door into an abandoned chamber where a great table was set for dinner. The food had long since crumbled to dust.

So had the diners, whose dry skeletons were slumped in their chairs in the remains of their finery. Here, there was room to fight properly and Rudi's sword counted. Gargoyles fell.

The bandit chief held the doorway, swinging his blade about him and the creatures flew to fragments. Finally, with a grunt, he kicked the door shut on the last of the enemy. Veidt and Oswald piled in with heavy chairs that could be stacked against the wood. Efficiently, they barricaded themselves into the dining hall of the dead.

Genevieve gripped her aching hand and tried to set the bones in their proper places. She managed to push her fingers back in joint. Her wound was bleeding slightly as she smoothed it over. She hoped no silver traces were caught inside. That could cause gangrene and she would have to have the hand, or the limb, amputated. It might be a hundred years before she grew a new one. It had taken Chandagnac an entire generation to regain an ear lopped off by an overzealous priest of the Old Faith.

She looked down at herself. Her britches, boots and jerkin were filthy and stinking, as if she had crawled through the mud of a plague-pit. The others were in no better condition, although Oswald bore his dirt and rags as if they were perfumed silks. And Veidt had never looked any different; the only clean things about him were his weapons.

'What happened here?' Rudi asked.

'A poison feast,' said Oswald. 'It's one of the worst Drachenfels stories. He appeared alone, on his knees, at the court of the Emperor nearly six centuries ago, and offered to make penance for his sins. He paid generous reparations to all his living victims and abased himself at the graves of many others. He renounced evil and swore allegiance to the gods he had previously cursed. He vowed his loyalty to the Empire. Everyone was convinced he had changed. In ten thousand years, anyone might repent, might wish to cleanse his heart. Any *man*, that is. He invited the Emperor Carolus and all his court to this place to celebrate his new life, and decreed that Drachenfels would forever be open as a shelter for the destitute. Some of Carolus's advisers spoke against the feast, but the Emperor was a kindly man, and too young to remember Drachenfels's worst deeds. They came here, all of them, the

Emperor, and the Empress Irina, their children, and all the nobles of the court. My own ancestor, Schlichter von Konigswald, sat here among them...'

They looked at the abandoned corpses, and saw the jewels lying under cobwebs. One smiling dowager corpse had rubies in her eye-sockets, and a silver-set net of pearls, sapphires and diamonds on her bare ribs. Genevieve picked a tarnished gold circlet from a broken skull.

'The old crown,' Rudi said, eyes alight with avarice. 'It's priceless.'

'We'll return it, my outlaw friend,' Oswald said. 'There'll be plunder for you, but this crown we will return.'

Oswald had promised Rudi Wegener a pardon when they returned to Altdorf in triumph, but knew, as Genevieve knew, the bandit would not accept it. Once this good deed, this honourable revenge, was done, he would be returning to the forests, to the outlaw life.

Genevieve looked at the corpses and saw flashes of a long-ago day. The chamber was clean and new and brightly-lit. She heard laughter and music. She saw dishes being served. Handsome gentlemen were charming, beautiful ladies fluttered fans. And at the head of the table, a regal man with a crown was attended by a plainly-dressed man in a simple tin mask. She blinked and the dark present was back.

'He poisoned them, then?' Menesh asked Oswald.

'Yes. Only, they didn't die. They were paralyzed, turned to feeling statues. Years later, one of Drachenfels's minions made a confession before he went to the gallows. He told the whole story of the obscenities that took place before the helpless eyes of Carolus and his court. They had brought their children, you see, those foolish and trusting nobles. Heinroth would have understood the horror. After the entertainments were over, Drachenfels left his guests frozen. With a feast laid out before them, they starved to death.'

Oswald struck the table with his sword-hilt. It shook. Brittle crockery broke, a candelabrum fell over, a rat burst from its nest in a ribcage, a skeleton still bedecked in the robes of the high priestess of Verena fell apart. Tears stood out on the prince's face. Genevieve had never seen him betray such emotion.

'Fools!'

Genevieve laid a hand on his shoulder and he calmed instantly.

'After this night, Drachenfels will prey on no more fools.'

He strode across the chamber and pulled open a set of double doors.

'Come on, the minion also drew maps. He bought himself a quick death. Drachenfels's chambers lie beyond these passageways. We're near him.'

IV

THE FORTRESS WAS the man, Genevieve thought. The towers and battlements, the corridors and chambers, the very mountain crag which the bowels of Drachenfels were carved from: they were the Great Enchanter's arteries and organs, his blood and bones. Oswald's band might as well be penetrating Drachenfels's body like knives, striking for his heart. Or they might be fragments of food tumbling down his gullet. And wasn't that a comforting thought?

Erzbet alone was doubtful as they followed Oswald. She was talking to herself, reciting the names of her dead. The corridors were wider here and hung with tapestries. One depicted the Great Enchanter at play and a deal of red thread had had to be employed. Even Veidt paled at what was shown here.

Oswald glanced at the central panels of the hanging and slashed out with his sword. The entire dusty tapestry fell and lay on the floor like a fen-worm's cast-off skin. Menesh touched his torch to it and in an instant the fire spread along its length. The next tapestry, a group portrait of the certain dreaded gods, caught too.

27

'Very clever, stunted lackwit,' spat Veidt. 'Burning us up now, is it? That makes a change from the traditional dwarfish knife in the small of the back.'

The dwarf pulled his knife and held it up. Veidt had his dart pistol out. There were fires all around them.

'A traitor, eh? Like dead-and-damned Ueli?'

'I'll give you dead-and-damned, scavenger!'

Menesh stabbed up, but Veidt stepped out of the way. Flames reflected in the bounty hunter's dark eyes. He took careful aim.

'Enough!' Oswald cried. 'We've not come this far to fall out now.'

'Veidt cries "traitor" too much,' Rudi said sourly. 'I trust no one who can be bought as easily.'

The outlaw heaved his sword up and Veidt turned again.

'Ethics from a bandit, that's rich–'

'Better a bandit than a trader of corpses!'

'Your corpse is hardly worth the seventy-five gold crowns the Empire has offered for it.'

The pistol came up. The sword wavered in the air.

'Kill him and be done with it,' said Menesh.

This was like Veidt, and like the hot-tempered Rudi. But Menesh had been quiet until now, dodging Veidt's taunts with good humour. Something was working on them. Something *unnatural*. Genevieve staggered forward as someone landed on her back, pushing her face to the floor.

'Hah! Dead bitch!'

Erzbet's noose was about her neck and drawing in. She had taken her by surprise. Genevieve had to struggle to brace her hands against the flagstones, to give herself the leverage to heave Erzbet off her. The wire constricted. The assassin knew her business: beheading would work, all right. Immortality is so fragile: beheading, the hawthorn, silver, too much sun…

Genevieve got her hand under her, palm flat against the stone and pushed herself up. Erzbet tried to ride her like an unbroken pony, her knees digging into the ribs. Genevieve corded her neck muscles and forced breath down her windpipe.

She heard the wire snap and felt Erzbet tumble from her seat. She stood and struck out. The other woman took the blow heavily and fell. Erzbet rolled on the floor and came up, a knife in her hand. Did it gleam silver like Ueli's?

'The dead can die, leech woman!'

Genevieve felt the urge to kill. *Kill the stinking living slut! Kill all these warmblood bastard vermin! Kill, kill, KILL!*

'Fight it,' shouted Oswald. 'It's an attack, an enchantment!'

She turned to the prince. *Whoreson noble! Sister-raping, wealth-besotted scum! Drenched in perfume to cover the stench of his own ordure!*

Oswald held her, shaking her by the shoulders.

Blood! Royal blood! Rich, spiced, hot-on-the-tongue, youthfully-gushing blood!

The vein throbbed in his throat. She took his wrists in her strong hands, feeling their pulses. She heard his heart beating like a steady drum and saw him as a student of anatomy might a dissected corpse. Veins and arteries laid through flesh and over bone. The blood called to her.

How long since she had fed? Properly?

Oswald broke her grip and slapped her.

She found herself and saw only his clear eyes in the dark. He kissed her on the cheek and stood back. The thirst could wait.

Oswald went to each of them in turn, calmed them. Erzbet was the last. She had pressed herself into a corner of the passageway and refused to come out unless coaxed. She waved her knife. Oswald took her hand and pulled the knife out of it. The woman was mad, Genevieve realized, and had been for hours.

Erzbet emerged from her bolt-hole when Oswald talked to her in a low, soothing voice. She clung to the prince like a frightened child to its mother during the daemon king's scenes of a puppet play. Oswald detached the dancer-assassin from his shoulder and passed her to Rudi. The chastened, suddenly serious bandit took her on his arm – had they been lovers, Genevieve wondered? – and Erzbet pressed herself to his side. She sensed Veidt about to make a remark about their new burden, but he kept quiet. Good for him.

The fires were dying. They walked again.

Erzbet was useless now. And Veidt – weather-beaten and hardy Veidt – was ailing. He had sustained a wound during the battle with the gargoyles. It was just a scratch on his face, a newer scar among so many old ones, but it was still bleeding steadily and he had a greyish look. He was moving slowly now, lagging behind them. His sharpness was going and he blundered too often against the walls.

Genevieve heard a clattering and looked back. Veidt had dropped his trifurcate crossbow, his dart pistol and his swordbelt. He was trudging on, trailing them like a prisoner his ball and chain.

This was unthinkable. Veidt would never drag his beloved weapons through the dirt.

Menesh, who had taken so many insults from the bounty hunter, went to him and offered a shoulder to be leaned on. Veidt put out a hand to steady himself, but missed Menesh and fell clumsily against the wall. He crawled on and finally came to rest, gasping for breath, at Oswald's feet. Menesh pulled him upright and propped him against the wall. His face was ashen and he was drooling. He went into convulsions. The dwarf held him down.

'He can't go on, highness.'

Oswald picked up Veidt's dart pistol. It was a fine piece of workmanship, a coil spring-powered gun that could drive a six-inch nail through an oak door. The prince checked it for dirt and blew a cobwebby lump off the barrel. He thrust the weapon into Veidt's hand and he gripped it. The bounty hunter had come through the convulsions.

'We leave him,' said Oswald. 'We'll pass this way again.'

Veidt nodded and weakly raised his hand in salute. He wasn't holding the pistol correctly, Genevieve realized. His finger wasn't on the trigger. If he wasn't helped, he'd be dead by dawn. But they could all be dead by dawn.

Menesh took a stone from his pocket and handed it to Veidt. The bounty hunter tried to pick it up from his lap, but it just lay there. A crude pick was carved on the rounded piece of rock.

'It's the mark of Grungni, dwarf god of the mines. Good luck.'

Veidt nodded. Rudi patted his head as he passed. Erzbet swept her skirts over his legs. Oswald saluted him.

Genevieve looked him in the eyes and saw his future in them.

'Tell me, Mistress... Dieudonné,' Veidt said, each syllable an effort. 'What is it... like?... Being... dead?'

She turned away and followed the others.

Rudi was struck down next, by a simple mechanical device Genevieve would have thought unworthy of the Great Enchanter. A mere matter of a hinged stone set in the floor, of counter-weights and balances, of oiled joints and three iron-hard pieces of wood the length and size of a heavy man. They sprang out of the wall. Two – one at chest height, one at knee height – swung out in front of Rudi, the last – between the others – from behind. They meshed like a three-fingered fist, and the bandit was bent forwards and back between them. They could all hear his bones snapping.

He hung there in the wooden grip, dripping blood and screaming oaths. Then the wooden arms drew back as suddenly as they had leaped out, and he fell in a jellied heap.

Oswald jammed a sword into the wall to hold the arms back and went to him. It was worse than Genevieve had thought. He was still alive. Inside him, whenever he moved, his broken bones would be a hundred knives.

'One by one,' he said. 'The devil is clever, my prince. You must leave old Rudi as you left Veidt. Come back if you can...'

There was blood on the prince's hands. Erzbet was kneeling by the bandit, feeling for his wounds, trying to find the broken places.

'Stay with him,' Oswald told her. 'Be alert.'

So, only three came to the heart of Drachenfels.

V

THIS WAS A throne-room for a king of darkness. The rest of the fortress had been ill-lit and dilapidated, but this was spotless and illumined by jewelled chandeliers. The furniture was ostentatiously luxurious. Gold gleamed from every edge. And silver. Genevieve shuddered to be near so much of the stuff. There were fine paintings on the wall. Rudi would have wept to see so much plunder in one place. A clock chimed, counting unnatural hours as its single hand circled an unfamiliar dial. In a cage, a harpy preened herself, wiping the remains of her last meal from her feathered breasts. Genevieve's heart fluttered as it had not done since she was truly alive.

Oswald and Genevieve trod warily on the thick carpets as they circled the room.

'He's here,' said the prince.

'Yes, I feel it too.'

Menesh kept to the walls, stabbing at tapestries.

One wall was a floor-to-ceiling window, set with stained glass. From here, the Great Enchanter could gaze down from his mountain at the Reikswald. He could see as far as Altdorf and trace the glittering thread of the River Reik through the forests. In the stained glass, there was a giant image of Khorne, the Blood god, sitting upon his pile of human bones. With a chill, Genevieve realized that Drachenfels didn't so much worship Khorne as look down upon him as an amateur in the cause of evil. Chaos was so undisciplined... Drachenfels had never been without purpose. There were other gods, other shrines. Khaine, Lord of Murder, was honoured in a modest ossuary. And Nurgle, Master of Pestilence and Decay, was celebrated by an odiferous pile of mangled remains. From this stared the head of Sieur Jehan, its eyes pecked out.

Oswald started to see his tutor so abused and a laugh resounded through the throne-room.

Six hundred years ago, Genevieve had heard that laugh. Amid the crowds of Parravon, when the First Family's assassin was borne aloft by daemons and his insides fell upon the citizenry. A laugh somehow amplified by the metal mask from behind which it came. In that laughter, Genevieve heard the screams of the damned and the dying, the ripples of rivers of blood, the cracking of a million spines, the fall of a dozen cities, the pleas of murdered infants, the bleating of slaughtered animals.

He loomed up, enormous, from his chair. He had been there all the time, but had worked his magics so none could see.

'I am Drachenfels,' he said mildly, the deathly laugh still in his voice, 'I bid you welcome to my house. Come in health, go safely and leave behind some of the happiness you bring...'

Menesh flew at the Great Enchanter, a dwarfish miner's pick raised to strike. With a terrible languor, moving as might a man of molten bronze, Drachenfels stretched out and slapped him aside. Menesh struck a hanging and fell squealing in a heap. Blood was spurting from him. The harpy was excited and flapped her wings against the bars of her cage, smelling the blood.

Drachenfels was holding the dwarf's arm in his hand. It had come off as easily as a cooked chicken's wing. The enchanter inclined his head to look at his souvenir, giggled and cast it away from him. It writhed across the floor as if alive, trailing blood behind it and was still.

Genevieve looked at Oswald and saw doubt in the prince's face. He had his sword out, but it looked feeble set against the strength, the power of the Great Enchanter.

Drachenfels opened a window in the air and the stink of burning flesh filled the throne-room. Genevieve peered through the window and saw a man twisting in eternal torment, daemons rending his flesh, lashworms eating through his face, rats gnawing at his limbs. He called out her name and reached for her, reached through the window. Blood fell like rain onto the carpet.

It was her father! Her six-centuries-dead father!

'I have them all, you know,' said Drachenfels. 'All my old souls, all kept like that. It prevents me from getting lonely here in my humble palace.'

He shut the window on the damned creature Genevieve had loved. She raised her sword against him.

He looked from one to the other and laughed again. Spirits were gathering about him, evil spirits, servant spirits. They funnelled around him like a tornado.

'So you have come to kill the monster? A prince of nothing, descendant of a family too cowardly to take an Empire for themselves? And a poor dead t1hing without the sense to lie down in her grave and rot? In whose name do you *dare* such an endeavour?'

Oswald tried to be strong. 'In the name of Sigmar Heldenhammer!'

Oswald's words sounded weak, echoing slightly, but gave Drachenfels pause. Something was working behind his mask, a rage building up inside him. His spirits swarmed like midges.

He threw out his hand in Genevieve's direction and the tide of daemons engulfed her, hurling her back against the wall, smothering her, weighing her down, sweeping over her face.

Oswald came forward and his sword clashed on the enchanter's mailed arm. Drachenfels turned to look down on him.

She felt herself dragged down, the insubstantial creatures surging up over her. She couldn't breathe. She could barely move her limbs. She was cold, her teeth chattering. And she was tired, tired as she shouldn't be until dawn. She felt bathed in stinging sunlight, wrapped in bands of silver, smothered in a sea of garlic. Somewhere, the hawthorn was being sharpened for her heart. Her mind fogged, she tasted dust in her throat and her senses dulled.

Unconscious, she missed the battle all the ballads would be about. The battle that would be the inspiration for poets, minstrels, sculptors, painters. The battle that would make Prince Oswald von Konigswald a hero famed throughout the Old World. The battle that would cause some to see in the prince the very spirit of Sigmar reborn.

The battle that would put an end to Constant Drachenfels.

ACT ONE

I

It wasn't so much that the food in Mundsen Keep was *bad*, but that there was so little of it. Detlef Sierck was used to far more substantial daily fare than a measly piece of cheese and a hunk of rough, unbuttered bread served with a half-pitcher of oily water. Indeed, his current accommodations entirely lacked the comforts and services his position entitled him to. And those with whom he was compelled to share his circumstances did not come up to the standards of decorum and intellect he usually expected of his companions.

'I do believe,' he said to Peter Kosinski, the Mad Mercenary, 'that were I to own Mundsen Keep and the Chaos Wastes, I would live in the Wastes and rent out the keep.'

The sullen fellow grunted, belched and kicked him in the head. This was not the sort of treatment usually accorded those of his genius.

The room in which he found himself confined was barely twice the size of the average privy and smelled three times worse. He shared quarters with five others, none of whom he would have, given the choice, selected for his entourage. Each had a blanket, except Kerreth, the smallest, who had, upon

the application of some little force, generously given his away
to Kosinski, the largest. And they each had a piece of cloth
with a number chalked on it.

The cloth was important. Detlef had heard the story of the
two comrades who playfully exchanged their cloths, with the
result that a clerk who had mischanced to cough loudly during a speech by the high priest of Ulric was sent to the
headsman, while a murderer of small children was required
to throw three schillings into the poor box at the temple in
Middenheim.

'If you can afford it,' he said to nobody in particular, 'never
go to debtors' prison in Altdorf.'

Someone laughed and was slapped down by a soul too far
gone in misery to see the humour.

When Detlef woke up on his first morning in Mundsen
Keep, he found his boots and embroidered jacket taken from
him.

'Which of you louts is responsible?' he had asked, only to
discover the culprit was not a fellow convict but Szaradat, the
turnkey. Guglielmo, a bankrupt Tilean wine importer,
explained the system to Detlef. If a man were to stay alive and
well-behaved long enough, he stood a good chance of being
promoted from ordinary prisoner to trusty.

Szaradat was a trusty. And trusties were entitled to work off
the debt that had originally brought them to the Keep by
filching whatever could be pawned, sold or bartered from
lesser prisoners.

The next night, his shirt and britches disappeared and
smelly rags were left in their place. The only thing he had left
to call his own, Detlef reflected, was the iron collar welded in
place around his neck for the convenience of the warders. But
the night after that, he woke up to find himself being held
down by uniformed officials while Szaradat hacked away at
his hair.

'He sells it to Bendrago, the wig-maker on Luitpoldstrasse,'
explained Guglielmo, who was himself sporting an enthusi-
astic but hardly competent fresh haircut. Detlef knew there
were magicians or students desperate for certain other, less
dispensible, parts of the human anatomy. He hoped fervently
that Szaradat didn't know any of them.

Kosinski, with his wrestler's physique and sore-headed bear's temper, was the only one of the cell-mates not shorn. He was well on his way to being a trusty, Detlef assumed. He had the attitude for it. The others, all of whom sported the identical cropped style, were Manolo, a dusky sailor with an unfortunate fondness for games of chance; Justus, a devotee of Ranald fallen upon hard times; and Kerreth, a cobbler driven to ruin by three or four wives. Kerreth had lost his blanket and much else to Kosinski. Detlef guessed the brawny giant only let the cobbler have a mouthful of his bread and water on the principle that if Kerreth died Kosinski would stop getting the extra ration.

There wasn't much to do in the cell. Justus had a deck of Ranald-blessed cards, but Detlef knew better than to play 'Find the Empress' with him. Manolo had obviously been a blessing for Justus, and had already wagered away a year's worth of food to the trickster-priest. Kerreth had a three-inch sliver of hardwood he had smuggled in, and was working away in vain at the mortar of the walls. He'd barely scraped out half a cupful of dust and the stone blocks were as solid as ever. Detlef had heard the walls were fifteen feet thick.

It was only a question of time before someone turned Kerreth and his sliver in to Szaradat for an extra privilege. Sometimes, he wondered who would betray the sailor. Kosinski, who didn't care about anything, was the obvious choice, but if he hadn't seen this opportunity to grease his way to trusty status by now, he probably never would.

Detlef was honest enough to suspect he would be the one eventually to take Szaradat aside during their monthly exercise period and point out Kerreth's sliver. And decent enough to hope to put off that treachery for as long as possible. But there was only so much an artist could take.

There was a question that always came up. It was about the only conversation the prisoners – the talkative Guglielmo excepted – really took to. There were many ways of approaching the question: What did you do on the outside? Will you ever get out of here? How deep is your hole? How wide your river? How high your wall? How long your life? What these were all getting at was simple: How much do you owe?

After three weeks, Detlef knew to the penny how much his cell-mates owed. He knew about the sixteen gold crowns Manolo had staked on the unbeatable hand of cards dealt him in the back room of the Gryphon and Star on the Sacred Day of Manann, god of the seas. And the three shillings and fourpence, compounded with interest to eighteen gold crowns, that Kerreth had obtained from a moneylender to purchase a trinket for his latest fiancée. And the ninety-eight crowns Kosinski had spent before learning that he had hired on to an expedition to the Northern Wastes even the most crazed of the other mercenaries thought suicidal. And the two hundred and fifty-eight crowns, twelve shillings and sixpence Guglielmo had borrowed from a certain Tilean businessman to purchase a ship's cargo of fine wines that had gone to the bottom of the Sea of Claws.

He knew about the five hundred and forty crowns Justus had duped out of a spice merchant's wife in return for a course of cream treatments guaranteed to restore her to the full bloom of youth and beauty. He had been lucky to be arrested before the woman's sons returned from overseas to sharpen their swords. Detlef knew about all their debts. And they knew about his.

'One hundred and nineteen thousand, two hundred and fifty-five gold crowns, seventeen shillings and ninepence.'

That was Manolo. But it could have been any of them. They all said it from time to time, sometimes with reverence like a prayer, sometimes with anger like an oath, and sometimes with awe like a declaration of love.

'One hundred and nineteen thousand, two hundred and fifty-five gold crowns, seventeen shillings and ninepence.'

Detlef was getting fed up with the tune. He wished the sum could alter, one way or another. Preferably another. If he had friends outside, patrons or sponsors, he hoped they would feel a generous impulse. But it would take a supernaturally generous impulse to do anything worthwhile to the figure.

'One hundred and nineteen thousand, two hundred and fifty-five gold crowns, seventeen shillings and ninepence.'

'Enough. I'm tired of hearing that.'

'I know,' said Kosinski, with grudging respect, 'but *one hundred and nineteen thousand, two hundred and fifty-five gold crowns, seventeen shillings and ninepence*. Why, it's an achievement. I've tried to think of it, to see it in my mind, but I can't…'

'Imagine a city built of gold crowns, Kosinski,' said Justus. 'Towers piled high as temples, stacks pushed together like palaces.'

'One hundred and nineteen thousand, two hundred and fifty-five gold crowns, seventeen shillings and ninepence.' There it was again. 'Why, I'll bet the Emperor Karl-Franz himself couldn't lay his hands on one hundred and nineteen thousand, two hundred and fifty-five gold crowns, seventeen shillings and ninepence.'

'I rather think he could. Quite a bit of it was his in the first place.'

Guglielmo shook his head in wonder. 'But how did you do it, Detlef? How could you conceivably spend such a sum? In my entire life, I've barely had five thousand crowns pass through my hands. And I'm a man of business, of trade. How could you possibly spend one hundred and nineteen–'

'…thousand, two hundred and fifty-five gold crowns, seventeen shillings and ninepence? It was easy. Costs kept going up and expenses arose that weren't foreseen in my original budget plan. My accountants were criminally negligent.'

'Then why aren't they in this cell with us?'

'Ahem,' Detlef was shamed, 'well, most of them were… sort of… um… killed. I'm afraid that some of the parties involved were unable to take the long view of the affair. Small minds and money-boxes are the blight of the artistic spirit.'

There was a drip of water at the back of the cell. Kerreth had been trying to catch it in rolled cones made from the pages of a book Szaradat hadn't bothered to steal, but Kosinski kept eating the soggy paper. A mouse had found its way in yesterday and Kosinski had eaten that too. He said he'd tasted worse when campaigning in the Northern Wastes.

'But still,' wondered Guglielmo, 'to spend all that money just on a play…'

'Not *just* on a play, my dear Guglielmo! On *the* play. The play that, had it ever been produced, would have lived forever in the minds and hearts of those mortals lucky enough to see it. The play that would have sealed my reputation as the premier genius of my day. The play that would, not to put too sharp a point on it, have earned back tenfold the meagre cost of its staging.'

It was called *The True History of Sigmar Heldenhammer, Founder of the Empire, Saviour of the Reik, Defier of the Darkness*. Detlef Sierck had written it on a commission for the Elector of Middenland. The epic was to have been staged in the presence of Emperor Karl-Franz himself. Detlef had planned to call upon the full resources of three villages in the Middle Mountains for the production. The entire populations would have been drafted in to serve as extras, a castle of wood was to be erected and burned down during the course of the action and wizards had been engaged to present state-of-the-art illusions during the magical sequences.

The natural amphitheatre in which the play was to have been staged was twelve days' ride from Middenheim, and the Emperor and electors would have to be conveyed there in a magnificent procession. There would have been a two-day feast merely as a prologue for the drama, and the action of the epic would have unfolded over a full week, with breaks in the story for meals and sleep.

Detlef himself, the greatest actor of the age as well as the premier dramatist, had cast himself in the role of Sigmar, one of the few in literature large enough to contain his personality. And Lilli Nissen, the famous beauty and – it was rumoured – sometime mistress of six out of fourteen electors, had consented to take the role of Shallya, goddess of healing and mercy. Mercenaries had been engaged to fight nearly to the death during the battle scenes, an enormous homunculus had been bred especially by skilled wizards to stand in for Constant Drachenfels, an army of dwarfs had been hired to portray Sigmar's dwarf allies and another engaged to stand in under masks for the goblin hordes the hero was to drive out of the Empire – Detlef would have insisted on real goblins, but his cast baulked at working with them. The crops of three successive harvests were stored up to fuel the cast and audience, and almost one thousand professional actors, singers, dancers, animal trainers, jugglers, musicians, jesters, combatants, prostitutes, conjurers and philosophers retained to play the major parts in the great drama.

And it had all been ruined by something as petty and uninteresting as an outbreak of plague among the battlefield extras. Lilli Nissen would not budge from Marienburg when the news of the epidemic reached her, and hers was merely the first of the many returned invitations. Finally the elector himself pulled out and Detlef found himself forced to deal with a seeming army of angry creditors whose notes against the electoral coffers were suddenly refused. Under the circumstances, he had found it necessary to disguise himself as a priestly type and flee to Altdorf, where the elector's ambassadors unfortunately awaited his appearance. There had been considerable expenses already, and those who had laid out the thousand gold crowns he had been asking for a reserved ticket were clamouring for the refund of their money. Furthermore, the three villages were rumoured to be clubbing together to petition the assassins' guild.

'It would have been magnificent, Guglielmo. You would have wept to see it. The scene where I was to best the forces of evil with only my hammer and my noble heart would have lived eternally in the annals of great art. Picture it: as Sigmar, all my allies are dead or flown, the dwarfs have not yet committed to my cause, and I stride – my massive shadow cast before me by a miracle of ingenious lighting effects – to the centre of the field of corpses. The goblins creep from their holes. For a full two hours, I stand immobile as the goblins gather, each more fantastically hideous than the last. Women and children were to have been barred from this section of the drama, and entertained elsewhere by acrobats. I had commissioned a choral work of surpassing power from my regular composer, Felix Hubermann. I had personally designed the monstrous masks for each of the goblin extras. When the hordes were finally assembled before me, I would have produced my hammer – my glowing, holy, singing metal warhammer – and it would have given off lights the like of which you've never seen. You would have been struck dumb for weeks by Hubermann's Hammer Theme, and have felt your youth return as I displayed my heroism and courage in battle against the goblins and the Great Enchanter. It would have been the triumphant crowning moment of my altogether glorious career.

'*The Tragedy of the Bretonnian Courtesan* would have been forgotten, *The Loves of Ottokar and Myrmidia* would have been completely eclipsed, and the critics who so sneered at my experimental production of Kleghel's *Great Days of Empire* would have slit their throats for shame.'

'If words were pennies, you'd have gone free long ago,' said Justus.

'Pennies! That's all I can hope to earn here. Did you note my visitor yesterday? The fellow with the evil eye and the frightful twitch?'

Guglielmo nodded.

'That was Gruenliebe the Greasy. You may remember him. He used to be court jester in Luitpold's day. His speciality was a nauseating little act with trained lambs. When he became too old and fat and slimy to entertain any more, he expanded his business. Now, he owns a string of so-called entertainers who clown and juggle and caper in taverns, and turn over a good three-fourths of their earnings to him for the privilege. If the fumbler drops the balls, the minstrel sounds like a basilisk in pain or the comedian uses lines that might just have been topical in the days of Boris the Incompetent, then you can be certain he belongs to Gruenliebe. Anyway, this piece of offal wrapped up in a human form, this veritable orc in a clown's apparel, had the nerve to propose I work for him...'

The drip dripped, and Detlef burned with the memory of the humiliation, the anger that still boiled...

'What did he want you to do?'

'He wanted me to write *jokes* for him. To turn out satirical lyrics at a penny a line, to supply his army of witless incompetents with the stuff of laughter, as if one could teach a skaven to play the fiddle or a grave robber to discourse on the cuisine of Cathay. I, whose poems have moved princes to crying fits that will be with them their lives through. I, whose mere offhand remarks have caused hermits under a vow of silence literally to split their sides suppressing laughter...'

'A penny a line,' mused Justus. 'Do you know how many lines it would take to pay off one hundred and nineteen thousand, two hundred and fifty-five gold crowns, seventeen shillings and ninepence at a penny a line?'

'As it happens...'

Justus looked at the ceiling, and his eyes rolled. 'You don't want to know. The great library at the university doesn't have that many lines.'

'Do you think I'd make a good trusty?' Detlef asked.

Kosinski laughed, nastily.

'It was just a thought.'

II

FROM THE TERRACE of the convent, Genevieve could see the deep, slow, glass-clear waters of the River Talabec, hundreds of feet below. Bordered with thick, sweet-smelling pine forests, the river was like the central artery of the Empire. Not as long as the Reik, which ran a full seven hundred and fifty miles from its rise in the Black Mountains to its mouth at Marienburg, but still cutting across the map like a knife-slash, from the rapid streams of the World's Edge Mountains through the heart of the Great Forest, swelled by its confluence with the Urskoy, to the inland port of Talabheim and then, heavy and thick with the black silt of the Middle Mountains, into the Reik at Altdorf. If she were to cast her kerchief from the terrace, it could conceivably travel the length of the Empire to the sea. Just now, a riverboat – unusual this far up – was pulling in to the jetty that served the convent. More supplies for the Order of Eternal Night and Solace.

Here, secluded from all, she liked the idea of the waters running like the bloodstream. She had come to the convent to be out of the world, but her centuries among men had given her a taste for their affairs. A taste that Elder Honorio discouraged, but which could still not be suppressed. As the comforting dark fell, she saw the tall trees dwindle into shadows and the risen moon waver in the waters. How were things in Altdorf? In Middenheim? Did Luitpold still rule? Was the Crescent Moon still doing business? Was Oswald von Konigswald yet the elector of Ostland? These were not her concerns, and Elder Honorio dismissed her interests as 'a prurient liking for gossip,' but she couldn't be without them. The boat below would be bringing animals, clothes, tools, spices. But no books, no music, no news. In the convent, one was supposed to be content with the changelessness of life, not caught up in its chaotic tumble of events, of fads, of trends. A quarter-century ago, Genevieve had needed that. Now, perhaps she needed to return to the world.

The convent had been founded in the time of Sigmar by Elder Honorio's father-in-darkness, Belada the Melancholy, and had remained unchanged in its isolation down through the centuries. Honorio still wore the buckles and pigtail of a long-gone era, and the others of the order favoured the fashions of their lifetimes. Genevieve felt herself the child again, and sensed censorious eyes criticizing her dresses, her hairstyle, her longings. Some of the others, the Truly Dead, disturbed her. They were the creatures in the stories who slept by day and would burst into flame at cock-crow if not safely packed in a coffin layered with their native soil. Many bore the marks of Chaos: eyes like red marbles, wolfish fangs, three-inch talons. Their feeding habits offended her polite sensibilities, and caused much hostility between the convent and the few nearby woodland villages.

'What's a child, more or less?' Honorio asked. 'All who live naturally will die before I next need to razor the bristles from my chin.'

Genevieve had been feeding less of late. Like many of the old ones, she was outliving the need. In some ways it was a relief, although she would miss the rush of sensations that came with the blood, the moments when she felt most truly *alive*. One thing she might regret was that she had never given the Dark Kiss; she had no get, no young vampires to look to her as a mother-in-darkness, no progeny to seed the world.

'You should have had your get while you were still young enough to appreciate them, my dear,' said the graceful, stately Lady Melissa d'Acques. 'Why, I've birthed near a hundred young bloods in my centuries. Fine fellows all, devoted sons-in-darkness. And all handsome as Ranald.'

Chandagnac had been the Lady Melissa's get, and so the vampire noblewoman treated Genevieve as a granddaughter-in-darkness. She reminded Genevieve of her real grandmother in her manner of speech and in her fussiness, although the Lady Melissa would always physically be the golden-haired twelve-year-old she had been eleven hundred years ago. One night then, her coach had been held up by a nameless brigand thirsty for more than money.

According to the grimoires of the order, Genevieve would lose her ability to procreate with the passing of the red thirst. But maybe not: in the libraries of the convent, and through a simple observation of her companions in the order, she had learned that there were as many species of vampire as there were of fish or cat. Some abhorred the relics and symbols of all the gods, others entered Holy Orders and lived the most devout of lives. Some were brutish predators who would drain at a draught a peasant girl, others epicures who would sip only, and treat their human meals as lovers rather than cattle. Some, skilled in sorcery and wizardry, could indeed transform themselves into bats, wolves or a sentient red mist; others could barely tie their own bootlaces. 'What kind am I,' Genevieve would occasionally wonder to herself, 'what kind of vampire am I?'

The thing that marked her bloodline – the line of Chandagnac, reaching ultimately back to Lahmia – from the vampires of dark legend was that they had never died and lain in the earth. The transformation had been wrought lovingly while they still drew breath. She might have no reflection and feel the need for blood, but her heart still beat. The Truly Dead – sometimes known as the Strigoi – were more dead than alive, essentially walking corpses. Few of them were decent, they were the bad ones, the child-stealers, the throat-tearers, haunters of the grave...

Genevieve and the Lady Melissa played cards on the terrace as the sunset faded, the quality of the game improving as their night-senses awoke. Genevieve ran her tongue over her sharp teeth, and tried to think two or three hands ahead.

'Now, now, my girl,' said the Lady Melissa, her child's face grave, 'you shouldn't try to read your granny's mind like that. She's much older and wiser than you, and could easily give you the vision of the wrong cards.'

Genevieve laughed, and lost again, trumped from nowhere.

'You see.'

The Lady Melissa laughed, as she scooped the trick. For the moment, she was genuinely a giggling child; then she was the old lady again. Inside the convent, the Truly Dead were rising. Wolves howled in the forests. A large bat flapped lazily across the sky, blotting the moon for a moment.

Twenty-five years ago, Genevieve had been in at the death of the most evil man alive. The effects had been calamitous, and unforeseen. Throughout the Known World, the agents of evil – some of whom had masqueraded for years as ordinary or even exemplary citizens – were transformed into their true, monstrous selves, or struck down by invisible arrows to the heart, or blasted to pieces by explosions. A castle in Kislev fell silently to the ground, crushing a coven of witches to a paste. Thousands of spirits were freed from their ties to the earth and passed on, beyond the ken of mediums and necromancers. In Gisoreux, the statue of a martyred child came suddenly to life, speaking in an ancient dialect no one could understand, the spell upon him at last lifted. And Prince Oswald and his companions became the heroes of the age.

Emperor Luitpold, shamed by his initial refusal to aid Oswald's expedition, had sent in a troop of the Imperial Guard to clear out the pathetic remnants of Drachenfels's foul servants from his castle. Goblins, orcs, trolls, hideously altered humans, degenerates and hordes of unclassifiable creatures had been put to the sword, or burned at the stake, or hanged from the battlements. The Emperor had wanted to raze the place to the ground, but Oswald interceded, insisting that it should stay standing and desolate as a reminder of the evil that had been. Drachenfels's books, papers and possessions were argued over by the grand theogonist of the cult of Sigmar and the high priest of the cult of Ulric, but eventually found their way into shrines and libraries throughout the

Empire, accessible only to the most esteemed and unblemished of scholars.

Genevieve, meanwhile, had refused all offers of reward and returned to the Crescent Moon. Her part in the adventure was over, and she wanted to hear no more of it. There were too many dead and worse for her to make light of the story. But the tavern had changed, and was thronged now with the curious and the disturbed. Balladeers wanted her story, the devout wanted relics of her person, relatives of the monster's victims inexplicably wanted reparations from her, politicians wanted her name to lend to their causes, a clandestine group of young sons-in-darkness wanted to form a vampires' guild around her to lobby the Emperor for the lifting of certain laws against the practices of their kind.

Those loyal to the cause of Drachenfels tried several times to assassinate her. And those narrow-minded worthies who couldn't bear the thing she was decried her part in the fall of the Great Enchanter and tried to make her out as his secret ally.

Most unnerving of all were the flocks of young men who became her admirers, who would bare their throats and wrists to her, begging her to drink deeply, who would sometimes take an edge to their veins in her presence. Some were of that sorry type who plague all the undead, those who crave the Dark Kiss and all it brings. But others claimed they would be content simply to bleed their last for her, to die twitching and ecstatic in her arms.

There was only so much she could stand, and eventually she embarked upon a riverboat for the convent. She had heard such a place existed, and various of her cousins-in-darkness had given her contradictory stories about a remote refuge for vampirekind, but only now did she make the effort to find the truth behind the stories, to petition for admittance into the Order of Eternal Night and Solace. When she had needed to find them, they had got in touch with her. Evidently, they had their agents in the world.

'You're troubled,' the Lady Melissa said. 'Tell me your troubles.'

It was not a helpful suggestion. It was a command.

'I've been dreaming.'

'Nonsense, girl. Our kind don't dream. You know as well as I do that we sleep the sleep of the dead.'

Genevieve saw the masked face in her mind, heard the chilling laughter. 'And yet I've been dreaming.'

They were joined on the terrace by Honorio, the vampire dwarf who was the current elder of the order, and a party of others. One of the party was alive, and nervous. He was a young man, well enough dressed, but obviously not of the first rank. Something about him struck her as being not quite right.

Wietzak, the Truly Dead giant who had once ruled Karak Varn with unparalleled savagery, eyed the young man with obvious bloodlust. Wietzak was Honorio's favoured attendant and would do nothing unsanctioned by the elder, but the visitor wasn't to know that.

'My ladies, I hope you will pardon this interruption,' began Elder Honorio. 'But it seems that though we have left the world behind, the world is not quite ready to abandon all its interest in us. A message – a summons – has been brought here. This gentleman is Henrik Kraly, from Altdorf, and he would have words with you, Genevieve. You may see him or not, as you wish.'

The messenger bowed to her, and presented her with a scroll. She recognized the seal, a crown against trees, and broke it at once. Wietzak ground his teeth as she read. In the forest, there was a commotion as a bat took a wolf.

Within the hour, she was aboard the riverboat, prepared for a long journey. The Lady Melissa gave her a long lecture of farewell, cautioning her against the perils of the world outside and reminding her of the difficulties she would face. Genevieve loved the old lady-child too much to tell her that the hawthorn-wielding Inquisitors she spoke of were three centuries gone and that the cities she remembered as thriving sources of lifesblood were abandoned ruins. Lady Melissa had been with the order for an apparent eternity. They embraced, and the Lady Melissa returned to the jetty where Wietzak, one of those who couldn't bear running water, awaited to accompany her back to the heights of the convent. As her grandmother-in-darkness waved goodbye to her, Genevieve had the disturbing feeling that they were both alive again, and that they were just dearest girlfriends, sixteen and twelve, being separated for a summer.

The next day, prone in her bunk as the oarsmen propelled the craft through the forests, she dreamed again.

The iron-masked man with the hellish laugh would not leave her sleep. Gone he might be, but forgotten was another matter entirely.

She was travelling now to Altdorf. But eventually, she knew, her journey would take her back to the Grey Mountains, back along the course she had followed twenty-five years ago.

Back to the fortress of Drachenfels.

III

WHEN SZARADAT CAME round with the rations, Kosinski let Kerreth keep a little less than usual. Detlef realized the little cobbler was going to die after a few more months of this treatment, and Kosinski would grow stronger. Then, the mad mercenary would need a new source for his extra rations. Guglielmo was nearly an old man, and his legs were spindle-thin. He would be Kosinski's next supplier, his next victim. But, after that…? Manolo was still tough from the seas, and Justus had all the skills one would expect of a follower of the patron god of tricksters and thieves. Detlef knew he was out of condition. His weight only really got down to a comfort-able level when he was in the middle of a production, and exercising vigorously every day. He was decidedly flabby now, even on short rations. And Kosinski kept looking stronger and meaner each morning. After Kerreth and Guglielmo died, Kosinski would start taking food from him. And Manolo and Justus would let him, just as he was letting Kosinski steal from Kerreth. As he would let the brute steal from Guglielmo, who was his closest friend in the cell. And if Kosinski took enough, Detlef would himself die.

It hardly seemed a fit fate for the author of *The History of Sigmar*, the brightest star of the Konigsgarten Theatre in Middenheim. He tried counting the broken hearts he had left among the daughters of Middenheim society, but he was still not cheered. He pondered the roles he had not yet played, the classics he had not yet staged, the masterpieces he had not yet written. Perhaps, if he were ever by some miracle, to get out of the keep, he should consider staging Tarradasch's *The Desolate Prisoner of Karak Kadrin* as a starring vehicle. Only now, he felt, did he truly understand the plight of the disconsolate Baron Trister.

Someone prodded him out of his reverie. It was Szaradat, rattling his keys in his face.

'What do you want? More hair? Fingers and toes, perhaps, for a cannibal cookpot, or to use as corks for foul wines?'

The trusty spat in the corner.

'You've got a visitor, play-actor.'

'Ach! Gruenliebe again! Tell him I'm unwell, and unable to see him. No, that my social diary is overfull and that I can't squeeze him in. No, that–'

Szaradat pulled Detlef upright, and slapped him across the face with the keys. He drew blood.

'You'll see your visitor, or I'll have you transferred to the punishment wing. You won't have the *luxuries* you have here…'

Detlef did not relish the prospect of learning through their absence precisely with which luxuries his current cell was indeed invisibly equipped. To some, he supposed, it might be deemed a luxury to be in a cell without a ravening wolf in it. Or to have one's bodily wastes taken away once a week. Or not to be neck-deep in the rotten waters of an oubliette.

Szaradat attached a chain to Detlef's iron collar, and dragged him through the door. The genius was led like a dog through the prison, and exposed to the cries and pleas of the other inmates. The keep was centuries out of date, and still equipped with the torture chambers employed during the reign of Hjalmar the Tyrannical, Didrick the Unjust and Bloody Beatrice the Monumentally Cruel. Szaradat looked with longing at a dilapidated rack, and then with disgust at Detlef. It wasn't hard to guess what the trusty was thinking.

As emperors go, Karl-Franz was almost reasonable, but who knew what the electors would come up with next. Even Beatrice, to the historian's eye an obvious maniac, had been voted into office by the unanimous decision of the Great and the Good. There was no guessing if or when Szaradat would get to dust off the Tilean boot, oil the spikes of the iron maiden of Kislev, or heat up again the array of tongs and branding implements that now hung forgotten under cobwebs. And when that happened, the trusty would be delighted as a new father... and Detlef would have further cause to regret the day the plausible elector of Middenland came calling at his theatre.

The Great and the Good, pah! Small-minded and Snakelike was more to the point. Vindictive and Verminous! Mean-spirited and Miserly!

At length, Detlef was pushed and jostled into a tiny courtyard. His bare feet froze on the icy stones. It was an overcast day, but the light still hurt his eyes. It was as if he were gazing directly at the sun. He realized how used he had become to the gloom of the cell.

A figure appeared on a balcony overlooking the courtyard. Detlef recognized the black robes, gold chains and superior expression of Governor van Zandt, who had upon his admission given him a lecture on self-denial and peace through suffering. He was one of those officials whose religiosity is such that Detlef suspected them of having taken a vow of stupidity.

'Sierck,' Van Zandt said, 'you may be wondering what that smell is you've been unable to get rid of these last few weeks...'

Detlef grinned and nodded, just to keep in with the governor.

'Well, I'm sorry to have to be the one to tell you this, but I'm afraid the stink is you.'

Gargoyles just below the balcony disgorged streams of water, which fell like a rain of rocks upon Detlef. He was knocked to the ground, and floundered in the jets. He tried to get out of the way, but the streams were redirected and struck him down again. His rags fell apart under the pressure, and great swatches of dirt were scraped painfully from his body.

He found fist-sized chunks of ice in the water, and realized he was being washed with melted snow from the roofs. Szaradat threw him a stiff-bristled brush that could well have been one of his prized instruments of torture, and ordered him to scrub himself.

The streams died away. Szaradat tore the remains of Detlef's rags from his body, and prodded him in the bulge of his stomach. He smiled like a rat, showing unpleasantly yellowed teeth. Still dripping, and with the gooseflesh standing out all over, he was marched down a corridor into another room. Szaradat produced a plain robe, hardly stylish but better than nothing, and allowed Detlef to towel himself off before getting into it.

'Gruenliebe must be getting squeamish in his old age,' Detlef said, 'to be offended by a smell far less unhealthy than that given off by his clients' acts.'

Van Zandt came into the room. 'You aren't to see Gruenliebe today, Sierck. Your caller is far more distinguished.'

'Distinguished enough to require the personal attention of the governor of this deathpit?'

'Indeed.'

'You intrigue me. Lead on.'

Detlef waved imperiously, summoning some of the grandeur he had practiced for the roles of the seven emperors in Sutro's great *Magnus the Pious* cycle. Van Zandt took Detlef's arm impatiently, and steered him through another door. Warmth engulfed him as he stepped, for the first time since his incarceration, into a room properly heated by an open fire. There were unbarred windows to let in the light, and a bowl of fruit – yes, *fruit!* – stood casually on the table awaiting anyone who might chance to desire a bite or two between meals.

A man of perhaps forty was sitting at the table, polishing a red apple on his generous sleeve. Detlef was struck by his aristocratic bearing and his piercingly clear eyes. This was no ordinary charitable visitor.

'Detlef Sierck,' began Governor van Zandt, an awed quaver in his voice deferring to the man, 'may I present you to Oswald von Konigswald, Defier of the Darkness, Adept of the Cult of Sigmar, Crown Prince and Acting Elector of Ostland.'

The crown prince smiled at Detlef. Detlef had a presentiment that his disasters were only beginning.

'Sit down,' said the man who defeated Drachenfels. 'We have much to talk about, you and I.'

IV

THE FATE OF the Empire was at stake. And the castle was the point that must be held, that must not fail. There were only twenty knights arrayed on the battlements, their plumes stiff on their helms, and barely a hundred common soldiers behind the walls, stoutly prepared to die for the Emperor. Set against them were an orcish horde of some five thousand, reinforced with giants, minotaurs, ogres, undead horsemen, snotlings, greater and lesser daemons and all manner of creatures of darkness. It all fell to the decision of the commander of the castle, His Highness Maximilian von Konigswald, Grand Prince of Ostland.

He pondered the situation, looked about him, and consulted the general. After a brief conference, he knew his plan of action. Maximilian returned the general to his top pocket and gave the order.

'Rain down fire upon the enemy.'

He touched a burning candle to his goblet of Bretonnian brandy, and cast it down at the battlefield. The flames spread, and a thousand or more of the forces of evil were engulfed. They melted, peeling, and the battlefield itself was eaten up by the fire. The smell was quite frightful, and Maximilian himself started back as the orcs hissed and exploded.

The commander-in-chief of the horde looked up and burst into tears.

'Mama, mama,' cried the orcish commander. 'He's burning my soldiers again.'

The commander's mother, the grand prince's nurse, came to the rescue with a pail of water. The soldiers were washed this way and that by the flood, but the fires were put out. The table-top castle became soggy and collapsed, tipping the grand prince's painted lead forces into the melee. Maximilian giggled his high-pitched giggle, and picked out his favourite knights from the mess. Water cascaded onto the marble floors of the palace games room.

'Now, now, highness,' clucked the nurse, 'we mustn't burn down the palace must we? The Emperor would be most upset.'

'The Emperor,' shouted Maximilian, standing to attention despite the pains in his back and limbs, snapping a smart salute. 'To die for the Emperor is the highest honour one can expect.'

The orcish commander, an outsize soldier's helmet strapped to his undersize head, returned the elector's salute.

'Yes, yes, quite,' said the nurse, 'but don't you think it's time for your nap, highness? You've been fighting for the Emperor all morning.'

Maximilian bristled.

'Don't want to nap,' he said, sticking out his lower lip, sucking in his white moustaches and holding his breath. His cheeks went red.

'But an elector needs his rest. You'll be no use to the Emperor if you're falling asleep all over the battlefield.'

'All right. Nap then.' Maximilian began to unbutton his uniform. The nurse stopped him before he dropped his trousers.

'It might be a good idea if you didn't get undressed until you were in your bedchamber, highness. The corridors of the palace are drafty at this time of year and you might catch a nasty chill.'

'Chill? Nasty? Reminds me of the time the Emperor sent me to Norsca. Bloody chilly, Norsca. Lots of snow and ice and white wolves. But cold, mostly. Yes, mostly cold. Norsca is like that. Will there be eggs for supper?'

The nurse manoeuvred the elector away from his battle table as he talked, walking him through the hallways to his daybed room. Behind her, her son wailed. 'Can I be the Emperor's armies next time? I always have to be the orcs. It's not *fair*.'

Maximilian coughed, deep, racking coughs that came from his lungs and brought stuff up with them. He missed the spittoon, and the nurse had to wipe his moustaches again. He was a very sick elector, they told him, and he needed his rest.

'Eggs, woman,' he thundered. 'Will there be eggs?'

'I think cook had planned on quail, but if you're good and nap until three I think eggs could be arranged.'

They passed a ticking pendulum clock, its face a smiling sun, its workings exposed under glass.

'Nap 'til three! That's hours and hours and hours off.'

'Well, it'll be quail then.'

Two distinguished men, priests of Ulric, saw Maximilian coming and bowed low to him. He poked his tongue out at them, and they passed on without passing comment. He didn't care for priests of Ulric, dried-up old fools who looked down their long noses at heroes of the Empire and tried to get him to read boring papers and things.

'Don't like quail. Like eggs. Good battle food, eggs. Keep you going all day, eggs for breakfast.'

The nurse helped the grand prince into his room. It was decorated with big, bright-coloured pictures of the old emperor, Luitpold, and of glorious battlefields. There was even a portrait of Maximilian von Konigsberg as a young man, with his wife and young son, dressed up for a court affair. Maximilian's hand was on his sword-hilt.

'Sleep 'til three, highness, and perhaps eggs can be found.'

'Half past two.'

'Three.'

The nurse wiped dribble from the elector's moustache.

'A quarter to three.'

'Done.'

The elector bounced on his bed, whooping for joy. 'Eggs, eggs! I'm getting eggs for supper. You can't have eggs, but I can, 'cause I'm a hero of the Empire. The Emperor himself said so.'

The nurse pulled the elector's uniform off, and pulled his bedclothes up over him.

'Don't forget the general.'

'So sorry, highness.' She took the lead soldier out of the elector's jacket pocket and put it on the bedside table where he could see it from beneath his covers. He saluted the figure, who was perpetually saluting him back.

'Say sweet dreams to the general, highness.'

'Sweet dreams, general…'

'And remember, when you've had your nap, you're to see Crown Prince Oswald. You're to put your seal to some papers.'

Oswald. As Maximilian fell asleep to dream of battles and wars, he tried to think of Oswald. There were two Oswalds. His father, the old grand prince, had been an Oswald. And there was another, a younger fellow. It must be his father he was to see, because Old Oswald was important, another hero of the Empire.

But still… *eggs!*

V

DESPITE HIS HARD-WON distrust of the Great and the Good, Detlef Sierck was impressed with Crown Prince Oswald. Those who carve their names in the annals of history usually turn out to be drooling idiots. The general who kept back the hordes of darkness smells like a cesspool, picks his nose and has pieces of onion in his beard. The courtesan who decided the fate of a city has a missing tooth, a grating laugh and the habit of digging you painfully in the ribs whenever a *double entendre* creeps into the conversation. And the philosopher whose propositions changed the entire course of Imperial Thought is locked in an infantile battle with his neighbour over a barking dog. But Crown Prince Oswald still looked in every particular the hero who slew the monster, won the lady, saved the kingdom and honoured his father.

He was more handsome than any matinee idol, and his relaxed but alert posture suggested an athleticism superior to most professional swordsmen or tumblers. Detlef, used to being the object of all eyes in company, realized sadly that were a party of ladies to be introduced into the room, they would all, even if unaware of his position in society, flock to

Oswald. Detlef would be left to make embarrassed conversation with the inevitable bespectacled, bad-complexioned frump all groups of pretty women haul about with them to throw their attributes into the spotlight.

There was a woman in the story of Oswald and Drachenfels, Detlef was sure. A beautiful woman, of course. What had her name been? He was certain the crown prince was unmarried, so she must have passed out of the story soon after the death of the Great Enchanter. Perhaps she died. That was the fashion in melodrama, for the hero's beloved to die. Heroes had to be free of such attachments if they were to continue their adventuring. During his own dashing hero phase, Detlef had lost count of the number of dying damsels he had vowed eternal love over, and the number of justified revenges he had later claimed.

The crown prince bit into the apple with perfect, even teeth, and chewed. Detlef was conscious that his own teeth were rather bad. He had even taken to wearing his moustaches unfashionably long to cover them up. But he was also conscious now of the hunger that had been with him for months. He knew the crown prince was looking him over, getting the measure of him, but he could only look, with a craving that amounted to lust, at the plain bowl of fruit. He swallowed the saliva that had filled his mouth, and forced himself to meet his visitor's gaze.

What must he look like after these months of Mundsen Keep? He assumed that, even without Oswald to make him seem the male answer to the proverbial frump, he would break no hearts for the while. His stomach groaned as the crown prince threw his apple core into the fire. It hissed as it burned. Detlef would have exchanged a week's bread and cheese for the fruitflesh that had remained on that core.

Evidently, his hunger was all too obvious to his visitor. 'By all means, Mr Sierck, help yourself…'

Crown Prince Oswald waved a gloved hand at the bowl. Pearl buttons at his wrist caught the light. He was, of course, dressed impeccably and in the latest style. Yet there was no showiness about his costume. He wore rich clothes with ease and wasn't overwhelmed by them. There was, indeed, a princely simplicity about his outfit that would look all the better by comparison with the gaudy gorgeousness and over-ornamentation favoured by too many of the nobility.

Detlef touched an apple, relishing the feel of it, like a picky housewife in the marketplace testing for ripeness before making a purchase. He took it out of the bowl, and examined it. His stomach felt as if it had never been full. There were sharp pains. He bit into the fruit, and swallowed a mouthful down without tasting it. The apple was gone in three bites, core and all. He took a pear, and made a hasty meal of that too. Juice dribbled down his face. The crown prince watched with an eyebrow raised in amusement.

Oswald was still a young man, Detlef realized. And yet his famed exploit was some twenty-five years behind him. He must have been little more than a boy when he bested Drachenfels.

'I have read your works, Mr Sierck. I have seen you perform. You are prodigiously talented.'

Detlef grunted his agreement through a mouthful of grapes. He spat the pips into his hand, and felt foolish that there was nowhere else to put them. He made a fist, intending to swallow them later. If Kosinski could eat mice, then Detlef Sierck wouldn't baulk at grapestones.

'I was even granted access to the manuscript of your *History of Sigmar*. It is held, as you must know, by the elector of Middenland.'

'My greatest work? Did you like it?'

The crown prince smiled, almost slyly. 'It was… ambitious. If impractical…'

'The manuscript would tell you little, highness. You should have seen the production. That would have convinced you. It would have been epoch-making.'

'No doubt.'

The two men looked closely at each other. Detlef stopped eating when there was no more fruit. The crown prince was in no hurry to disclose the purpose of his visit to Mundsen Keep. The fire burned. Detlef was aware of the pleasantness of simple warmth and space. An upholstered chair to sit on, and a table for his elbows. Before he came to the keep, he had insisted on mountains of embroidered pillows, maidservants waiting forever in attendance to gratify his needs, lavish meals served at any hour of the day or night to fuel his genius, and the finest musicians to play for him when he needed inspiration. His theatre in Middenheim had been more imposing, more *monumental*, than the Collegium Theologica. Never again would he demand such luxuries if he could but have a bed with a mattress, a fireplace and an axe to get wood, and a sufficiency of humble but honest fare for the table.

'The courts have found you responsible for quite a considerable sum of money. You have more creditors than a Tilean kingdom has illegitimate claimants to the throne.'

'Indeed, crown prince. That is why I am here. Through no fault of my own, I assure you. It is not my place to criticize an elector of the Empire, but your honoured colleague from Middenland has hardly acted in the spirit of fairness and decency over my situation. He undertook the responsibility for my production, and then had his lawyers find a way of breaking his contract with me...'

In fact, Detlef had been forced at knife-point to sign a statement absolving the elector of Middenland of any financial liability for *The History of Sigmar*. Later, the Konigsgarten Theatre had been burned to the ground by a rioting mob of tailors, carpenters, bit-part-players, musicians, ticket-holders, saddlers, bawds, merchants and inn-keepers. When faced with the choice between a pit of lime and a barrel of boiling tar, his trusted stage manager had denounced him. Everything he had had was seized by the elector's bailiffs and thrown to the creditors. And Middenland himself had elected to make an official visit to some southern state with a decent climate and an official edict against stage plays not of a tediously religious nature. No amount of petitioning could recall the former patron of the arts to the aid of the greatest actor-dramatist to put on a false nose since Jacopo Tarradasch himself. And since Detlef had always felt Tarradasch somewhat overrated, the calumny stung even more. He could conceive of no tragedy greater than that his art should be stifled. It was not for himself that he railed against the injustice of his life in prison, but for the world that was deprived of the fruits of his genius.

'Middenland is the beggar among electors,' said the crown prince. 'He has no elephants from the east, no golden idols from Lustria. Set beside the riches of the emperor, his fortune would barely pay for a pot of ale and a side of beef. Your debts are nothing.'

Detlef was astonished.

Seriously, Oswald said, 'Your debts can be taken care of.'

Detlef felt the tripwire coming. Here were the Great and the Good again, smiling and reassuring him that all would be taken care of, that his worries were thrown out with yesterday's slops. He had learned from his dealings with patrons that the rich are a different species. Money was like the fabled warpstone; the more contact you had with the stuff, the less like a human being you became.

His presentiment troubled him again. He was supposed to have a touch of magic in him through some wrong-side-of-the-blanket great-grandfather. Once in a while, he had intuitions.

'You could walk out of Mundsen Keep this afternoon,' the crown prince said, 'with crowns enough to set you up in fine style at any hostelry in Altdorf.'

'Highness, we are straightforward men, are we not? I would indeed relish the prospect of quitting my current accommodations. Furthermore, it would please me greatly to have the burden of my innocently-acquired debts lifted from me. And I have no doubt that your family has the wherewithal to accomplish such miracles. But, as you may know, I am from Nuln, a beneficiary of that city's famed houses of learning. My father began life as a street vendor of vegetables and rose through his own efforts to great wealth. Throughout his life, he remembered the lore of his initial calling, and he taught me a lesson far greater than any the priests and professors were able to impart. "Detlef," he said once to me, "nobody ever gives anything away. There is always a price." And that lesson comes back to me now…'

Actually, Detlef's father had always refused to talk about the days before he assembled the strong-arm gang who enabled him to corner the Nuln vegetable market by smashing the other traders' stalls. He had been too much of a miserable bastard to give his son any advice beyond 'don't go on the stage or I'll cut you off without a penny!' Detlef had heard that his father died of apoplexy during a meeting with the

Nuln tax collectors, at precisely the moment when it was suggested that his returns for the last thirty years would bear a close re-examination. His mother had decamped to the coastal city of Magritta in Estalia and taken up with a much younger man, a minstrel more noted for the contour of his tights than the sweetness of his voice. She hadn't exactly encouraged his genius either.

'In short, highness, I would know now, before accepting your generous offer of aid, what is the price for your intervention in my case? What do you want of me?'

'You're a shrewd fellow, Sierck. I want you to write and stage a play for me. Something less unwieldy than your *History of Sigmar*, but nevertheless a work of some standing. I want you to write and perform my own story, the story of my quest to Castle Drachenfels, and of the fall of the Great Enchanter.'

ACT TWO

I

IT TOOK A FULL week to negotiate the contract. During that time, Crown Prince Oswald arranged, much to Governor van Zandt's cold fury, that Detlef have his collar struck and be transferred to more comfortable quarters within the keep. Unfortunately for the administration of the prison, the only quarters that even approximated Detlef's idea of comfort were the governor's own official chambers in the central tower. Van Zandt was booted out to seek refuge in a nearby hostelry and Detlef took over his offices for his own business. Although still technically a convicted debtor, he took the opportunity to rearrange his circumstances. Instead of a single dirty blanket, he had an Imperial size bed brought to the governor's rooms; instead of Szaradat's rough treatment, he was attended by a poor unfortunate girl in whose case he took an interest and whose gratitude was memorable and invigorating; and instead of the cheese, bread and water, he was served a selection of the finest meats, wines and puddings.

Even for a week, however, he could not tolerate the drab and tasteless furnishings van Zandt evidently chose to live

with. It was hardly the governor's fault that his parents had
been a pair of pop-eyed uglies with little judgement when it
came to commissioning portraits from cross-eyed mounte-
banks, but it seemed odd that he should compound the
family shame by hanging over his desk an especially revolting
daub of the van Zandts, senior, bathed in the golden light of
some idiot's palette. After a morning in the room with the
thing, imagining the governor's fish-faced mother frowning
upon him with disapproval, Detlef personally threw the
painting off the balcony and had it replaced with a magnificent oil of himself in the role of Guillaume the Conqueror in
Tarradasch's *Barbenoire: The Bastard of Bretonnia*. He had a
generous impulse to leave it behind when he left, to cheer up
the cold-hearted official's surroundings with a daily reminder
of the keep's most notable past tenant, but then thought better of it. The oil, executed by the Konigsgarten Theatre's art
director, was too valued an item to leave for such a poor fellow to gaze dully upon while shuffling parchments and
sanctioning the mindless brutality of his staff.

Normally, he would have entrusted the business of the contract to his valued associate, Thomas the Bargainer. But
Thomas had been the first to turn on him, and stood at the
head of the list of creditors, with his hand out for repayment.
Therefore, Detlef took care of the tedious business himself.
After all, Thomas had bargained him into his contract with
the elector of Middenland. This time, he was certain, there
would be no hidden clauses to catch him later.

The agreement was that Oswald pledged to underwrite the
production of Detlef's *Drachenfels* to the depths of his trea-
sury, provided the dramatist himself lived modestly. Detlef
hadn't been sure about that particular condition, but then
reasonably assumed that the crown prince's idea of a modest
living would probably shame a sybarite's decadent dream of
total luxury. As Detlef put it, between sips of van Zandt's
Estalian sherry, 'all a man like me requires is food and drink,
a warm bed with a stout roof over it, and the means to repre-
sent my genius to the public.'

Detlef also decided to share his good fortune with his erst-
while cellmates, and insisted that Oswald settle their debts
too. In each case, the release could only be obtained if Detlef

promised to vouch for their good character and provide them with employment. That was no problem: Kosinski and Manolo were brawny enough to shift heavy scenery, Justus's previous occupation suggested he would make a fine character actor, Kerreth could cobble for the whole company, and Guglielmo would, his bankruptcy notwithstanding, make an admirable substitute for Thomas the Betrayer as business manager. Detlef even arranged, anonymously, for Szaradat's release, confident that the turnkey's base qualities would swiftly return him to prison. It would take years of suffering for him to regain, if he ever did, his unmerited position of privilege within the order of misery that was Mundsen Keep.

Meanwhile, Crown Prince Oswald had a ballroom in his palace reopened as a rehearsal hall. His mother had been fond of lavish parties, but since her death the position of the Empire's premier hostess had fallen to the Countess Emmanuelle von Liebewitz of Nuln. The old grand prince, struck down by ill-health and grief, pottered about with toy soldiers, refighting all his great battles in his private rooms, but the business of the von Konigswalds was done exclusively now by his son. Oswald's men were sent to seek out those remaining members of the Konigsgarten Theatre company who hadn't turned traitor. More than a few actors, stagehands and creative personnel who had sworn never again to be involved in a Detlef Sierck production were wooed back to the Prodigy of Konigsgarten by the von Konigswald name and the sudden settling of outstanding wages they had long ago written off as another loss in the notoriously hard life of the stage.

Word of Detlef's return spread throughout Altdorf, and was even talked about in Nuln and Middenland. The elector of Middenheim took advantage of the sudden interest to have *The History of Sigmar* published along with a self-composed memoir blaming the dramatist for the disaster of the production that had never taken place. The book sold well, and thanks to his ownership of the manuscript, the elector was able to avoid paying a penny to Detlef. One of Gruenliebe's balladeers composed a ditty about the foolishness of entrusting another major theatrical event to the architect of the *Sigmar* debacle. When the song came to the attention of

Crown Prince Oswald, the balladeer found his license to jest summarily revoked, his merry face no longer welcome in even the lowest dives and a passage paid for him on a trading expedition to Araby and the South Lands.

Eventually, the contract was drawn up, and Detlef and the crown prince put their seals to it. The greatest dramatist of his generation strolled through the open gates of the debtors' prison, dressed again in flamboyant finery, his grateful comrades a respectful twenty paces behind. It was the first good day of spring, and the streams of melting snow cleaned the streets around the depressing edifice of the keep. He looked back, and saw van Zandt fuming on one of his balconies. Two trusties were carrying a bent and muddy painting up the outside staircase of the tower. Van Zandt shook his fist in the air. Detlef swept the ground with his longfeathered cap and bowed low to the governor. Then, straightening, he gave a cheery wave to all the miserable souls peering out through the bars, and turned his back forever on Mundsen Keep.

II

'NO,' SCREAMED Lilli Nissen in her dressing room at the Premiere Theatre in Marienburg, as the fourth of the four priceless jewel-inset cut-glass goblets given her by the Grand Duke of Talabecland shattered into a million pieces against the wall. 'No, no, no, no, no!'

The emissary from Altdorf quaked as the famed beauty's cheeks burned red, and her haughty nostrils flared in unnatural fury. Her large, dark eyes shone like a cat's. The minute lines about her mouth and eyes, totally unnoticeable when her face was in repose, formed deep and dangerous crevices in her carefully-applied paint.

It was entirely possible, Oswald's man supposed, that her face would fall off completely. He wasn't sure he wanted to see what lay beneath the surface that had so enchanted sculptors, painters, poets, statesmen and – it was rumoured – six out of fourteen electors.

'No, no, no, no, no, no.'

She looked at the seal on the letter again, the tragic and comic faces Detlef Sierck had taken for his emblem, and tore it off with lacquered fingernails like the claws of a carrion bird. She had gone into her rant without even scanning the substance of the message, simply at the mention of the name of the man from whom it came.

Lilli's trembling dresser cringed in the corner, the bruises on her face eloquent testimony to the great beauty's hidden ugliness. The dresser had a lopsided face, and one of her legs was shorter than the other, forcing her to hobble on a thick-soled boot. Given the choice, Oswald's man would have at that moment chosen the dresser to warm his bed at the Hotel Marienburg this night, and left the actress who could inspire love in millions to her own devices.

'No, no, no, no.' The screaming was less shrill now, as Lilli digested the meat of Sierck's proposal. Oswald's man knew she would relent. Another starring role more or less meant nothing to the woman, but the name of Oswald von Konigswald must stand out on the page as if written in fire. He would be elector of Ostland soon, and Lilli had a collection to complete.

'No, no...'

The actress fell silent, her blood-red lips moving as she re-read the letter from Detlef Sierck. The dresser sighed, and came out of her corner. Without a complaint, she got painfully down on her knees and started picking up the pieces of the goblets, separating the worthless glass shards from the redeemable jewels.

Lilli looked up at Oswald's messenger and flashed a smile he would remember every time he saw a pretty woman for the rest of his life. She put her fingers to her temples, and smoothed away the cracks. Again, she was perfect, the loveliest woman who ever lived. Her tongue flicked over one sharp eyetooth – the dramatist had cast her well as a vampire – and her hand went to the jewelled choker at her throat. Her fingers played with the rubies, and then went lower, parting her negligee, revealing a creamy expanse of unrouged skin.

'Yes,' she said, fixing Oswald's man with her glance. 'Yes.' He forgot the dresser.

III

'HAVE I EVER told you about the time when the Crown Prince Oswald and I bested the Great Enchanter?' roared the fat old man.

'Yes, Rudi,' said Bauman, without enthusiasm. 'But this time you'll have to pay for your gin with coin, not the same old story.'

'Surely there's someone...' Rudi Wegener began, sweeping a meaty arm about.

The solitary drinkers of the Black Bat Tavern took no notice of him. His chins shook under his patchy grey beard, and he lurched from his stool at the bar, enormous belly seeming to move independently of the rest of his body. Bauman had reinforced the stool with metal braces, but knew that Rudi would still crush it to splinters one day.

'It's a fine tale, my friends. Full of heroic deeds, beautiful ladies, great perils, terrible injuries, treachery and deceit, rivers of blood and lakes of poison, good men gone bad, and bad men gone worse. And it ends nobly, with the prince destroying the monster, and Good Old Rudi there to guard his back.'

The drinkers looked down into their tankards. The wine was vinegary, and the beer watered down with rat's pee, but it was cheap. Not cheap enough for Rudi, though. Two pence a pint might as well be a thousand gold crowns if you don't have two pence.

'Come on, friends, won't anyone hear the story of good old Rudi? Of the prince and the Great Enchanter?'

Bauman emptied the remains of a bottle into a pot and pushed it across the polished and scarred wood towards the old man. 'I'll buy you a drink, Rudi…'

Rudi turned, alcoholic tears coursing down the fatty pockets of his cheeks, and put a huge hand around the pot.

'… but only on the condition that you *don't* tell us about your great adventures as a bandit king.'

The old man's face fell and he slumped on the stool. He moaned – he had hurt his back long ago, Bauman knew – and peered into the pot. He looked down at himself in the wine, and shuddered at some unspoken thought. The moment was a long one, an uncomfortable one, but it passed. He raised the pot to his mouth, and drained it in a draught. Gin flowed into his beard and down onto his much-stained, much-patched shirt. Rudi had been telling his lies in the Black Bat ever since Bauman had been old enough to help out his father behind the bar. As a boy, he had swallowed every story the fat old fraud dished out, and he had loved more than anything else to hear about Prince Oswald and the Lady Genevieve and the monster Drachenfels. He had believed every word of the tale.

But, as he grew up, he came to know more about life, and he discovered more about his father's clientele. He understood that Milhail, who would boast for hours of the many women he pursued and won, went home each night to his aged mother and slept alone in a cold and blameless bed. He learned that the Corin the Halfling, who claimed to be the rightful Head of the Moot dispossessed by a jealous cousin, was, in fact, a pick-pocket expelled from his home when his fingers got too arthritic to lift a purse unnoticed.

And Rudi, so far as he knew, had never adventured beyond Altdorf's Street of a Hundred Taverns. Even in his long-gone youth, the old soak couldn't have found a horse willing to go under him, hefted a weapon any more dangerous than a beer bottle – and then only to his lips – or stood up straight to any foeman who came his way. But, Rudi the Bandit King had been Bauman's childhood idea of a hero, and so now he generally had a drink or two to spare for the old fool whenever he hadn't the price in his pouch. He probably wasn't doing the old man that much of a kindness, since Bauman was certain Rudi was floating himself to a coffin on his wines and ales and the burning Estalian gin only he of all the Black Bat's patrons could stand.

It wasn't much of a night. Of the talkative regulars, only Rudi was in. Milhail's mother was sick again and Corin was in Mundsen Keep after a brief and unsuccessful return to his old calling. The others just nursed their miseries and drank themselves into a quiet stupor. The Black Bat was the losers' tavern. Bauman knew there were places with worse reputations – brawlers favoured the Sullen Knight, the unquiet dead flocked mysteriously to the Crescent Moon and the hard core of Altdorf's professional thieves and murderers could be found at the Holy Hammer of Sigmar – but few quite as depressing. After five straight years at the bottom of the street's dicing league, Bauman had withdrawn the tavern from the competition. Somewhere else could lose for a while. The only songs he ever heard were whines. And the only jokes he ever heard were bitter.

The door opened, and someone new came in. Someone who had never been to the Black Bat before. Bauman would have remembered him if he'd seen him. He was a handsome man, dressed with the kind of simplicity that can be very expensive. He was no loser, Bauman knew at once from the set of his jaw and the fire in his eyes. He was at his ease, but he was not the sort to be used to taverns. He would have a coach and horses outside, and a guard to protect them.

'Can I help you, sir?' Bauman asked.

'Yes,' the stranger's voice was deep and rich. 'I'm told that I can generally find someone here. An old friend. Rudolf Wegener.'

Rudi looked up from his pot, and turned on his stool. The wooden legs creaked and Bauman thought that this was finally going to be the tumble he had expected all along. But no, Rudi lurched upright, wiping his dirty hands on his dirtier shirt. The newcomer looked at the old man, and smiled.

'Rudi! Ulric, but it's been a long time…'

He extended a hand. A signet ring caught the light.

Rudi looked at the man, with honest tears in his eyes now. Bauman thought he was about to fall flat on his face in front of his old friend. With a painful thump, Rudi sank to one knee. Buttons burst from his shirt, and hairy rolls of belly fat surged out from behind the cloth. Rudi bowed his head, and took the outstretched hand. He kissed the ring.

'Get up, Rudi. You don't have to be like this. It is I who should bow to you.'

Rudi struggled upright, trying to push his gut back into his shirt and tighten his belt over it.

'Prince…' he said, struggling with the word. 'Highness, I…'

Recovering himself, he turned to the bar, and thumped it with his huge fist. Glasses and tankards jumped.

'Bauman, wine for my friend, Crown Prince Oswald. Gin for Rudi, King of the Bandits. And take yourself a pint of your best ale with my compliments.'

IV

ONCE ESTABLISHED IN the palace of the von Konigswalds, Detlef set to work. As usual, the play would grow into its final form as it was rehearsed, but he had to get a structure for it, cast the parts and rough out the characterizations.

He was allowed access to the von Konigswald library, and all the documents relating to the death of Drachenfels. Here was de Selincourt's *The House of von Konigswald*, with its flattering portrait of Crown Prince Oswald as a youth. And Genevieve Dieudonné's surprisingly slender *A Life. My Years as a Bounty Hunter in Reikwald, Bretonnia and the Grey Mountains* by Anton Veidt, as told to Joachim Munchberger; *Constant Drachenfels: A Study in Evil* by Helmholtz; *The Poison Feast and Other Legends* by Claudia Wieltse. And there were all the pamphlets and transcribed ballads. So many stories. So many versions of the same story. There were even two other plays – *The Downfall of Drachenfels* by that poltroon Matrac and *Prince Oswald* by Dorian Diessl – both, Detlef was delighted to find, appalling rubbish. With *The History of Sigmar*, he had found himself up against too many masterpieces on the same subject. Here, he had new dramatic ground to mark out as his own. It would especially amuse him to trounce his old critic and rival Diessl, and he worked in a lampoon of some of the more shabby mechanisms of the old man's terrible play into his own outline. He wondered if Dorian was still infecting the drama students at the Nuln University with his outmoded ideas, and if he would venture to Aldorf to see himself outstripped by the pupil he had dismissed from his lecture on Tarradasch when Detlef had pointed out that the great man's female characters were all the same.

The title bothered Detlef for some time. It had to have 'Drachenfels' in it. At first, he favoured *Oswald and Drachenfels*, but the crown prince wanted his name out of it. *The History of Drachenfels* was impossible: he didn't want to remind audiences of *Sigmar*, and, also, he was dealing only with the very end of a history that spanned thousands of years. Then he considered *The Death of Drachenfels*, *The Fortress of Drachenfels*, *The Great Enchanter*, *Defier of the Dark* and *Castle of Shadows*. For a while, he called it *Heart of Darkness*. Then, he experimented with *The Man in the Iron Mask*. Finally, he settled down with the simple, starkly dramatic one-word title, *Drachenfels*.

Oswald had promised to set aside an hour each day to be interviewed, to be questioned about the truth of his exploits. And he had endeavoured to track down those of his companions in adventure still living, to persuade them to come forward and discuss their own parts in the great drama with the writer who would set the seal on their immortality. Detlef had the facts, and he had a shape for his play. He even had some of the speeches written down. But he still felt he was only beginning to grasp the truths that would lie behind his artifice.

He began to dream of Drachenfels, of his iron face, of his unending evil. And after each dream, he wrote pages of dark poetry. The Great Enchanter was coming to life on paper.

Oswald was not without the aristocrat's traditional vanity, but he was strangely reticent on some subjects. He had commissioned Detlef's play as part of a celebration of the anniversary of his enemy's death, and he knew very well that the event would serve to increase his renown. Detlef gathered that it was important to Oswald to be in the public eye after some years as a background presence. He was already the elector in all but name, and his father wasn't expected to last out the summer. Eventually, he would have to be confirmed in his position and be, after the Emperor, one of the dozen most powerful men in the Empire. Detlef's *Drachenfels* would silence any voices that might speak out against the crown prince. Yet, for all Oswald's political canniness in backing a production that would remind the world of his great heroism just as he was ready to take part in the running of the Empire, Detlef still found the crown prince occasionally a little too modest for his own good. Incidents that in the accounts of others were hailed as mightily heroic he shrugged off with a simple 'it was the only thing to do' or 'I was there first, any of the others would have done the same.'

It wasn't until Rudi Wegener came forth to speak that Detlef began to understand what had happened in the Reikwald on the road to Castle Drachenfels, and how Oswald had bound together his companions in adventure almost by sheer force of will. And it wasn't until the cult of Sigmar finally allowed him to examine the *Proscribed Grimoires of Khaine* that Detlef realized quite how monstrously potent Drachenfels's age-spanning evil had been. He began to connect with the research he had done for *The History of Sigmar*, and – with a nauseating lurch in his stomach – tried to get his mind around the concept of a man, a mortal man born, who could have been alive in the time of Sigmar two-and-a-half thousand years ago and yet who was still walking when Detlef Sierck had been born. He had been four years old when Drachenfels died, exhibiting his prodigious genius in Nuln by composing symphonies for instruments he never got round to inventing.

Detlef wrote speeches, sketched settings, and whistled musical themes to Felix Hubermann. And *Drachenfels* began to take monstrous shape.

V

THE TALL, GAUNT man who stuttered too badly crept away, his moment in the spotlight over.

'Next!' shouted Vargr Breughel.

Another tall, gaunt man strode onto the make-shift stage in the von Konigswald ballroom. The crowd of tall, gaunt men shuffled and muttered.

'Name?'

'Lowenstein,' said the man in deep, sepulchral tones, 'Laszlo Lowenstein.'

It was a fine, scary voice. Detlef felt good about this one. He nudged Breughel.

'What have you done?' asked Breughel.

'For seven years, I was the actor-manager of the Temple Theatre in Talabheim. Since coming to Altdorf, I have played Baron Trister in the Geheimnisstrasse Theatre production of *The Desolate Prisoner*. The critic of the Altdorf *Spieler* has referred to me as "the premier Tarradaschian tragedian of his, or indeed any other, generation".'

Detlef looked the man up and down. He had the height, and he had the voice.

'What do you think, Breughel?' he asked, so low that Lowenstein couldn't hear him. Vargr Breughel was the best assistant director in the city. If there wasn't a prejudice against dwarfs in the theatre, Detlef thought, he'd be the second best director in the city.

'His Trister was good,' said Breughel. 'But his Ottokar was outstanding. I'd recommend him.'

'Have you prepared anything?' Detlef asked, addressing a tall, gaunt man for the first time this morning.

Lowenstein bowed, and launched into Ottokar's dying declaration of love for the goddess Myrmidia. Tarradasch had claimed to be divinely inspired the day he wrote it, and the actor gave the best reading Detlef had ever heard of the speech. He himself had never played in *The Loves of Ottokar and Myrmidia*, and if he had to be compared with Laszlo Lowenstein, he might consider putting it off a few decades.

Detlef forgot the tall, gaunt actor, and saw only the humbled Ottokar, a haughty tyrant brought to the grave by an obsessive love, dragged into bloody deeds by the most noble of intentions, and only now conscious that the persecution of the gods will extend beyond his death and torment him for an eternity.

When he finished, the crowd of tall, gaunt men – hard-bitten rivals who would have been expected to look only with hatred and envy upon such a gifted performer – applauded spontaneously.

Detlef wasn't sure, but he thought he'd found his Drachenfels.

'Leave your address with the crown prince's steward,' Detlef told the man. 'We'll be in touch.'

Lowenstein bowed again, and left the stage.

'Do you want to see anyone else?' Breughel asked.

Detlef thought a moment. 'No, send the Drachenfelses home. Then let's have the Rudis, the Meneshes, the Veidts and the Erzbets…'

VI

THE MADWOMAN was quiet. In her early days at the hospice, years ago, she had shouted and smeared the walls with her own filth. She told all who would listen that there were enemies coming for her. A man with a metal face. An old-young dead woman. She was constrained for her own good. She used to attempt suicide by stuffing her clothing into her mouth to stop her breathing, and so the priestesses of Shallya bound her hands by night. Eventually, she settled down and stopped making a fuss. She could be trusted now. She wasn't a problem any more.

Sister Clementine made the madwoman her especial concern. The daughter of rich and undeserving parents, Clementine Clausewitz had pledged herself to Shallya in an effort to pay back the debt she felt her family owed the world. Her father had been a rapacious exploiter of his tenants, forcing them to labour in his fields and factories until they dropped from exhaustion, and her mother an empty-headed flirt whose entire life was devoted to dreaming of the time when her only daughter could be launched in Altdorf society. The day before the first great ball, to which a pimply nine-year-old boy who was distantly related through marriage to the Imperial family was *almost* certainly going to come, Clementine had run off and sought the solace of a simple, monastic life.

The Sisters of Shallya devoted themselves to healing and mercy. Some went into the world as general practitioners, many toiled in the hospitals of the Old World's cities, and a few chose to serve in the hospices. Here, the incurable, the dying and the unwanted were welcome. And the Great Hospice in Frederheim, twenty miles outside Altdorf, was where the insane were confined. In the past, these cloisters had been home to two emperors, five generals, seven scions of electoral families, sundry poets and numberless undistinguished citizens. Insanity could settle upon anybody, and the sisters were supposed to treat each patient with equal care.

Clementine's madwoman couldn't remember her name – which was listed in the hospice records as Erzbet – but did know she had been a dancer. At times, she would astonish the other patients by performing with a delicacy and expressiveness that belied her wild, tangled hair and deeply-etched face. At other moments, she would recite a long list of names to herself. Clementine didn't know what Erzbet's litany meant, and – as one dedicated to a cult which forswore the taking of any intelligent life – would have been horrified to learn that her patient was recalling all those she had murdered.

Erzbet was supported in the hospice by generous donations. A person named Dieudonné who had never visited had ordered the banking house of Mandragora to set aside a hundred crowns a year for the hospice as long as the dancer was in its custody. And one of the first families of Altdorf also took an interest in her case. Whoever Erzbet had been, she had had some influential friends. Clementine wondered if she was the maddened daughter of some ashamed nobleman. But then again, her only regular caller was a remarkably fat and unsightly old man who smelled of gin and was clearly no one's idea of a leading light in high society. Who she had been was less important to the sister than who she would be.

Now, even Clementine had to admit Erzbet would most likely never again be anybody. Over the years, she had withdrawn into herself. During the hours she spent in the sunny quadrangle at the hospice, she simply stared into emptiness, not seeing the sisters or the other patients. She neither sewed nor sketched. She could not or would not read. She had not danced for over a year. She didn't even have nightmares any more. Most of the priestesses thought of Erzbet's quietness as a sign of merciful healing, but Sister Clementine knew this wasn't so. She was sinking fast. Now, she was a convenient patient – unlike some of the raving creatures the order had to deal with – but she was further into her own darkness than she had been when she was brought to the hospice.

The ravers – the biters, scratchers, kickers, screamers and resisters – got all the attention, while Erzbet sat still and didn't say anything. Sister Clementine tried to reach her, and took care to spend as much as an hour every day talking to her. She asked unanswered questions, told the woman about herself and brought up general topics. She never had the impression Erzbet heard her, but knew she had to try. Occasionally, she admitted to herself that she talked as much for her benefit as for Erzbet's. The other sisters were from a very different background, and were too often impatient with her. She felt a kinship with this troubled, silent woman.

Then, the man came from Crown Prince Oswald. A suave steward with a sealed letter for High Priestess Margaret. Somehow, Sister Clementine was disturbed by the steward's sleekness. His carriage was black, and had discreet bars fitted on it – incongruous next to the generous upholstery – specifically for this mission. The von Konigswald arms – a three-pointed crown against a spreading oak tree – reminded her of her silly mother's silly dreams. She didn't know if her parents had given up searching for her, or simply never cared enough to make the effort in the first place.

Margaret called her to the chapel, and told her to make Erzbet ready to take a trip. Clementine protested, but a simple look from the high priestess of mercy chilled her blood enough to dissuade her. The steward was with her when she went to see the madwoman in the courtyard. She thought the madwoman took notice of the man, and saw the old fears creeping back. Erzbet clung to her, kissing the silver dove on Sister Clementine's robe. She tried to soothe her patient, but couldn't be convincing. The steward stood aside, seeming not impatient, and didn't say anything. Erzbet had no personal possessions, had no clothes outside the white robe the hospice's residents all wore. All she had was herself, and now, it seemed, she belonged to another, to the whim of a prince.

Clementine took the dove-pin from her robe, and gave it to Erzbet. Perhaps it would be a comfort to her. She stroked some semblance of tidiness into the woman's hair, kissed her forehead and said her goodbyes. The steward helped detach Erzbet's fingers from Clementine's robe. That night, the sister of Shallya cried herself to sleep. The next morning, she was surprised and a little ashamed to find her pillow stiff with dried tears. She made her devotions and returned to her duties.

High Priestess Margaret never told Clementine that in the coach on the road to Altdorf, Erzbet had found uses for the two-inch steel pin on the back of the dove the sister had given the madwoman. She gouged out the steward's eye and, while he was screaming and floundering in his own blood, jammed the pin into her own throat.

As the dancer-assassin died, she named her dead for the last time. The steward had never introduced himself, so she had to miss him out. But, as she finally slipped into the darkness where evil things were waiting for her, she remembered to list her last victim.

'Erzbet Wegener…'

VII

KERRETH HAD PROVED skilled with more than simple shoe-making. When he had brought Detlef the samples of his other work, he had been promoted to head of the wardrobe department in what was now being called the Von Konigswald Players' Theatre. He had seamstresses and tanners working under him, and was coming up with impressive designs for the special costumes. His leather suits of armour looked like iron, but weighed a fraction of what they ought to. The battle extras loved wearing them. And, on his own time, he came up with five separate leatherwork masks for Drachenfels. Detlef realized he was lucky to have found the little cobbler in the keep. Otherwise, he would have fainted under the weight of his costume half-way through the first act. At the last estimate, twenty-five per cent of the actresses who had been up for the role of Erzbet had fallen in love with Kerreth, and, after those months in Mundsen Keep, he had been only too happy to oblige them. Detlef felt the barest touch of envy, but ignored it. There was so much to do.

VIII

LILLI NISSEN MADE an entrance while Detlef was busy shouting at Breughel about prop swords.

'Darling!' he screamed, his voice rising a full octave.

'Dearheart,' she answered. They flew into each other's arms and kissed noisily. Everyone stood and watched the greatest actor and actress in the Empire play an impromptu love scene.

'You're twice as lovely as you were the last time I saw you, Lilli. Your radiance knows no bounds!'

'And you, my genius, you have written me the greatest part any actress could hope to fill. I kiss each of your supremely talented fingers!'

Afterwards, Detlef told Breughel, 'It's a good thing that cow is playing a six hundred year-old in this one. It's the first time she's ever done anything near her real age.'

And Lilli shouted at her dresser, 'That fat, smug, oily monster! That foulest of worms! That viper-tongued tyrant! Only a personal summons from the grand prince of Ostland would persuade me to step into a room with that pus-oozing vermin, let alone play opposite him in another of his rot-awful shitguts melodramas!'

IX

Laszlo Lowenstein met his patron at dead of night in the back room of a supposedly empty house. He did not care who the man was, but often wondered what he hid behind his mask. Lowenstein's career had had its ups and downs since he was forced to quit Talabheim a few paces ahead of the witch hunters. A man of his talents and his habits was too easy to find, he reflected. He needed friends. Now he was in the Von Konigswald Players, he was protected by his association with the crown prince, even by his work with Detlef Sierck. But still he returned to his old patron, his original patron. Sometimes, years would go by without the man in the mask. Sometimes, they would meet on a daily basis.

Whenever Lowenstein needed him, the man got in touch. Usually through an intermediary. It had never been the same intermediary twice. Once, it had been a warpstone-altered dwarf, with a cluster of tentacles around his mouth and a jellied-over eye just opening in his forehead. This time, it had been a slender little girl dressed all in green. He would be given an address, and would find the man in the mask waiting for him.

'Laszlo,' the even, expressionless voice began, 'it's good to see you again. I hear you have been having a run of fortune lately.'

The actor was tense now – not all his patron's requests had been pleasant – but sat down. The man in the mask poured him some wine, and he drank. Like all the food and drink his patron had served him, it was excellent, expensive stuff.

'An indifferent house, don't you think?'

He looked at the room. It was undistinguished. Bare plaster, discoloured except where icons had hung. There was a rough table and two chairs, but no other furniture.

'I do believe it's due to be accidentally burned down tonight. The fire may spread to the whole street, the whole quarter…'

His mouth was dry now. He took more wine, and sloshed it around in his mouth. Lowenstein remembered another fire, in Talabheim. And the screams of a family trapped in the upper storeys of a fine house. He remembered the look of blood in the moonlight. It was red, but it seemed quite black.

'Wouldn't that be a tragedy, my dear friend, a tragedy?'

The actor was sweating, imagining expressions on the man's mask, imagining inflections in his voice. But there was nothing. Lowenstein's patron might just as well have been a tailor's dummy brought to life as a real man. He spoke as if he were reading his lines without any effort, just to get the words right.

'You have won yourself a fine role in the crown prince's little exercise in vanity, have you not?'

Lowenstein nodded.

'The *title* role?'

'Yes, but it's still a supporting part. Detlef Sierck, the playright, is taking the leading role, the young Prince Oswald.'

Lowenstein's patron chuckled, a sound like a machine rasping. 'Young Prince Oswald. Yes, how apt. How, thoroughly apt.'

Lowenstein was conscious of the lateness of the hour. He had to be at the palace early tomorrow, to be fitted by Kerreth the cobbler with his leather-iron outfit. He was tired.

'And you play…?'

'Drachenfels.'

The chuckle came again. 'Ah yes, the man in the iron mask. That must be uncomfortable, don't you think? An *iron* mask?'

The actor nodded, and the man in the mask laughed outright.

'What do…?'

'Come on now, Laszlo, spit it out.'

'What do you want of me?'

'Why, nothing, my friend. Just to congratulate you, and to remind you of your old attachments. I hope you shan't forget your friends as you achieve the fame you so richly deserve. No, I hope you shan't forget…'

Something small was crying softly in the next room. It bleated like a goat. Lowenstein felt the uncertain stirrings of his old desires. The desires that had led him to his nomadic life, that had made him a wanderer from city to city. Always cities, never towns, villages. He needed a population large enough to hide in. But he needed to hide while putting his face before audiences every night. It was not an easy situation. Without his mysterious patron, he'd have been dead seven times over.

Lowenstein controlled himself. 'I don't forget.'

'Good. You've enjoyed your wine, I trust?'

The crying was quite loud now, not like a goat or a lamb at all. Lowenstein knew what awaited him next. He wasn't as tired as he had thought. He nodded his head to his patron's question.

'Excellent. I like a man who enjoys his pleasures. Who relishes the finer things in life. I enjoy rewarding them. Over the years, I've greatly enjoyed rewarding you.'

He got up and opened a door. The room beyond was lit by a single candle. The thing that cried was tied to a cot. On a table beside it were laid out a trayful of shining silver implements such as Kerreth the cobbler might have, or one of the barber surgeons in Ingoldtstrasse. Lowenstein's palms were slick now, and his nails dug into them. He finished his wine with indecent haste, wiping a trickle from his chin. Trembling, he got up and walked into the other room.

'Laszlo, your pleasure awaits you…'

X

DETLEF WAS DISCUSSING sets with Crown Prince Oswald's architects. The crown prince had managed to arrange for the purchase of the actual fortress of Drachenfels, with the intention of staging the play in its great hall. The advantages were obvious, but so were the drawbacks. Some parts of the castle would have to be restored to their original condition, and others remade as dressing rooms, scenery docks and actors' quarters. A stage would be built in the great hall. Initially, Detlef was tempted by the idea of having the play take place in real time, with the audience tagging along after the characters as they made their way to the fortress and then penetrated its interior. But the scheme was too reminiscent of *The History of Sigmar* for Oswald to authorize.

Besides, while the audience would be few enough in number – only the most important citizens of the Empire would be privileged to attend the performance – they were not likely to be in the first bloom of youth. It would be difficult enough to transport the creaky and antique dignitaries to the fortress by the gently sloping road that had been impassable and daemon-haunted in Oswald's days, let alone the vertiginous path the adventurers had taken. Even if Detlef's cast could brave the perils, it would be likely that some high priest or lord chamberlain would take a nasty tumble from the sheer cliffs on top of which the fortress stood.

This would be the crowning achievement of his career, this single performance. But, all the while, Detlef was planning to prepare a less lavish version of his text more suited to ordinary theatres. He saw no reason why *Drachenfels* shouldn't enter the repertoire of every company in the Empire, on the condition that substantial royalties were paid him. He already had Guglielmo putting out feelers for a theatre in Altdorf where the play could have a good run after its much-publicized premiere. There was already much interest, with the involvement of the crown prince doing a good deal to off-set Detlef's bad reputation. Detlef was waiting for a good bid from a house which would let him stage his play by his own lights, and take the central role himself. Currently, he favoured Anselmo's on Breichtstrasse, but the more experimental Temple of Drama was running a close second. Anselmo's was just a bit too wrapped up in regurgitating two-hundred-year-old productions of Tarradasch's lesser works for the burghers and merchants who came to Altdorf and felt they had to snore through a play while in the city.

Detlef glanced over the architects' sketches, and put his initials to them. He was satisfied with their suggestions, although he would have to go himself to Castle Drachenfels before making any final decisions. After all, it should be safe now. The Great Enchanter had been dead for twenty-five years.

'Detlef, Detlef, a problem…'

It was Vargr Breughel, waddling into Detlef's chambers with his usual perpetual expression of anxiety. It was always a problem. The whole art of drama was nothing but a succession of problems solved, ignored or avoided.

'What now?' Detlef sighed.

'It's the role of Menesh…'

'I thought I'd told you to settle with Gesualdo. I trust you in matters dwarfish, you know. You ought to be an expert.'

Breughel shifted on his feet. He was not a true dwarf, but the stunted offspring of human parents. Detlef wondered if his trusted lieutenant didn't have a touch of the warpstone in his nature. A lot of people in the theatrical profession had an iota or two of Chaos in their make-up. Detlef himself had had an extra little toe on his left foot which his lamented father had personally amputated.

'There's been some controversy over your selection of the Tilean jester for the part,' said Breughel, waving a long curl of paper covered in blotty signatures. 'Word got out, and some of the dwarfs of Altdorf are presenting this petition. They're protesting against the representation of all dwarfs on the stage as comic relief. Menesh was a great hero to the dwarfs.'

'And what about Ueli the Traitor? Is he a great hero to the dwarfs?'

'Ueli wasn't a real dwarf, as you well know.'

'He's also not likely to be the source of much comic relief, is he? I can't think of many stab-in-the-back gags.'

Breughel looked exasperated. 'We can't afford to upset the dwarfs, Detlef. Too many of them work in the theatre. You don't want a scene-shifters' strike. Personally, I hate the smug bastards. Do you know what it's like being turned out of taverns for being a dwarf when you aren't one, and then being turned out of dwarf taverns for not being a real dwarf?'

'I'm sorry, my friend. I wasn't thinking.'

Breughel calmed down a little. Detlef looked at the illegible petition.

'Just tell them I promise not to make any unwarranted fun of Menesh. Look, here, I'm making some cuts…'

Detlef tore up some already discarded pages. Accidentally, the petition was among them.

'There, no more "short" jokes. Satisfied?'

'Well, there's another objection to Gesualdo.'

Detlef thumped his desk. 'What now? Don't they know that geniuses need peace of mind to create?'

'It's the one-armed dwarf actor we saw. He's insisting he have the role, that he's the only one who can play the part.'

'But Menesh only gets his arm torn off at the very end. I admit we could do some clever trickery with a fake limb full of pig's guts and have a convincing horror scene. But he'd never be able to go through the whole drama without the audience noticing the stiff and inactive hand. Besides, the fool was at least twenty years too old for the part.'

Breughel snorted. 'He would be, Detlef. He's the real Menesh!

XI

THE PRISONER WAS going to make an escape attempt. Anton Veidt could see Erno the burglar tensing himself for the break-away. They were only three streets away from the town house of Lord Liedenbrock, the citizen who had posted reward on the man. Once Veidt dropped his charge off and collected his bounty, Liedenbrock would be free to do whatever he wanted to get his property – twenty gold crowns, some jewels belonging to the countess and a gilded icon of Ulric – back. And since the thief had fenced the merchandise in another town and drunk away all the money, Liedenbrock would probably turn his mind towards extracting repayment in fingernails or eyes rather than more common currency. The lord had a reputation for severity. If he hadn't, he would have hardly employed Veidt.

The bounty hunter could tell precisely when Erno would make his run for freedom. He saw the alleyway coming a hundred yards away, and knew his man would try to duck into it, hoping to outdistance Veidt and find some willing blacksmith to get the chains off his arms and legs. He must think the old man wouldn't be able to run after him.

And, of course, he was right. In his youth, Veidt might have raced after Erno and brought him down with a tackle. But, then again, he would more likely have done exactly what he was going to have to do now.

'Veidt,' said the burglar, 'couldn't we come to some arrangement...'

Here was the alley.

'Couldn't we...?'

Erno swung his chains at the bounty hunter. Veidt stepped back, out of range. The burglar pushed aside a fat woman nursing a child. The baby started bawling, and the woman was in Veidt's way.

'Get down,' he shouted, drawing his dart pistol.

The woman was stupid. He had to shove her aside and take aim. The child was squealing like a roasting pig now.

The alleyway was narrow and straight. Erno couldn't weave from side to side. He slipped on some garbage, and fell, chains tangling about him. He rose again, and ran, reaching for a low wall. Sharply conscious of the pain in his twice-broken, twice-set wrist, Veidt brought his pistol up and fired.

The dart took Erno in the back of the neck, lifted him off his feet, and brought him down in a heap of limbs and chains amid the filth of the gutter. Evidently, the alley was used mainly by the inhabitants of the upper storeys of the adjacent houses as a receptacle for their wastes. The stones were thickly-grimed, and a smell of dead fish and rotting vegetables hung like a miasma in the air.

Veidt had been trying for the thighs. That should have brought Erno down, but kept him breathing. The money was the same, dead or alive, but now he would have to haul the deadweight carcass to Liedenbrock's house. And he was breathing hard already. He leaned against a slimy wall, and fought for breath.

A physician had told him that something was eating him up from the inside, a sickness that might be the result of his life-long addiction to the strong cigars of Araby. 'It's like a black crab feeding inside you, Veidt,' the man had said, 'and it'll kill you in the end.'

Veidt didn't mind. Everybody died. If it came to a life without cigars or death with them, he'd not have hesitated about his choice. He took out a cigar now, and his tinderbox. He drew in a double lungful of smoke, and had a coughing fit. He hawked black, ropy phlegm, and made his way down the alley, steadying himself against the walls.

Erno was dead, of course. Veidt pulled out his dart and wiped it clean on the corpse's rags. He reloaded the pistol, setting the spring and the safety catch. Then, he unlocked the chains, and slung them over his shoulder. Chains were an expensive item in his line of work. He'd been using these, forged especially by dwarf blacksmiths, for over ten years. They were good chains, and had kept far more dangerous men than Erno in his custody.

He took the dead man by his bare feet – he'd sold the boots after chaining him up – and dragged him back to the street. As he pulled, there were sharp pains in his chest. The black crab was settling on his ribs, he thought, eating away at the muscles holding bone together, and now his skeleton was grinding itself to dirt inside him. It wouldn't be much longer before he collapsed like a jellyfish, useless to himself.

His aim wasn't so good these days, either. Good enough, he supposed, but he used to be a champion shot. When bounty hunting had been slow, he'd been able to pick up extra income from winning contests. Longbow, crossbow, pistol, throwing knife: he'd been the best with them all. And how he'd taken care of his weapons! Each was honed to the perfect sharpness, oiled if need be, polished, and ready to kiss blood. He still tried to keep up, but sometimes things were more difficult for him than they had been.

Twenty-five years ago, briefly, he had been a hero. But fame passes quickly. And his part in the downfall of Drachenfels had been minor enough to be overlooked by most balladeers. That's why he had allowed Joachim Munchberger to publish Veidt's own account as a book. The mountebank had disappeared with all the profits, and it had taken him some years – working between jobs – to track him down and extract payment. Munchberger must have had to learn to write with his left hand.

Now, the whole thing was about to start up again. Crown Prince Oswald's emissaries had found him, and asked him to come forward and talk to a fat actor for some new version of the tale. Veidt would have refused, but money was offered, and so soon he would have to go through the whole dull story again for this Detlef Sierck – a runaway debtor himself, by all accounts – and again be overlooked while young Oswald luxuriated in the golden glow of glory.

Oswald! He had come a long way down the road since his days as a snot-nosed boy. Soon, he'd be picking his first emperor. While blubber-bellied Rudi Wegener was drowning himself in gin, crazy Erzbet was raving in some cell and Lady Eternity was gorging herself on virgins' blood. And Anton Veidt was where he'd always been, out on the streets, searching for the wanted and unwanted criminals, converting the guilty into crowns. Oswald was welcome to his position.

Erno was getting heavier. Veidt had to sit down in the street and rest. A crowd gathered around him as he watched over his goods, but soon went away again. Flies were buzzing about the dead man's face, crawling into his open mouth and nostrils. Veidt hadn't the strength to shoo them away.

So, haloed by insects, the two proceeded together towards the house of the fine gentleman.

XII

DETLEF WOKE UP to find himself face down in a sea of manuscript pages. He had fallen asleep at his desk. By the clock, it was three in the morning. The palace was cold and quiet. His candle had burned low, spilling wax onto the desk, but the flame still burned.

Sitting upright, he felt the dull throbbing in his head that always came with periods of extreme overwork. Sherry would help. He always had some nearby. He pushed his chair back, and took a bottle from the cabinet near the desk. He swigged a mouthful from the bottle, then poured himself a glass. It was fine stuff, like all the luxuries of the von Konigswald palace. He rubbed together his chilled hands to get the warmth back into them.

He ordered the pages on the desk, shuffling them together. His working text was nearly complete. All the alterations prompted by his interviews with Rudi Wegener, Menesh the dwarf and the crown prince were pencilled in, and he doubted whether the testimony of the bounty hunter Veidt or the vampire lady Dieudonné would make much difference. Research was the skeleton of the play, but the flesh on it was all Detlef

Sierck's. His audience would expect no less. Oswald had even
encouraged him to depart from history at a few points, the
better to reach the truth of the matter. Would that all patrons
were as enlightened in the matter of artistic license.

His headache began to fade, and he re-read a few pages. He
had been working on his curtain speech, the summation of
the drama, when he had fallen asleep, and an ink-trail
scratched across the bottom of the last sheet of paper.

He'd blotted his soliloquy with his cheek, and guessed the
ink would be dried in by now. He must look a fool.

His own words still moved him. He knew only he could do
justice to such a speech, only he could convey the triumph of
good over evil without falling into bathos or melodrama.
Strong men would weep as Detlef-as-Oswald spoke over his
fallen foe, finding at last a touch of sorrow for the ending of
even a life such as Drachenfels had led. He had planned to
have Hubermann underscore the scene with a solo gamba,
but now he decided that the music wouldn't be necessary.
The lone voice, the stirring words, would be enough.

> *'Let joyful towers a tintinnabulation sound*
> *That the Enchanter Great is under good ground,*
> *And let th'infernal churches sound their bells*
> *To welcome Constant Drachenfels.'*

Outside the window lay the grounds of the palace, and
beyond them the sleeping city. There was a full moon, and he
could see the immaculately laid-out lawns as if in a mono-
chrome etching. The crown prince's ancestors, the previous
electors of Ostland, stood in a row on pedestals, seeming
staid and monolithic. Old Maximilian was there, in his
younger days, waving a sword for the Empire. Detlef had seen
the current elector being assisted about the place by his
nurses, blathering to all who would listen about the great old
days. Everyone in the household knew the time of
Maximilian was drawing to an end, and that the days of
Oswald would soon be beginning.

The architects Oswald had engaged to assist in the settings
for the play were also planning to remodel some of the
palace. More and more, the crown prince was taking over the
business of the von Konigswalds. He spent most of his days
closeted with high priests, chancellors, Imperial envoys and

officials of the court. The succession should be smooth. And Detlef's *Drachenfels* would mark the start of the Oswaldian era. An artist is not always set aside from the course of history, he supposed. Sometimes, an artist could as much make history as a general, an emperor or an elector.

He scratched his moustache, and drank more sherry, savouring the quiet of the palace by night. It was so long since he had known sustained quiet. The nights of Mundsen Keep had been filled with terrible groans, the screams of those who slept badly and the incessant drip of the wet walls and ceilings. And his days now were a total cacophony of voices and problems. He had to interview actors and the leftovers of Oswald's adventurers. He had to argue with those too hidebound to see how to convert his ideas into actuality. He had to put up with the shrill complaints and the nauseating cooing of Lilli Nissen. And, through it all, there was the clumping of booted feet on wood as actors stamped through rehearsals, the hammerings of the workmen constructing devices for the play and the clatter of the cast members learning to fence for the fight scenes. Most of all, there was Breughel, always roaring 'Detlef, Detlef, a problem, a problem...'

Sometimes, he asked himself why he had chosen the theatre as an outlet for his genius. Then, he remembered...

There was nothing to compare it with.

A cold hand caressed his heart. Out there in the gardens, things were moving. Moving in the shadows of the electors' statues. Detlef wondered if he should raise the alarm. But something suggested to him that these shapes were not assassins or robbers. There was an unearthly languor to their movements, and he thought he detected a faint glow, as of moonlight, to their faces. There were a column of them now, robed like monks, their shining faces deeply shadowed. They moved in complete silence towards the house, and Detlef realized with a chill that they weren't displacing the grass and gravel as they walked. They trod on the air, floating a few inches above the ground, the cords of their robes trailing behind them.

He was frozen to the spot, not with fear exactly, but with fascination, as if under the influence of one of that species of venomous serpent that chooses first to charm, then to bite.

The window was open, but he did not remember unfastening it. the night air was cold on his face.

The monkish figures floated higher now, feet above the ground, drifting upwards towards the palace. Detlef imagined sharp eyes glittering in their indistinct, half-seen faces. He knew with a sudden burst of panic that whatever these beings might be they were here for a purpose, to visit him, to communicate specifically with Detlef Sierck.

He prayed to the gods he'd neglected. Even to the ones he didn't believe in. Still, the figures rose into the air. There were ten or twelve of them, he thought, but perhaps more. Perhaps as many as a hundred, or a thousand. Such a crowd couldn't assemble in the gardens of the palace, but perhaps they were there despite all possibility. After all, men didn't float.

A group of the figures came forward and hovered outside the window, barely out of Detlef's reach. There were three, and the one in the centre must be the spokesman. This figure was more distinct than the others. Its face was more defined, and Detlef could make out a forked, black beard and a hooked nose. It was the face of an aristocrat, but whether a tyrant or a benevolent ruler he could not tell.

Were these the spirits of the dead? Or daemons of darkness? Or some other variety of supernatural creature as yet uncatalogued?

The floating monk looked at Detlef with calm, shining eyes and raised an arm. The robe fell away and a thin hand appeared, its forefinger extended towards the playwright.

'Detlef Sierck,' said the figure in a deep, male voice. 'You must go no further into the darkness.'

The monk spoke directly into Detlef's mind, without moving his lips. there was a breeze blowing, but the apparition's robes weren't moving in it.

'You should beware…'

The name hung in the air, echoing in his skull before it was uttered…

'Drachenfels.'

Detlef could not speak, could not answer back. He was being warned, he knew, but against what? And to what purpose?

'Drachenfels.'

The monk was alone now, his companions gone, and fading away himself. His body suddenly caught the wind and was twisted this way and that, coming apart like a fragile piece of cloth in a gale, and wafted away on the air currents. In a moment, there was nothing left of him.

Covered in a cold sweat, his head hurting more than ever, Detlef fell to the floor, and prayed until he fell into a swoon.

When morning came, he discovered he had watered and fouled himself in fear.

ACT THREE

I

IT WAS A typical riverboat romance. Sergei Bukharin had travelled down the Urskoy from Kislev, an ambassador to the Empire from Tsar Radii Bokha, Overlord of the North. He joined the *Emperor Luitpold* just after the confluence of the Urskoy and the Talabec. Genevieve was immediately taken with the tall, proud man. He had won his scars championing the tsar against the altered monstrosities of the Northern Wastes, and wore his hair and moustaches in long braids threaded with ceramic beads. He radiated strength, and his blood was richer than any she had tasted since her retirement to the convent.

Aside from Henrik Kraly, Oswald's steward, Sergei and Genevieve were the only passengers on the *Luitpold* travelling the length of the Talabec to Altdorf. There was a glum and withdrawn elven poet who had come down from Kislev with Sergei and debarked at Talabheim, but he kept his purposes to himself and was shunned and mistrusted by Captain Iorga and his oarsmen. Of course, Genevieve was shunned and mistrusted too, but they seemed better able to deal with her condition than this alien, unknowable creature. At

Talabheim, the cabins were swelled by an influx of merchants, a pair of Imperial tax collectors and a major in the service of Karl-Franz who insisted on debating military matters with Sergei.

Genevieve spent the long, slow days on the long, slow river belowdecks, dreaming restlessly in her bunk, and her dizzying nights with Sergei, delicately picking off his scabs and sampling his blood. The Kislevite seemed to enjoy the vampire kiss – as most humans do if only they allow themselves – but was not otherwise all that interested in his deathless lover. When not in her arms, Sergei preferred the company of Major Jarl or Kraly. Genevieve had heard that the tsar's people put little store by women in general, and vampire women in particular. There was the famous example of the Tsarina Kattarin, who had sought the Dark Kiss and extended her reign over Kislev. A conspiracy of her great-great-grandchildren, frustrated at the block she represented to the dynastic succession, had led to her well-merited assassination. The vampires of Kislev and the World's Edge Mountains were all like Wietzak, self-important Truly Dead monsters who at once looked down on humankind as cattle and feared the day-dwellers for their hawthorn and silver.

She never pressed the matter with Sergei, but she guessed the brave warrior was a little afraid of her. That could well be the attraction for him, the desire to overcome a breath of fear. For her part, she was pleased to pass the dull journey – mile after mile of tree-lined banks, and the eternal grunting and straining of the bonded oarsmen – with a strong taste in her mouth and a roughly handsome face to look at. By the time they were within a few days of Altdorf, she was already growing bored with her Kislevite soldier-diplomat, and although they exchanged accommodation addresses, she knew she would never see him socially again. There were no regrets, but there were no really pleasant memories either.

The *Luitpold* upped oars as it was hauled to the quayside, between two tall-masted ocean-going merchant ships down from the Sea of Claws with goods from Estalia, Norsca and even the New World. Sergei strode down the gangplank, saluted her from the docks and marched off to court, presumably intending to stop off with Major Jarl at the first bawdy house along the way to remind himself of the feel of a real woman. To her surprise, Genevieve found a tear welling in her eye. She wiped the red smear away and watched her lover walk off with his friend.

'My lady,' said Kraly, impatient now the trip was ended. 'The crown prince's coach is waiting.'

It was an impressive vehicle, and out of place on the malodorous docks of Altdorf, between the stacked-up goods and the dray-carts. Liveried servants waited by the black and red carriage. The arms of von Konigswald were picked out in green and gold. Kraly gave a dock-worker a crown to carry Genevieve's luggage from the *Luitpold* to the coach. She refrained from mentioning that, for all her girlish appearance, she could best the emissary's bruiser in an arm wrestling contest and pick up a heavy trunk one-handed.

Genevieve bade a respectable farewell to Captain Iorga, who looked relieved to be rid of his half-dead passenger but wasn't afraid enough not to suggest she book a return passage with him if she intended to go back to the convent in a month or so.

After years in the convent, the scents and sounds of Altdorf were again a revelation. The *Luitpold* had pulled into the docks just after sunset. Torches had been lit to facilitate late workers, and Genevieve could smell, taste and hear as well as any creature of the night. Here was the largest city in the Empire; indeed, in the Known World.

Built upon the islands of the Reik and the Talabec, but extending widely on the banks, Altdorf was a city of bridges and mudflats, surrounded by tall, white walls with distinctive red tiles. Hub of the Empire, home of the Imperial court and the great Temple of Sigmar, and known, so the guidebooks say, for its universities, wizards, libraries, diplomats and eating houses. Also, as the guidebooks omit to mention, its cutpurses, spies, scheming politicians and priests, occasional outbreaks of plague and ridiculous overcrowding.

None of this had changed in twenty-five years. As they pulled into the city, Genevieve noticed that yet another layer of dwellings had been built upon the mudflats, creating a permanently wet, permanently unhealthy beehive structure in which the poor – dock labourers, dwarf wall engineers, street traders – lived in a distinct counterpoint to the fine houses of Altdorf's rich.

There weren't many vampires, because of the bridges. Wietzak and his kind would have found themselves penned in on all sides by running water. Were she ever fully to die and become like them, one of the Truly Dead vampires, a walking corpse with an eternal bloodlust, she would have to avoid this city for ever. For now, she drank in all the sensations, seeking out the pleasant scents of good Altdorf cooking and a ready-to-be-loaded cargo of herbs and ignoring the mud, the rotting fish and the sheer press of unwashed humankind. Left to herself, she would be glutted on blood tonight, but she supposed other arrangements had been made for her. A shame, for here there was life in the night. The Crescent Moon would be opening for business, and other taverns, the theatres, concert halls, circuses, gaming houses. All the rich, gaudy, rotten, beguiling pursuits of the living. The things which, in six-and-a-half centuries, Genevieve had been unable to put behind her.

The door of the carriage swung open, and an elegant man got out. He was so simply dressed that, for a moment, Genevieve took him for another steward. Then, recognition came…

'Oswald!'

The crown prince grinned and stepped forward. They embraced, and she heard again the call of his blood. She touched his bare neck with her wet tongue, connecting electrically between beard and collar with his life force.

He broke the embrace and took a good look at her.

'Genevieve… my dear… it's so hard to get used to it. You're the same. It could have been yesterday.'

Twenty-five years.

'To me, highness, it *was* yesterday.'

He waved her formality away. 'Please, no titles. It's always Oswald to you, Genevieve. I owe you so much.'

Recalling herself unconscious and at the mercy of the iron-faced fiend of her dreams, she responded, 'Surely, it is I who owe you, Oswald. I still live only by your sufferance.'

He had been a beautiful boy, with his golden hair and his clear eyes. Now, he was a handsome man, with darker colouring, lines of character and a man's beard. He had been slender and wiry, surprisingly strong and agile in battle, but still slightly awkward with a sword in his hand. Now, he was as well-muscled as Sergei. His body felt hard and healthy beneath his jerkin, and his tights revealed well-shaped calves and thighs. Oswald von Konigswald had grown up. He was still barely a prince, but he looked every inch the elector he was soon to become. And his eyes were still clear, still bright with integrity, with emotion, with adventure.

Impulsively, he kissed her. She tasted him again, and this time it was she who drew back, for fear that her red thirst would overwhelm decorum. He helped her into the coach.

'There's so much to tell, Genevieve,' he began, as they trundled through the crowds of the docks towards the city thoroughfares. 'So much has happened…'

A street singer was performing by the Bridge of Three Towers, a comic song about a woodcutter's daughter and a priest of Ranald. When he sighted the arms upon the approaching carriage, he switched to the ballad that told of the death of Drachenfels. Oswald reddened with embarrassment, and Genevieve couldn't help but be a little satisfied to see his flush. This version of the tale was entitled 'The Song of Bold Oswald and Fair Genevieve' and imputed that the prince had taken on the Great Enchanter 'for the love of his long-dead lady.' She wondered, not for the first time, whether there had ever really been anything between them. Looking back on it, Genevieve supposed it would have been strange had they *not* fallen in love on the road to Castle Drachenfels. But, in his terms if not hers, that was half a life ago. Even Oswald was not about to present a vampire barmaid at court.

When the bridge and the song were behind them, Oswald began to talk of his theatrical venture.

'I have engaged a very clever young man. Some call him a genius and some a damned fool. Both factions are right, but generally the genius outweighs the fool, and perhaps it is the foolery that fuels the genius. You will be impressed with his work, I'm sure.'

Genevieve allowed herself to be lulled by the creak of the wheels, the clap of hooves on cobbles and the pleasant fire of Oswald's voice. The carriage was nearing the Altdorf palace of the von Konigswalds now. They were in the wide streets of the city's most exclusive area, where the mansions of the foremost courtiers stood in grounds spacious enough to accommodate a veritable army of lesser men. Smartly uniformed militiamen patrolled the streets to keep out the bad elements, and torches burned all night to light the way home for the weary aristocrat after a hard evening's toadying and prancing in the corridors of the Imperial palace. Genevieve had not often been in this quarter during her century in Altdorf. The Crescent Moon was back near the docks, in a bustling, lively, dirty avenue known as the Street of a Hundred Taverns.

'I'd like you to talk to Detlef Sierck, to give him the benefit of your recollections. You play a leading part, of course, in his drama.'

Genevieve was amused by Oswald's enthusiasm. She remembered him as a boy declaring that were he not expected by his family to take the role of elector after his father passed on, he would have chosen to be a travelling player. His poetry had won many plaudits, and she sensed that the grown man regretted that the demands of public life had prevented him from continuing to wield his quill. Now, by association, he could return to the arts.

'And who, Oswald, is to play me?'

The crown prince laughed. 'Who else? Lilli Nissen.'

'*Lilli Nissen!* That's ridiculous. She's supposed to be one of the great beauties of the age, and I'm...'

'...barely pleasing to look upon. I knew that'd be your reaction. In Kislev they say "beware the vampire's modesty". Besides, all is equal. I'm to be played by a dashing young genius who has broken more hearts than the emperor's militia have heads. We are speaking here of the theatre, not of dry-as-dust historical tomes. Thanks to Detlef Sierck, we'll all live for ever.'

'My darling, I'll already live for ever.'

Oswald grinned again. 'Of course. I had forgotten. I might also mention that I have met Lilli Nissen, and, startling through she undoubtedly is, she cannot compare to you.'

'So flattery is still considered an accomplishment at the court of the Emperor?'

The coach paused, and there was a rattling of chains.

'Here, we're there.'

The great gates, inset with a wrought-iron von Konigswald shield, swung open, and Oswald's coach turned into the wide driveway. There was some commotion up ahead, outside the palace itself. Trunks were piled high, and people were arguing loudly. An imposing, slightly overweight, young man in an elaborate and undeniably theatrical outfit was shouting at a quavering coachman. Beside them, a dwarf was hopping from one foot to another. There were other outlandishly dressed characters present, all serving as an audience for the great-voiced shouter.

'What's this?' Oswald cried. He clambered out of the still-moving coach and strode towards the knot of arguers. 'Detlef, what's happening?'

The shouter, Detlef, turned to the crown prince and fell briefly silent. In an instant, Genevieve felt the young man – the young genius, if Oswald was to be trusted – catch sight of her. She was leaning from the coach. They exchanged a look each was to remember for a long time thereafter, and then the moment was past. Detlef was shouting again.

'I'm leaving, highness! I don't need to be warned twice. The play is off. I'd rather be back in Mundsen Keep than persecuted by ghosts. My company and I are withdrawing from the project, and I strongly suggest that you drop the matter yourself unless you want to be visited by floating monks who speak without speaking and carry with them the odour of the grave and a strong suggestion that anyone who defies them will be joining them in the afterlife!'

II

DETLEF HAD TAKEN hours to calm down. But Crown Prince Oswald had spoken reasonably and at length, trying to put some less threatening interpretation upon the monkish manifestations.

'Ghosts can be petty, misleading even, and yet they are not known for their intervention in mortal matters.' He waved an elegant hand in the air, as if conjuring the harmless spirits of which he spoke. 'The palace is old, haunted many times over.'

That was all very well, Detlef thought, but Oswald hadn't stared the deathly things in the face and been given direct orders by the dead.

'It is said that whenever a von Konigswald draws near death, the shades of his ancestors return to bear him away with them. When the grandfather for whom I am named lay comatose with the brain fever, the noseless spectre of Schlichter von Konigswald was seen waiting implacably at his bedside…'

Detlef was unconvinced. He still remembered the ghost monk's piercing eyes and bony forefinger. 'You'll pardon me for mentioning it, highness, but in this case, you seem to be

in the pink of good health while it is I, who can boast no relationship to your noble house, who has been placed under the
threat of death.'

A grave look came over the prince. 'Yes, Detlef,' he said gently, 'but my father, the elector…'

The crown prince nodded towards the corner of the room,
in which the elector of Ostland was coughing gently as he
played with his toy soldiers, mounting an assault on the coal
scuttle.

'Hurrah for the general,' cried Elector Maximilian. It must
have been near his bed-time.

Oswald looked at Detlef, and Detlef felt suitably chastened.
The old man was indeed on the point of expiry. His mind had
long since crumbled under the sieges of age, and his body was
rapidly failing. But there was still the matter of the daemon
monks and their levitation tricks.

'A drink, Detlef?'

Detlef nodded, and Oswald poured out a generous measure of Estalian sherry. Detlef took the goblet, and ran his
thumb over the embossed von Konigswald shield. Here, in
the warmth of a well-lit room, with the calm, unaffected
Oswald and a battery of well-armed servants, the phantoms
of the night seemed less menacing. If he came to think about
it, the monks were far less impressive a manifestation than
the tricked-up appearance of Drachenfels's daemon-pig servitors he was planning for the play. If it came to it, the afterlife
could not compete with a Detlef Sierck production for supernatural spectacle.

'So, that's settled? Your production will continue?'

Detlef drank, feeling better. There was still something that
troubled him, but he instinctively trusted the crown prince.
Anyone who could walk alive out of the fortress of
Drachenfels must have some experience with the unearthly.

'Fine. But I'll want you to detail some of your guards to
watch over the company. There have been too many "accidents," you know…'

Kosinski had broken his ankle thanks to a carelessly
anchored – or tampered with – piece of scenery. Gesualdo the
Jester had been struck down with a mysterious sweating sickness, and Vargr Breughel was having to read his lines in

rehearsal. Someone had broken into Laszlo Lowenstein's rooms and shredded his collection of playbills. And every bit player and scene shifter was telling a spook story of some sort. The only thing that was running as expected about the production was that Lilli Nissen was proving awkward and hiding in her rooms most of the time. She had expended more energy on fluttering her doubtless counterfeit eyelashes at Oswald than on learning her speeches. Detlef had heard of blighted productions before, and none could have been more thrice-cursed than *The History of Sigmar*, but there were more tripwires and hidden pits along this route than he had a right to expect. And the company had not even made its way to Castle Drachenfels yet.

'That might not be ill-advised, Detlef. We both have more than enough enemies in Altdorf.'

Oswald summoned a servant, and gave him brief instructions.

'There'll be twenty men, under the command of my trusted aide Henrik Kraly, at the disposal of your company tomorrow. Your rooms will be guarded by night.'

The servant hurried off.

'And I'll have your chamber exorcized by the priests of whichever god you favour. I don't hold out much hope, though. This place is too old for exorcisms to take. It's been tried many times, I believe, and there are always new ghosts springing up. There's a story about a bleeding child who trails his grave garments behind him, and there's the skull-faced governess who radiates an eerie blue light, not to mention the phantom dog who recites passages from Tarradasch...'

Oswald seemed to warm to the subject, and was displaying an unhealthy, childish relish in the dark history of his home.

'There's no need to elaborate, highness. I believe I appreciate the situation.'

'And our ghosts are as nothing to the ghosts of the Imperial palace. The first Emperor Luitpold was reputed to have been witness to no fewer than one hundred and eighty-three spectral manifestations in his lifetime. And Albrecht the Wise's hair was white before he was thirty thanks to the sudden apparition of a daemon of the most frightful appearance dressed in the uniform of the Imperial Guard...'

'The general has triumphed again!' shouted the elector, holding high one particular lead hero. 'Eggs all round! Eggs for the troops!'

The old man's nurse quieted him down, and led him away by the hand to his bedroom. Oswald was embarrassed, but clearly felt for his father's condition.

'You should have seen him as he was when I was a boy.'

Detlef bowed slightly. 'Men are not responsible for their dotage, any more than they are for their infancy.'

There was a brief silence. The troubles passed from Oswald's face, and he turned to his other guest.

'And now, you must meet the heroine of your piece... Genevieve Dieudonné.'

The pale girl came forward, curtsied prettily, and offered her slim, white hand to Detlef. He bowed to her, and kissed her knuckles. She was cool to the touch, but didn't have the dead, slightly rancid appearance of the two other vampires Detlef had met. It was difficult not to think of her as the equal in age and experience of any of the young actresses and dancers Detlef had known in the theatre. She hardly seemed more than a year or two at most out of her schooling, ready to embark upon her first freedoms, fully prepared to be young. And yet she had seen six and a half centuries go by.

'Enchanted,' he said.

'Likewise,' she replied. 'I've been hearing about you. I trust that my reputation is in good hands with your quill.'

Detlef smiled. 'I shall have to rewrite several speeches now that I have seen you. It would be unnatural for anyone to chance across such beauty and not remark upon it.'

Genevieve smiled too. Her eyeteeth were a fraction longer and sharper than a normal girl's would have been. 'Evidently, you and Oswald have studied bottom-kissing flattery under the same tutors.'

The crown prince laughed. Detlef, to his surprise, found the bizarre woman charming.

'We must talk,' Detlef said, suddenly keener on an interview. 'Tomorrow, in the daytime, we could take tea and go through my text. It is still developing, and I would greatly appreciate your thoughts upon the drama.'

'Tomorrow it shall be, Mr Sierck. But let's make it after sunset. I'm not at my best in the daytime.'

III

HIS PATRON HAD done so much for him. It was about time Lowenstein did something for his patron. Even something as distasteful, dangerous and illegal as grave robbery.

Besides, it wasn't really grave robbery; the woman wasn't yet buried. His patron had told him she could be found packed in ice at the shrine of Morr. The corpse was awaiting the Emperor's coroners. And Lowenstein's pleasure. The tall, gaunt actor passed through the door of the shrine, glancing up at the black stone raven that stood on the lintel, its wings spread to welcome the dead, and those whose business was with the dead.

Opposite the shrine was the Raven and Portal, the tavern favoured by the priests of Morr. The black bird on its sign swung in the wind, creaking as if squawking to its cousin across the way. Nearby were the Imperial cemeteries, where the richest, the most lauded, the most famed were interred. In Altdorf, as in every city, Morr's Town was the district of the dead.

The man in the mask had smoothed Lowenstein's way considerably. A guard had been drugged, and lay in the foyer of the low, dark building, his tongue protruding from a foamy mouth. The keys hung precisely where his patron had told him they would be. He had been in mortuaries before, for recreational purposes, and had no undue fear of the dead. Tonight, leather against his face, he had no undue fear of anything.

He pulled the watchman out of the way, so he could not be seen by any late passerby. The shrine smelled strongly of herbs and chemicals. He supposed that if it didn't, it would stink of the dead. This was where those who died questionably were brought. The Emperor's coroners examined the bodies for traces of foul play, or hitherto unlisted disease. It was a shunned place. Just to make sure, he felt for the watchman's heart. It was strong. He pinched the man's nostrils and put a hand to his sticky mouth until the beat was stilled. His patron wouldn't mind. Lowenstein thought of it as an offering to Morr.

There were sounds outside, in the night. Lowenstein pressed himself into the shadows, and held his breath. A party of drunken revellers passed by, singing about the woodcutter's daughter and the priest of Ranald.

'Oh, my pretty laaaad, what you've done to me,
My father will do with his aaaaaxe to thee...'

One of them relieved himself loudly against the marble wall of the shrine, bravely cursing Morr, god of death. Lowenstein grinned in the darkness. The soak would come to know the god eventually, as do all, and his curse would be remembered.

Morr, god of death, and Shallya, goddess of healing and mercy, were the deities who really ruled the lives of men. The one for the old, the other for the young. You could placate the one or beg for the intercession of the other, but, in the end, Shallya would weep, and Morr would take his prize.

Lowenstein felt closer to Morr than all the other gods. In the Nuln production of Tarradasch's *Immortal Love*, he had played the god of death, and had been comfortable in the black robes. As he was comfortable now in the armour and mask of Drachenfels.

Tonight, he could meet his patron mask to mask, he thought. He had kept his costume with him, and worn the mask for his trip to the shrine. It served to shield his identity, but also he felt a strange ease when hidden behind it. Two days ago, he had noticed horny ridges budding under the skin of his forehead, and felt a roughening of his normally sunken cheeks. He must have caught a touch of warpstone. The mask served to conceal his alterations. With the leather over his face, he felt himself stronger, more alive, more powerful. If his patron had given him this mission in Nuln, he would have been anxious, jittery. Now, he was cool and decisive. He was changing, altering.

The drunks were gone. The night was quiet. Lowenstein proceeded to the back room of the shrine, where the bodies were kept. It was down a short stairway, its walls set into the earth. He touched tinder to a candle, and carefully descended the broad stairs. It was cold, and slow-melting ice dripped to the flagstone floor. Strong-smelling herbal possets hung from the beams, so the nostrils of visitors would not be offended. On raised biers lay the suspiciously dead of Altdorf. Or, at least, the suspiciously dead the Emperor's court cared about.

Here was a well-dressed young blood, his arm ending in a ragged stump, his throat torn out by some beast. Here was a little boy, his face flushed unnaturally red, his belly opened. Lowenstein stopped by the child, seized by a desire to place his hand on the apparently fevered brow, to find it hot or cool. He passed on, glancing at each in turn. Death by violence, death by illness, death by causes unknown. All death was here. The priests of Morr had placed amulets of the raven around the necks of all their charges, to signify the flight of the spirit. To the cult of Morr, remains were just clay. Bodies were revered for the sake of the living; the spirit was in the hands of the gods.

Finally, Lowenstein came to the bier he was looking for. The dead woman was out of place in such a wealthy shrine. In her drab and patched gown, she looked more the type to be left in the streets to rot than to be pored over by the coroners and troubled by the concern of Crown Prince Oswald. All deaths among such people were suspicious, and yet few attracted the attention of the priests of Morr. All the other corpses here were from the monied classes. This woman had clearly been poor.

Her throat had been raggedly cut, and the instrument lay on the ice beside the body. It was the dove of Shallya, blasphemously used in suicide. Lowenstein touched the open wound, and found it cold and wet. He brushed the lank, greying hair from the haggard face. The woman might have been pretty once, but that would have been long before her death.

As a young man, Lowenstein had seen Erzbet dance. It was in Nuln, in a travelling fair in the Grand Square. The woman had performed an exhausting solo, combining the high balletic techniques of the Nuln opera with the wild, primitive displays of the forest-dwelling nomads.

He had been aroused by the performance, by the tanned legs that kicked up her skirts, and by the dark eyes that caught the firelight. She hadn't paid him any notice. That had been the night Bruder Wiesseholle, king of the city's thieves and murderers, was killed. The next day, the fair was gone, and the criminals of Nuln were without a ruler. Erzbet had been good. Twenty-five gold crowns was her price. It had never varied, whether her intended was a mighty lord or a humble beadle. He had heard that – poor fool – she always insisted her clients debate ethics with her, and justify the removal from the world of those they wished to be rid of.

And here she was, Morr's meat at last. Her dead would be waiting for her, Bruder Wiesseholle and the numberless others. He hoped she remembered her ethical discussions now, and could justify each of her assassinations.

He put down his candle by the corpse's head and prepared to take what he had come for. If he were to plunder the other biers, he would doubtless find rings, coins, necklaces, stout boots, silver buttons, golden buckles. But Erzbet had no goods to lose, had nothing Lowenstein's patron could possibly want.

Except her heart.

Lowenstein took the small knives, honed to a razor's edge, from their oilcloth, and tested the one he chose against the ball of his thumb. It stung as it sliced with the merest touch.

And her eyes.

IV

GENEVIEVE TOOK OFF her tinted glasses and looked up at the fortress of Drachenfels. It seemed different now, smaller. It was a pleasant spring day, and the ride up from the village was almost easy. The last time she had been this way, they had avoided the road – it was littered with the bones of those who had thought they could just walk up to the castle and knock on the door – and scaled the precipitous cliffs. There were other abandoned castles in the Grey Mountains, and they were no more imposing, no more haunted than this one. There were none of the traditional signs of an evil place: birds sang, the local vegetation flourished, milk went unsoured, animals were not mysteriously agitated. Even with her heightened awareness, Genevieve could sense nothing. It was as if the Great Enchanter had never been.

Of course, Oswald's men had prepared the way. Henrik Kraly had sent out a squadron of cleaners, cooks, carpenters and servants to make the place ready for occupation. There had been some initial reluctance among the villagers who had lived all their lives in the shadow of Drachenfels to hire on with the company, but the crown prince's gold had overcome many objections. The lad who saw to her horse after she dismounted must have been born well after the death of Drachenfels. The young of the region were reluctant to believe the stories told by their parents and grandparents. And some of the old were impressed enough by the ballads of Oswald and Genevieve to conquer their aversion to the ruin and take positions with Detlef's troupe.

The genius was in good spirits as he rode at the head of his gypsy caravan of actors, musicians and show people. He was a good conversationalist, and eager to talk with Genevieve. They had been through the minutiae of Oswald's quest, of course, but the dramatist was also interested in the rest of her long life, and was skilled at drawing out incidents she hadn't spoken of for centuries. The breadth of his learning was impressive, and she found him well-informed about the great men and women of earlier eras. She had known Tarradasch, had seen his plays during their original runs, and cheered Detlef greatly with her opinion that the great dramatist was less skilled as an actor and director than as a writer.

'A regional touring company today could better the original Altdorf productions of Tarradasch's masterpieces without breaking a sweat,' she opined.

'Quite! Yes! Exactly!' he agreed.

It was a performance in itself, moving the company from the von Konigswald palace in Altdorf to the remote mountain fastness, and they had been on the road for some weeks. But the journey flew by, with stop-overs at the best inns, and leisurely evenings with the cast discussing their roles and practising their swordfights. By comparison, the original journey had been long, uncomfortable and fraught with danger. Genevieve felt nothing as she passed the sites of battles longsince won. She had made brief pilgrimages to the graves of Conradin – though there had only been bones to bury – and Heinroth, and found the markers Oswald had put up gone. There were no spirits lingering in the forests. Even the bandits had been cleared out years ago by the local militia. Despite it all, Genevieve found it difficult to be in company with Laszlo Lowenstein, the actor cast as Drachenfels. What she had seen of his performance was frighteningly good and, although he seemed offstage to be an ordinary, conscientious craftsman merely happy to be thrown a meaty role, she couldn't forget the impression he made when he pulled on the mask and tried to radiate evil. Even his voice took on the timbre she remembered, and his daemonic laughter, somehow amplified by a device inside his mask, was bone-chilling.

Rudi Wegener was with the caravan, Menesh the dwarf and Anton Veidt too. Veidt was old, lean and ill. He avoided her just as he had avoided her the first time. Rudi was also in poor health, she assumed, with his great girth weighing heavy on his heart and his great thirst similarly straining his liver and lights. Genevieve gathered he had suffered a loss recently, and approached him about it, but he hadn't been eager to talk of Erzbet. That had been a long time ago. It had been a difficult subject to bring up, for Genevieve still recalled the first sign of the dancer-assassin's madness, her unprovoked attack. Otherwise, Rudi was still prone to boasting and garrulousness. He regaled the company with fancifully embroidered accounts of his exploits as a bandit in these very woods, confident that all who might contradict him save Genevieve were dead and in their graves.

Only Menesh, the lack of an arm notwithstanding, was much as he had been. Dwarfs are more long-lived than humans. Genevieve understood that her one-time comrade had become something of a ladies' man since his injury forced him to abandon his life of wandering adventure. He was rumoured to have made several conquests among the girls of the chorus, and to be chasing the amorous record set by Kerreth, the fragile little costume master whose ways with the opposite sex were legendary. There was another dwarf in the company, Vargr Breughel, with whom Menesh was always arguing. Detlef told her that Breughel wasn't a true dwarf, but human born, and that he hated to be taken for one. Menesh was always thinking of cruel jests at Breughel's expense, and Detlef, who held his assistant in high regard, had several times turned uncharacteristically severe and threatened to throw out the one-armed swordsman along the way.

It wasn't the same trip, though. And Oswald wasn't with them. He would have to join the company later, at the head of the second caravan which would bring the audience to the play. Detlef was good company, and there was a spark between them she could not deny. But he was not Oswald, regardless of the role he was to take in the play.

Then again, Genevieve knew she was not Lilli Nissen. The star travelled in her own luxurious caravan, which was driven by a handsome, black-skinned mute from the South Lands who acted as her personal servant and bodyguard. By his scars, Genevieve recognized him as essentially the woman's slave. The vampire had been presented to the actress, and neither party wished to further the acquaintance. Genevieve saw Lilli's face as if it were a-crawl with worms, and the actress pointedly refused to touch the undead woman's outstretched hand. Detlef, too, obviously had little time for Lilli, but excused her on the grounds that, for all her foolishness and temperament, she could indeed be a goddess on stage. 'She had the ability to make audiences love her, even if they would, singly or in twos and threes, find her less appealing than the average monster of the night. She's probably possessed.'

The 'accidents' that had plagued the production in Altdorf abated, perhaps because of the presence of several of Henrik Kraly's pikemen. One inn along the way had been reluctant to accommodate the players, the owner having had bad experience in the past with the theatrical profession, but Kraly's men had quietly convinced him to change his ways. The only peculiar incident had taken place in a village at the foot of the Grey Mountains, where the caravan had been booked to stay overnight at a well-reputed traveller's rest stop.

Detlef had been sampling the excellent food on offer, and quizzing Genevieve about the Bretonnia of her girlhood, asking particularly about the still-remembered great minstrels of the day and the precise qualities of their voices. Breughel had come to their table in some state, accompanied by the owner of the hostelry.

'How many are we?' Breughel asked. 'In the caravan, I mean. Coaches, carts, wagons?'

'Um, twenty-five, I think. No, I was forgetting Lilli's boudoir on wheels. Twenty-six. What's the matter? Have we lost someone?'

'No,' said the hostelier, apologetically, 'quite the reverse. You have one too many.'

Detlef was taken aback. 'You've obviously miscounted.'

'No. The crown prince's messenger specified twenty-six vehicles, and so I set aside space in the yard for that number. The space is filled, and there is one carriage left over.'

'It's Lilli's,' said Breughel.

'It would be,' replied Detlef.

'And she's not happy about leaving it in the road.'

'She wouldn't be.'

The hostelier seemed unduly upset until Genevieve realized he must have recently been shouted at by Lilli Nissen. The famous beauty could be a mad gorgon at times. Detlef continued with his meal, complimenting the hostelier on his lamb chops in wine sauce. The man was from Bretonnia, and justly proud of his fare.

'The thing I can't understand, Detlef,' said Breughel, 'is that we've counted the caravan twice over. No matter where we start we get the same number.'

'Twenty-seven?'

'No, twenty-six. But there are still twenty-seven places filled in the yard.'

Detlef laughed. 'This is silly. You must just have arranged the wagons wrongly, taken up too much room.'

'You know what Kraly's ostlers are like. The wagons are as evenly spaced as old Maximilian's toy soldiers on a board.'

'Well, haul one of the scenery wagons into the road to make room for the human flytrap, and have a drink.'

The next day, at the off, Detlef and Breughel counted the wagons as they trundled up towards the mountain road.

'There, my friend, twenty-six.'

'And our own wagon, Detlef. Twenty-seven.'

It had been a puzzle, but certainly paled when set beside Detlef's experience at the von Konigswald palace. It was hard to take seriously an extra wagon as an omen of evil.

But the next night, Kosinski the scene-shifter, still hobbling on his broken ankle, came up to complain.

'I thought you wanted me to bring up the rear of the caravan.'

'I do, Kosinski. You've the heaviest, slowest wagon. It's the combination of your head and the scenery that keeps it back. You always have to catch up half an hour at the end of the day.'

'Then who's that behind me?'

Detlef and Breughel looked at each other and said in unison, 'The twenty-seventh wagon.'

'And who's that?'

'Who knows?'

They were camped in the open that night, the wagons together in groups. Four groups of six, with three left over. Twenty-seven. Detlef and Breughel independently counted the wagons again, and came up with only twenty-six. But there were still four groups of six, with three left over.

'Detlef,' concluded Breughel, 'there's an extra wagon with us we can't see all the time.'

Detlef spat into the fire. Genevieve had nothing to add.

'So, who is travelling with us?'

Detlef hadn't talked much that evening, and Genevieve hadn't been able to draw him out. He had had a conference with Kraly's men, and had them stand guard until dawn. When everyone else was asleep, Genevieve had counted the wagons. Twenty-six. She had an assignation with the youth playing Conradin that night, and fed well. He looked white and dazed the next morning, and avoided her for a while, so perhaps she had lost some of her control and taken too much.

But the journey was over now. She looked around for Detlef, but he was busy with Breughel and the architect, arguing over sketches. They could only see the castle as a giant stage set to be exploited for the maximum impact. Guglielmo, the Tilean business manager, was off with the local burgermeister, going over a list of provisions ordered and paid for. Genevieve put her glasses on again, and saw better through the tint.

The rest of the company were going merrily in through the great front gates, looking for their quarters, relieved to be off the road. Lilli Nissen swept past with her little retinue – slave, dresser, astrologer, face-paint adviser – and went into the castle like a queen making a call on the lesser nobility.

Genevieve stood on the road, hesitating. Looking behind her, she saw who else hesitated.

Rudi, Veidt, Menesh.

They each stood alone, looking at the fortress, remembering...

V

THE FIRST NIGHT in the fortress, Rudi threw a party and invited everyone. There would have been a party anyway, to mark the end of the journey, but Detlef Sierck was kind enough to let Rudi throw it. Of course, Crown Prince Oswald had provided the food and wine, not to mention the fortress itself, but Rudi was there to bring the party to life.

The last weeks, since Oswald found him in the Black Bat, had been good for Rudi. He hadn't been drinking less, but what he was drinking was of a better quality. He'd been telling the old stories again, with his usual 'improvements,' but now there was a marked difference in the interest of his audiences. Detlef had listened attentively to his accounts of the original quest to Drachenfels, and the theatre people encouraged him to recall his other exploits.

Rudi had always liked theatre people. Erzbet had been with her gypsy circus when they first met. He and his band had passed themselves off as strolling players on many occasions. Now, at his party, the company were enjoying his best theatrical story. He was remembering the time when, shortly after holding up a party of noblemen in the Drak Wald

Forest, he had been forced to stage a performance for his erst-
while victims in order to convince them that his band were
indeed show people rather than bandits. In his retelling, he
claimed that the Lord Hjalmar Poelzig had recognized him
straight away, but still insisted on the performance to humil-
iate Rudi. Surrounded by the lord's militiamen, Rudi's
bandits had improvised a tragedy about a bandit king and his
dancing queen and, at the close of the play, Poelzig had been
so moved that he decreed that Rudi should be rewarded and
allowed to go free under the lord's own protection.

Detlef roared with laughter as Rudi told his story, imper-
sonating the wily lord, and the brash young man he had
been.

Deep inside his drink-besotted brain, Rudi remembered the
real lord, and the five good men he had strangled with bow-
strings when he caught up with the bandits. He remembered
the lord's jailer – hardly more than a boy – and the way he had
screamed as Rudi battered him to death against the stones of
the prison before making an escape through the castle's stinking drains. Sobbing and befouled, the bandit king had crept
away in shame like an animal of the forest. Those had been
days of blood and filth and desperation.

The more he spoke of the days of plunder and glory and
adventure, the more Rudi came to know that this was the real
truth of the matter. What had happened didn't matter any
longer. Erzbet was dead, Poelzig was dead, the boy was dead,
his brains paste on the floor – the times were dead. But the
stories lived. Detlef understood that, with his histories and
his dramas. And Oswald too, with his play that would pass all
their names down to future generations. Rudi the dirty murderer, Rudi who howled in grief and fear as he smashed in the
skull of an innocent child, would be forgotten. Rudi the bandit king, Rudi the stalwart ally of brave Oswald, would be
remembered as long as there were stages to dress and actors
to walk upon them.

Reinhardt Jessner, the chubby young player cast as Rudi,
called for another story. Rudi called for another pot of gin.
The fires burned low, and the stories ran out. Eventually, Rudi
slumped insensible. He could see the others – Detlef laughing, the vampire Genevieve as pretty as she had ever been,

Veidt haggard and silent, Breughel arranging for more wine – but couldn't move himself from his spot by the fire. His belly weighed him down like an anchor. His limbs felt as if he were shackled to four cannonballs. And his back – his never-set-properly, never-right-again back – pained him as it had done for a quarter century, sending messages of agony up his spine.

Detlef proposed a toast 'to Rudolf Wegener, king of banditti' and everyone drank. Rudi belched, the turnip taste filling his mouth, and everyone laughed. Felix Hubermann, the master of the company's music, signed to a few of his players, and instruments were produced. Detlef himself took the shrill rauschpfeife, Hubermann the portative organ, and others the shawms, dulcian, fiddles, lute, curtal, cowhorn, cornett and gamba. The ensemble played, and the singers sang, untrained voices joining with the trained.

The old songs. 'The Miller of Middenheim,' 'Myrmidia's Doleful Lads,' 'Gilead the Elf King,' 'The Lament of Karak Varn,' 'The Goatherd of Appuccini,' 'Come Ye Home to Bilbali, Estalian Mariner,' 'The Reik is Wide,' 'A Bandit Bold' – this over and over, 'To Hunt the Manticore,' 'Sigmar's Silver Hammer,' 'The Pirate Prince of Sartosa.'

Then, the older songs, the near-forgotten songs. Menesh croaked an incomprehensible dwarfish ballad of great length, and six women burst into tears at its conclusion. Hubermann played an elven melody rarely heard by humans, let alone played by one, and made everyone wonder whether his ears weren't just a trifle too pointed and his eyes on the large side.

After some prompting from Detlef, Genevieve sang the songs of her youth, songs long dead except in her memory. Rudi found himself weeping with her as she sang of cities fallen, battles lost and lovers sundered. Bretonnia has always had a reputation for luxuriating in melancholia. Trickles of red ran down the vampire's lovely face, and she was unable to continue. There are precious few Bretonnian tales with happy endings.

Then the fires were piled high again, and the musicians played for dancing. Rudi was unable to stand up, much less dance, but he watched the others at their pleasure. Genevieve capered solemnly with Detlef, a courtly affair with many bowings and curtsies, but the music grew wilder, and dresses flew higher. Jessner took up with Illona Horvathy, the dancer cast as Erzbet, and swung her around in the air, so her skirts brushed perilously close to the fire. Rudi could have been watching his younger self. Illona was a spirited, athletic dancer, and she could perform acrobatic tricks the like of which Rudi had never seen. Jessner, who had taken Rudi into his confidence, assured him that Illona's imagination and physical stamina were not confined to the vertical brand of dancing. But she missed something of the grace, of the abandon, of the seriousness of the original. He had talked to her, and she was a cheerful girl, pleased to give pleasure. But there was none of Erzbet's passion. Illona had never taken a life, had never spared a life. She had not lived at the edge of experience the way Erzbet had.

…and Illona Horvathy wouldn't end her days in self-murder on the road from a madhouse.

A hand fell on his shoulder. It was Veidt's.

'It's over, Rudi. We're over.'

The bounty hunter was drunk, and his unshaven face was like a sagging skull. But he was right.

'Yes, over.'

'But we were here before, eh? Us old men. You and I and the dwarf and the leech girl. We were here when these play-actors were in their cribs. We fought as they'll never have to fight…'

Veidt trailed off, the light in his eyes going out, and keeled over sideways. Like all of them, he'd come out of Castle Drachenfels a different man than he had been outside the gates. Rudi regretted that he had not seen the bounty hunter in twenty-five years. They had shared so much, they should have been lifelong friends. The fortress should have brought them together, especially those hours injured in the dark, waiting for Oswald's return, knowing that the prince would die, and that things with claws and teeth would be coming for them.

The weight of wine shifted inside Rudi, and he desperately felt the need to piss. He shifted upright and staggered away from Veidt, his head spinning like a child's top. Jessner loomed before him, saying something he couldn't make out. The actor clapped him on the back, and sent him stumbling. The musicians were still playing. Illona was dancing alone now.

He made it into the next room, away from the light and the clamour. After he had relieved himself in a cold fireplace, he turned to make his way back to his place by the fire, to his friends.

She was in the doorway, between him and the party. He recognized her slim-hipped figure and long dark hair at once. She wore her dancing dress, slit to the thigh on one side and immodestly tight in the bodice.

'Rudi,' she said to him, and it was twenty-five, thirty years, ago. The days of plunder and glory and adventure.

'Rudi,' she extended an arm to him, her bracelets jingling.

He felt the weights falling away from him, and stood up straight. There was no pain in his back now.

'Rudi,' her voice was soft, yet urgent. Inviting, yet dangerous.

He lurched towards her, but she stepped aside, into the dark. She went to a door, and he blundered after her, pushing through it.

They were in a corridor. Rudi was sure this was where they had fought the living gargoyles, but Oswald's men had cleaned it up, put fresh candles in the sconces, laid down carpeting for the visiting dignitaries.

Erzbet led him on, into the heart of Drachenfels. In the chamber of the poison feast, a man waited for him. At first, because of the mask, he thought it was the actor, Lowenstein. It wasn't.

The man looked up from the table at him. His eyes shone through the slits of his mask. He had cutlery laid out before him, as for a meal. But there were no forks and spoons. Only knives.

The man picked up a knife. It shone like a white flame in his hand.

Rudi, cold inside, tried to push himself away, back through the door. But Erzbet stood before it, blocking his escape. He could see her better now. Her low-cut bodice disclosed the great red gash, like a crushed mouth sideways, in her breast.

She threw her head back, and her hair fell away from her face. He could see that she had no eyes.

VI

LILLI NISSEN'S FAVOURED method of communicating with her
director-writer-co-star was through Nebenzahl, her astrologer.
If she was unhappy with a line of dialogue, or the performance of some lesser light of the stage, or the food served in
her private rooms, or the noise made by the party she pointedly hadn't attended, or by the way the sun persisted on rising
in the east every single solitary morning, she despatched
Nebenzahl to whine at Detlef. Detlef was beginning to feel
quite sorry for the poor charlatan who was finding his easy
berth so unexpectedly rocky. It was the man's own fault, Detlef
supposed, for not foreseeing in the cards, stars or entrails what
a monster his employer would turn out to be.

The company were in the great hall of Drachenfels, which
had been converted into a theatre. Lilli chose to make her
entrance over the stage. As usual, she assumed there was no
business connected with the play more important than her
whim of the moment, and had herself borne in by her chair-
carrying giant in the middle of a rehearsal.

It was an early scene, where Oswald, in the palace at
Altdorf, is visited by the projected spirit of the Great

Enchanter. They debate in verse the conflict to come, and the major themes of the play are foreshadowed. Detlef was having Vargr Breughel read his own lines, so he could concentrate on Lowenstein's performance and the lighting effect that would make him seem insubstantial. With the mask, the thin actor seemed a different creature altogether. Genevieve, who was sitting in on the rehearsal, was shuddering – probably reminded nastily of the real Drachenfels – and Detlef took that to be a tribute to Lowenstein's skills. When he could get perspective on the play, Detlef realized he was in danger of being overshadowed by the villain, and resolved to make his own performance the more masterful. He didn't mind. While he took pride in his acting, he disdained those stars, of whom Lilli was most definitely one, who surround themselves with the most wooden, untalented supporting actors available in order to make themselves seem better.

During the journey to the fortress, Lilli had tried to persuade him through Nebenzahl to cast some of her favourite walking statues in the other female roles in Drachenfels and he had kicked the astrologer off his wagon. Having written, directed and conceived the play, Detlef felt he could afford to let others shine in it. He planned on taking last billing as an actor in the programme, allowing the weight of his name to be felt as the creator of the piece rather than as one of its interpreters.

Lowenstein-as-Drachenfels was towering over Breughel, vowing that his reign of evil would continue long after the puny prince's whited bones lay in forgotten dust, when Lilli made her unscheduled entrance, trailing her entourage. The black giant carried an oversized armchair without complaint. Lilli sat primly in it, like a child being carried by a fond parent. Her crippled dresser limped a few paces behind, bearing a basket of sweetmeats and fruit – part of the star's 'special diet' – and a few other functionaries whose exact purpose Detlef had never divined were also along to lend weight to their mistress's current gripe.

Nebenzahl strode up to Detlef, visibly embarrassed, but nerving himself to make the complaint. Lilli snarled imperiously, like a mountain cat with delusions of leonine grandeur, and fixed her flaming eyes on him. He knew it was going to be a bad one. If she chose to air the problem in front of the entire company, it was bound to involve a major row. The other actors on stage and in the audience shifted nervously, expecting a firestorm of holocaust proportions.

The foppish astrologer stuck out his fist, and opened his fingers. The teeth were in his hand.

'Lilli Nissen has no need of these, sir.'

He threw them on the ground. Kerreth had carved them especially, working away at scraps of boar's-tusk ivory. The wardrobe man was in the hall now, angry at the treatment of his work, but keeping quiet. He obviously had no wish to go back to being a cobbler, let alone a convict, and had correctly gauged the extent of Lilli Nissen's vindictiveness and influence.

'So, it's a toothless hag, you think I am now, Detlef Sierck!' shrieked Lilli, her face reddening. Her slave put her down, and she flew out of her chair, raging across the stage, knocking Breughel and Lowenstein out of her way. Detlef imagined angry eyes peering out from Lowenstein's mask. Lilli wasn't winning herself any more admirers this morning.

And, of course, it was such a *stupid* thing to bitch about!

'Lilli, it's no reflection upon your own teeth that I want you to wear these. It's the part you play…'

Lilli rose to the bait. 'The part I play! Ah yes, the part I play! And who cast me in such a role, who created such a disgusting travesty of womankind with me in mind, eh?'

Detlef wondered if Lilli had forgotten that Genevieve was with them. He suspected not. It was plain the women – vampire and vamp – didn't care for each other.

'Never in my career have I been asked to play such a part! Were it not for the involvement of my dear, dear friend Prince Oswald, who personally implored me to step in and fill out your petty little cast, I should have rent the manuscript to bits and flung it back into the gutter where it belongs. I've played empresses, courtesans, goddesses. Now, you want me to play a dead leech!'

Being reasonable wasn't going to help, Detlef knew, but it was the only tactic he could think of.

'Lilli, our play is a history. You play a vampire because Genevieve was… is… a vampire. After all, she *lived* this story. You only have to recreate it–'

'Pah! And is the drama invariably subject to history? Do you mean to tell me you have changed nothing for the sake of emphasis, to show yourself to the best advantage...'

There were mutterings at the back of the hall now. Nebenzahl was looking distinctly sheepish, patting down his ridiculous wig, self-conscious now he found himself on stage facing an unknown audience beyond the footlights.

'Of course, but–'

Lilli was unstoppable. Her bosom heaved as she drew breath and continued, 'For an instance, are you not somewhat too old and fat to play my good friend the future elector of Ostland as he was when but a boy?'

'Lilli, Oswald himself asked me to play him in this drama. Given the choice, I'd probably want – and no reflection upon you, Laszlo – to play Drachenfels.'

The star flounced towards the lights, and came so far forwards her face was in shadow. The house lights came up.

'Well, if you've rewritten Oswald as an ageing and overweight child prodigy, then you can rewrite Genevieve as something more suited to my personality.'

'And what, pray, might that be?'

'An elf!'

No one laughed. Detlef looked at Genevieve. Her face was unreadable. Lilli's nostrils flared and unflared. Nebenzahl coughed to break the silence.

Elven Lilli might once have been, but she inclined rather to the voluptuous these days. Her last husband had referred to her as having 'the breasts of a pigeon, the lungs of a bansidhe, the morals of an alleycat and a brain like Black Mountain cheese.'

Lowenstein laid a hand on Lilli's shoulder, and spun her round to face him. He was a full foot taller than her, and his built-up Drachenfels boots brought him up on a level with her silent giant.

Unused to such treatment, she raised a hand to slap the impudent actor, but he caught her wrist, and started whispering to her in a low, urgent, scary voice. Her colour faded, and she looked quite afraid.

Nobody else said anything. Detlef realized his mouth was hanging open in astonishment, and shut it.

When Lowenstein had finished his speech, Lilli blustered an apology – an unheard-of thing for her – and backed out, dragging her slave, her minions and astrologer with her. Nebenzahl looked appalled as he was yanked out of the great hall.

After a moment, there was a spontaneous round of applause. Lowenstein took a bow, and the rehearsal continued.

VII

MAXIMILIAN STOOD TO attention while the general was speaking. It was late, but the general had awoken him with secret orders. The general told him he must get out of bed, get dressed, and go down to the battlefield, where the fate of the Empire was to be decided. After the Emperor, the general was the most important military leader in the land, and Maximilian always wanted to impress him with his obedience, resourcefulness and courage. The general was the man Maximilian would like to be. Would have liked to have been.

When the orders were finished and understood, Maximilian saluted and put the general into his top pocket. This was a serious business. These were times of grave danger. Only Maximilian stood between civilization and anarchy, and he was determined to do his best or die.

The palace was quiet at this time of night. Quieter in the days too, now that Oswald's theatre friends had gone. Maximilian missed them a little. There had been one dancer who'd been sweet on him, and liked to join in with his battles, making suggestions and asking questions, even though nurse disapproved of her.

Nurse disapproved of a lot of things.

In his slippers, Maximilian was almost silent as he proceeded through the corridors and down the stairs. His breath was short, and he was getting a stitch, but the general would want him to continue. He would not let the general down, no matter what. He thought he saw robed figures in the shadows of one passageway, but ignored them. Nothing could keep him from the fray now he was needed.

The battle room was not locked.

There were several armies on the table. Goblins, dwarfs, elves and men. And in the centre was a castle, the objective. The Imperial standard was flying from the great tower of the castle. The flag was tattered, but waved proud. The armies were clashing already. The room was filled with the tiny sounds of their weapons clanging together, their cannon popping. When they were hit, the soldiers screamed like shrilling insects. The table-top battlefield was swarming with life. Miniature swords scraped paint from lead faces. The dead were melted in grey pools. Puffs of smoke rose. Battle trumpets sounded like echoes in Maximilian's head.

The general had ordered him to hold the castle for the Emperor. He needed a chair to step on before he could reach the table. He put his foot down on the battlefield, crushing a bridge to stickwood, pushing a platoon of wood elf wardancers into the painted stream. He pulled himself up, and stood like a giant on the table. He had to duck to avoid a chandelier as he stepped into the castle. The walls barely came to his ankles, but he was able to stand in the courtyard. The defenders of the castle cheered to have such a champion.

Moonlight came in through the tall, thin windows. The night battle swept across the table, backwards and forwards. The armies had lost all direction, and were turning upon themselves. Sometimes, all four forces appeared to combine to launch a new onslaught on Maximilian's castle. Mostly, every single soldier seemed at war with every other. He detected the claws of Chaos in this business. The felt of the hill was torn as charges fell back from the castle walls, and dark wood showed through the scratches.

The general kept up Maximilian's morale as a wave of goblins clambered up the hill and breached the walls. Dwarf engineers pushed a war-tower forwards. Cannonballs stung his shins. Still he held the fort, at attention, saluting. The castle was in ruins now, and the armies were attacking him, trying to bring him down. The defence forces were sought out and slaughtered. Maximilian stood alone against the enemies.

The wounds inflicted on his feet and ankles were fleabites. Bretonnian soldiers poured fire over his slippers, but he stamped it out, and the fires spread back to their ranks. He laughed. The sons of Bretonnia at war always were noted more for viciousness than valour. Then the battle-wizards came forward, and threw their worst spells at him. Frightful fiends swirled about his legs like fish, and he swatted them away with his hands. A three-headed creature with eyes and a maw in its belly flew for Maximilian's throat, and he caught it. It came apart like cobweb in his hand, and he wiped it away on his jacket.

Spears stuck to his calves, and he felt dizzy to be at such a height above the ground. Goblins were scaling his trousers, hacking through his clothes and sinking hooks into flesh and bone. There were more fires. A ballista and several mortars were deployed. There were explosions all around him. His right knee went, and he was pulled down. Small roars of triumph went up, and his back was riddled with a million tiny shots. Knives small as headlice sawed at him. Spears like needles jabbed. He fell across the battlefield, crushing the remains of the castle, flattening the hill, murdering hundreds beneath him. He rolled onto his back, and the armies reached his face. They set off charges in his eyes, and he was blind. Berserkers set fire to his hair. Warrior wizards opened up channels to his brain. Pikemen attacked his neck. Fresh-conjured daemons burrowed beneath his skin, excreting their poisonous filth.

The general told him he was doing well and that he must keep up the fight. In the dark, the Emperor Luitpold and all his court waited for him. Maximilian knew he would soon be permitted to leave the field of battle, to take his well-earned rest. There were medals and honours and eggs for him. He would receive his just rewards.

The armies moved over him, laying waste to whatever they found. They captured the general, and executed him. To the end, the man was a hero. His lead head rolled across Maximilian's chest and bounced lifeless onto the table.

Tired and relieved, Maximilian sank into the darkness…

The next morning his nurse found him, lying dead among his beloved toy soldiers. Physicians were called for, but it was too late. The old elector's heart had finally given out. It was said that at least his death was sudden and easeful. The sad news was delivered to the new elector with his breakfast.

Oswald von Konigswald wept, but was not surprised.

VIII

GENEVIEVE WAS ON the battlements, watching the sun go down, feeling her strength rising. There was a full moon, and the view was lightly shadowed. With her nightsight, she saw wolves loping in the forests and silent birds ascending to their mountain nests. There were lights burning in the village. She was stretching, tasting the night, wondering how she would drink this evening, when Henrik Kraly found her.

'My lady,' he began, 'if I might beg a favour…'

'Certainly. What do you wish?'

Kraly looked uncertain. This was not like Oswald's smooth and efficient catspaw. His hand rested casually on his sword-hilt in a manner that instantly disturbed Genevieve. During the long trip from the convent, she had gathered that not all his services to the von Konigswalds involved simple message-bearing.

'Could you arrange to meet me in half an hour, and bring Mr Sierck with you? In the chamber of the poison feast.'

Genevieve raised an eyebrow. She had been avoiding that particular place above all. For her, the fortress held too many memories.

'It is a matter of some urgency, but I would appreciate it if you could raise it without alerting anyone. The crown prince has charged me with discretion.'

Puzzled, Genevieve agreed to the steward's terms and left for the great hall. She supposed the dead must have been taken from the table by now and given their proper burial. She would probably barely recognize the poison room. Thus far, she had encountered no ghosts, even in her imagination, at Drachenfels. No ghosts, just memories.

Rehearsals had finished for the day, and the actors were being served in a make-shift canteen. Breughel was haranguing the Bretonnian cook about the lack of a certain spice in the stew, and the cook was defending the recipe handed down to him by his forefathers. 'Dwarfeesh buffeune, yiu 'ave not leeved unteel yiu 'ave taisted *Casserole à la Boudreaux!*'

Jessner and Illona Horvathy were all over each other in a corner, petting as they joked with other members of the cast. Menesh was talking intently to Gesualdo, the actor playing him, and gesturing extravagantly with his one arm while the other dwarf nodded. On the stage, Detlef and Lowenstein were stripped to the waist, towelling off the sweat they had worked up practising the duelling scenes.

'You've been giving me a fine dash-about, Laszlo. Where did you learn the sword?'

Without his mask and costume, Lowenstein was diminished, seeming rather dull. 'At Nuln. I took classes from Valancourt at the Academy.'

'I thought I recognized that vertical parry. Valancourt taught Oswald too. You'd be a formidable opponent.'

'I hope so.'

Detlef pulled on a jacket, and buttoned it. Although plump, his muscles were well-defined. Genevieve gathered that he too was skilled with the use of the sword. He would have to be, given his fondness for heroic roles.

'Detlef,' she said. 'Could we have a word? In private?'

Detlef looked to Lowenstein, who bowed and walked off.

'An odd fellow, that,' Detlef said. 'He's always surprising me. And yet, I get this feeling that there's something not all there about our friend Laszlo. Do you know what I mean?'

Genevieve did. To her heightened senses, Lowenstein registered as a complete vacuum, as if he were a walking shell waiting to be ensouled. Still, she had met many people like that. In an actor, it was hardly surprising. It did not really matter who Lowenstein was off-stage.

'Well, what's up, elf lady? Do you want me to dismiss Lilli and hire a human being for the role?'

'No, it's something mysterious.'

He smiled. 'You intrigue me.'

She smiled back, on the verge of flirting. 'Kraly wants to see you. Us. In the poison room.'

She caught his scent in the air, and felt the pricking of the old thirst. She wondered how his blood would flow.

'I wish you wouldn't lick your lips like that, Genevieve.'

She covered her mouth, and giggled. 'I'm sorry.'

He grinned. 'The poison room, eh? Sounds lovely.'

'You know the story?'

'Oh yes. Children tortured, parents left to starve. Another one of the Great Enchanter's charming little jokes. He'd have made a good match for Mistress Nissen, don't you think? Imagine the fun they could have had exchanging recipes for the best use of babies. "Yiu 'ave not leeved until yiu 'ave taisted *Enfant a la Boudreaux!*" Lead on.'

She took his arm and they left the great hall. Detlef winked at Kerreth the wardrobe master as they passed through the door. The little man laughed and rubbed his neck. Genevieve blushed. She could imagine the stories that would be told during rehearsals tomorrow. Oh well, after all these years, her reputation could hardly be more tarnished by an association with an actor.

In the corridor, they continued to talk. Detlef was making a conscious effort to be charming, and she wasn't putting up too much resistance. Perhaps if stories were to be told, she should make the effort to justify them.

'How does it feel to have those teeth anyway? Aren't you forever cutting your lips?'

A witty reply came to mind, but then they entered the poison chamber and saw the looks on the faces of the people grouped around the table. And the mess that lay on it...

When Detlef had finished vomiting, Kraly told him who it was.

IX

DETLEF WAS RELIEVED to learn that he wasn't the first to be sick. The body had been discovered by Nebenzahl the astrologer, and the little parasite had puked his breakfast at once. Even though he spent the greater part of his professional life peering into the entrails of chickens and cats, the exposed insides of a human being caused him much distress. Detlef wondered if there were a way of divining the future through the examination of vomit. Apparently, Nebenzahl had been looking for some trinket misplaced by his mistress and opened the wrong door. He had a talent for awkwardness and, as everyone had noticed but Lilli, absolutely no foresight.

Detlef looked from face to face. Henrik Kraly was expressionless, a hard man faced with a hard situation, intent on not giving anything of himself away. Genevieve seemed beyond caring, but she was not making jokes any more. Besides, it would be difficult to tell if a vampire were shocked pale. Nebenzahl was still sobbing quietly, clinging to one of Kraly's halberdiers, occasionally scraping at the regurgitated matter on his brocaded waistcoat. Vargr Breughel, whom Detlef had insisted on summoning, looked as he always did when faced with yet another problem, as if every disaster in the world were intended personally against him.

And Rudi Wegener did not look like much at all. His face was still there, but it hung loose like a soggy mask thrown over a skull.

Detlef's first thought was that the old bandit had been flayed, but Kraly had already performed the distasteful task of closely examining the corpse and knew exactly what had been done to Rudi.

'The eyes are gone, you notice. Fished out with a dagger or small knife, I'd guess. An unsqueamish man could do the job with his fingers, but he'd best wear gloves.'

Detlef had the unpleasant feeling that Kraly was talking from experience. Electoral houses needed a servant or two with more loyalty than scruples. It was hard to associate open, upright Oswald with this lizard-hearted iceman.

'But that's not what killed him?'

'No.'

'It looks like a wolf got at him, or a ravenous daemon. Something that attacked in a frenzy, devouring, tearing...'

Kraly smiled a one-sided smile. 'Yes, I thought that at first too, but look here.'

He pointed into the body cavity, lifting a flap of skin from the ribcage.

'No bones are broken. The organs are untouched. That, in case you're interested, is what a drinking habit like Wegener's does to your liver.'

The organ was red, swollen and covered with pustules. It was obviously rotted through, even to someone who didn't know what a healthy liver looked like. Detlef thought he was going to be sick again. Kraly poked at the wounds.

'Whoever did this, did it calmly and with great skill.'

Genevieve spoke. 'What exactly was done?'

'My lady, all the fat has been neatly cut out of his body.'

Kraly left the dead thing alone, and the group moved away from it by unspoken mutual consent.

Detlef was outraged. 'Why would anyone want to do that?'

The steward shrugged. Detlef realized that the man was enjoying this brief taste of command. For once, he was at the centre of things, not a simple creature of Oswald's.

'There are many possibilities, Mr Sierck. A religious ritual, dedicating the sacrifice to some dark god. A wizard needing the material for a spell. Many enchantments require peculiar ingredients. Or, it could be the work of a madman, an obsessive who kills in a bizarre manner in an attempt to tell us something...'

'Like "eat less and take more exercise," I suppose! This is insane, Kraly! A man is dead!'

Genevieve took his hand. That helped somehow. He calmed down.

'I'm sorry.'

The steward accepted his apology without sincerity. 'At the risk of being obvious, we must face facts. There is a murderer among us.'

They all looked at each other again, like participants in one of those dim haunted castle melodramas in which the cast drop dead at regular intervals until the high priest of Morr deduces who the killer is and the audience wakes up.

'And we must catch him without word of our troubles reaching the outside.'

'I beg your pardon?'

'Whatever we do must be done in secret. The crown prince would not want this to disrupt the smooth running of his play. I am here to deal with just such occurrences. You need not concern yourself. Know only this, that I will work to bring the murderer to justice as soon as possible.'

Breughel spoke up. 'Detlef, it might indeed be best to leave this to the prince's men.'

'But we can't just go on as if nothing has happened!'

'Can't we? By my interpretation of the crown prince's orders, we have no other course open to us.'

Nebenzahl was still shaking and moaning. Detlef nodded in his direction. 'And how do we keep the popinjay silent?'

Kraly's mouth did something that in another man might qualify as a smile. 'Mr Nebenzahl has just been recalled to Altdorf. He left early this afternoon, and has written to his employer severing their relationship...'

The astrologer started, and stared at the steward.

'I am given to understand that many who quit Miss Lilli Nissen's employ choose to leave in a similar manner.'

Nebenzahl looked like a man just informed of his impending death.

'Don't worry, gut-gazer,' said Kraly. 'You'll be better paid for shutting up and going away than you would have been for staying around and blabbering to everyone. I believe a position could be found for you in Erengrad.'

The halberdier left the room, pulling Nebenzahl along with him. Detlef wondered how the weedy little fraud would get by among the Norsemen and Kislevites of that cold port on the borders of the Northern Wastes. He was furious with Kraly by now, but had learned to be cool in his wrath. Nothing would be achieved if he threw a screaming fit like Lilli Nissen.

'And I'm supposed to continue with the play, and incidentally it is *my* play not Crown Prince Blessed Oswald's, while people are being slaughtered all the while?'

Kraly was resolute. 'If the crown prince so wishes it.'

'I wonder, my dear steward, if Oswald would entirely approve of your actions.'

This gave Kraly pause, but he soon snapped back. 'I'm sure the crown prince has every confidence in me. He did assign me these duties. I believe I have not been a disappointment to him in the past.'

Genevieve had walked back to the table, and was taking a close look at what was left of Rudi. For the first time, Detlef realized fully that, no matter how she seemed, the woman wasn't human. She had no fear of the dead, and indeed must have some familiarity with them.

'What are you doing?' asked Kraly.

'Feeling for something.'

Genevieve touched the corpse's head, and shut her eyes. She might be praying for his soul, Detlef supposed, or doing arithmetic in her head.

'No,' she said, after a time. 'He's gone. Nothing remains of his spirit.'

'Did you hope to read his murderer's face in his mind?' Kraly asked.

'Not really. I just wanted to say farewell. He was a friend of mine, in case you'd forgotten. He had a hard life, and was not well served by it.'

She left the body alone. 'One thing,' she said.

'Yes?'

'You are aware of the common superstition that a dying man's eyes hold the last sight he beholds? That a murderer may be betrayed by his image in his victim's pupils?'

They all looked at Rudi's face, at his empty eye sockets, and flensed cheeks.

'Of course,' Kraly was impatient now, 'it's rot. Physicians and alchemists no longer think...'

'Quite, quite. The foolishness of another age, like the belief that toad men from the stars ruled the world before the Coming of Chaos.'

'Besides, his eyes are gone.'

'That is precisely the point I wished to make. You and I know the story of the murdered man's eyes is nonsense. But Rudi's murderer might believe it. That would explain why he took the eyes.'

Kraly was taken with the thought. 'A superstitious man, then? A gypsy, or an Ostlander?'

'I make no accusations.'

'Perhaps a dwarf? They are known for their superstitious ways. Brass pennies for luck, black cats drowned at birth...'

Breughel bridled as Kraly turned to him.

'I'm no dwarf,' he spat. 'I hate the little bastards.'

Kraly waved his protest away. 'Still, the vampire lady has a point. My lady, your intuitions are as sharp as they are said to be.'

'There's another possibility,' said Detlef, 'that this was done by no human agency. The supernatural is no stranger to these walls. Drachenfels was famed as a conjurer of daemons and monsters. They were supposed to have been cleared out, but it's a huge building. Who knows what could have lived here all these years, festering in the dark, waiting for its master's murderers to return.'

Genevieve touched a finger to her chin, obviously following Detlef's train of thought. She shook her head slightly, unsure.

'And we have brought back all the survivors of Oswald's adventurers. As easy meat.'

Detlef was concerned for Genevieve – for Menesh and Veidt too – but Kraly had a single thought.

'The crown prince must be warned. He might not wish to come.'

Genevieve laughed. 'You really don't know your master very well, do you, Kraly? This would only make him the more determined to be here.'

'You could be right, my lady. Rest assured, I'll charge the guards with extra vigilance. This will not happen again. You have my word on it.'

X

ALONE IN HIS room, Vargr Breughel drank and looked at himself in the mirror. He did not know who had assigned the various quarters for the company, and assumed no cruel slight had been intended. But, his was the only bedroom he had seen here equipped with a floor-to-ceiling mirror. This must have been where some harlot witch painted and primped. The Great Enchanter had had many mistresses down through the millennia. Unlike Vargr Breughel in his meagre forty-seven years.

Moonbeams filtered down through the windows and lit the room, casting a baleful light over everything. Breughel sat in his chair, feet dangling a hand's-span above the carpet, and looked himself in the eye.

He remembered his parents, and the air of disappointment that always hung about them. His sisters, born before him, were above average height. His younger brother had been as tall, straight and handsome as anyone could wish until he fell in battle in the service of the Emperor, giving their parents another reason to be uncomfortable in his presence. His mother and father had blamed each other for his condition, and had spent their lives searching each other for signs of the deformity that had been passed down through their mating to their son. Of course, it had been embarrassing for them to explain to all callers at their home that, no, they didn't have a dwarf servant, they had a dwarf son. And he wasn't a true dwarf.

He was a midget.

He started his second bottle. He was drinking sloppily now. There were stains on his shirt. His skin itched under his clothes, and he wriggled.

He had run away and joined a travelling circus, become a clown. Soon, he was running his own circus – although he had full-sized men to deal with people – and branching out into the theatre. There had been true dwarf clowns working in his circus, but they had not accepted him as one of their own. Behind his back or to his face, they called him a freak, and a warped monstrosity.

Which is what he was.

He had no wife, no mistresses, and bathed in private. His body was a secret, and he kept it well. But he examined himself daily for new changes. Often, there were two or three a month. And with the changes, came new abilities, new senses. The tubers under his arms, held together by bat-like webbing, could tune in to people's emotions. He always knew how others felt, to what degree they were disgusted by him. So far his face had not been affected, but he had had to wear gloves for some years now, to cover the eyes in the palms of his hands. The eyes that could see sounds.

He was a midget. He was also an altered and a freak.

There was a new word for what he was. He had heard scholars use it, first of plants cultivated unnaturally, then of two-headed calves, wall-eyed dogs and the like. And now of humans affected by the warpstone, progressing beyond their flesh, becoming creatures of Chaos.

Vargr Breughel was a *mutant*.

XI

KARL-FRANZ I, of the House of the Second Wilhelm, Protector of the Empire, Defier of the Dark, Emperor Himself and the Son of Emperors, had come calling on the palace of von Konigswald. The foyer table was piled high with black-edged condolence cards delivered by messenger, but Karl-Franz laid his down in person. He brushed aside the stewards and guards, and walked briskly through the palace, in search of the new elector.

Others would have visited Oswald. The grand theogonist of the cult of Sigmar and the high priest of the cult of Ulric would have endeavoured to be polite to each other throughout the lying-in-state of the old elector, Maximilian.

Representatives of the city-states and the electoral provinces, emissaries from the major temples of Altdorf and the Halfling Moot would have called with messages of sympathy.

Karl-Franz came alone, without the usual pomp that accompanied his every move, and saw Oswald man to man. There were few others in the land who could warrant such treatment.

The Emperor found Oswald in Maximilian's study – Oswald's study, now – going through old papers. Oswald dismissed the secretaries and ordered wine to be brought.

'Your father was a great friend to me when I was a boy, Oswald. In many ways, he meant more to me than my own father. It's difficult to rule an empire and be the head of a family. As I know too well. Maximilian will be greatly missed.'

'Thank you.' Oswald was still withdrawn, moving as if in a dream.

'And now we must think of the future. Maximilian is buried with honour. You must be confirmed in the crown as soon as possible.'

Oswald shook his head. This must be difficult for him. Karl-Franz remembered the agonizing ceremony that had surrounded his own ascendance to the throne, the days of torture as the electors debated the succession. He had never believed the verdict would be for him. He understood through his own sources that the voting had been eight to four against on the first ballot, and that Maximilian had talked round all but one of the other electors by the end of the session. If he truly ruled, rather than held together a squabbling collection of principalities, then he ruled only on the sufferance of the House of von Konigswald.

'The coronation will be at Castle Drachenfels. After the play. The electors will all be there, and the other dignitaries. We should have no need to reassemble them a few weeks later for another of these stately ordeals.'

'You are right of course, Oswald, but an empire expects due ritual process. Ruling is not enough. One must be seen to rule.'

Oswald looked up at the portrait of his father in his prime. He had a falcon on his hand and stood in the woods, at the forefront of a group. A golden-haired child was by his side. The young Oswald.

'I never noticed before. That youth taking the bird. He's dressed as a falconer, but...'

Karl-Franz smiled. 'Yes, it's me. I remember those days well. Old Luitpold disapproved. "What if the future Emperor should fall from his horse, or lose an eye to an angry bird, or get stuck by a boar?" He thought the future Emperor should be treasured like a painted egg. Your father understood these things better.'

'Yes. I believe he did.'

'And already I see signs that young Luitpold thinks of you as I thought of your father. Maybe I too try to cosset and smother the future Emperor. I hope I'm not the domestic tyrant old Luitpold was, but I see all the signs around me. Circles come around between our houses.'

It was an impressive painting. Karl-Franz wished he could recall the artist. He must have been one of Maximilian's hunting friends. He had certainly had a feel for the forests. You could almost hear the wind in the trees, the cries of the birds.

'Soon, we'll be in the woods again, Oswald. On the road to Drachenfels. There'll be good hunting along the way. I must confess that when you proposed the trip, I wasn't sure about it. But I've always wanted to see the site of your great victory. And I'm weary of the stifling comforts of palaces and courtiers. It's been too long since we stalked a stag, or sang the old songs. And I was sorry that your friend Sierck's *History of Sigmar* fell apart. Middenland sank a sum of my money in it, you know. I've been looking forward to seeing the fellow act. The ladies of my court tell me he's quite the thing.'

'Yes, Emperor.'

'Emperor and elector, eh? I remember when we were just Karl-Franz and Oswald. There's one thing I've always wondered, though...'

'What, Emperor?'

'When we were young men, when our fathers said you were mad to go up against the Great Enchanter...'

'Yes?'

'Why did you not ask me to come along? I'd have danced for the chance of such an adventure, such a battle.'

ACT FOUR

I

DETLEF WAS NOT sleeping well. He had retired early, not wishing to be pulled back to the mundane business of the company and the play after having seen what was left of Rudi. Now, he lay awake in bed, wishing, as he had done more than once since this thing began, that he was back in his cell at Mundsen Keep. At least, Szaradat had been someone to hate. And he could see Szaradat, understand his petty nastiness. There weren't any phantom monks pointing their ghostly fingers in Mundsen Keep, and there weren't any fat-taking, eyeball-gouging killers either. Indeed, compared to the fortress of Drachenfels, the keep had been a resort. Perhaps Detlef would turn his prison experiences into the subject of a farce, one day, with the wily debtors outwitting the comically dim trusties and the pompous governor being for ever humiliated by his charges.

It was no use. He could not think of the comic mask tonight.

Not only might there be a madman among them, prowling the darkened corridors of Castle Drachenfels, but also he was worried that Henrik Kraly, Oswald's man, was a potential tyrant who would rather risk the lives of everyone in the company than inconvenience the crown prince in any way. Tarradasch had said "a patron is a man who watches you drowning for twenty minutes and, when you finally manage to drag yourself to the shore by your own efforts, burdens you with help." With the elector of Middenland and *The History of Sigmar*, and now the crown prince of Ostland and *Drachenfels*, Detlef appeared to be making a speciality of distinguished backers and doom-haunted productions. He liked Oswald, but he had no illusions about his own importance in the crown prince's ultimate schemes.

The only comfort he could take was that, apart from Lilli Nissen, the play was coming along startlingly well. If they all lived through it, *Drachenfels* would make their reputations. Laszlo Lowenstein was a revelation. When the play transferred to an Altdorf theatre, Detlef would insist that Lowenstein go with the package. After the performance, he would be a leading light of the stage. Next time, Detlef would consider stepping back to write and direct only, and create a real vehicle for the man's astonishing talents. There weren't any good histories of Boris the Incompetent, and Lowenstein might be right for such a tragic figure. There could even be a good story in the assassination of Tsarina Kattarin by her great-great grandson, the Tsarevich Pavel. If only Genevieve Dieudonné could be persuaded to play the Tsarina…

If only Genevieve Dieudonné could be persuaded to play herself. She'd certainly be less of a pain in the fundament than Lilli Nissen.

Detlef was thinking a great deal of the vampire. He guessed from the murder of Rudi that she was in some danger if she remained at the fortress, and he felt an obligation to her. Yet, how could he hope to protect a 660-year-old girl who could crush granite in her bare hands and had already faced the Great Enchanter and survived? Perhaps he would do better to ask her for protection?

And in addition to the unknown murderer, the ghostly monks and whatever daemons might still cling to the stones of Drachenfels, might they not also need protecting from Henrik Kraly?

Detlef wished Oswald were here already. He had bested the perils of this place once. Furthermore, Detlef hoped the crown prince would be interested to find out what Kraly was doing in his name.

When there came a scratching at his door, Detlef clutched the bedclothes to him like a child who has heard one too many ghostly bedtime stories, and his candle fell over. He knew that it was all going to end here, and the ballads would tell of the genius murdered in his bed before his best work could be done.

'It's me,' hissed a low, female voice.

Guessing he would regret it, he got up and unlocked the door. He had to pull a chair out from under the doorknob.

Genevieve was outside in the corridor. Detlef was at once relieved and excited by her presence.

'Genevieve,' he said, opening wide the door. 'It's late.'

'Not for me.'

'I'm sorry. I was forgetting. Do you ever sleep?'

Genevieve shrugged. 'Occasionally. In the mornings, usually. And not in a coffin filled with my native soil. I was born in Parravon, which was civilized enough even then to pave over their beaten earth roads, so that would be a problem.'

'Come in, come in…'

'No, you must come out. There are strange things happening here by night.'

'I know. That's why I'm staying locked up in my room with a silver throwing knife.'

Genevieve winced, and made a fist of her right hand. He recalled the story of the treachery of Ueli the dwarf.

'Again, I'm sorry. I should have thought.'

She laughed, girlishly. 'No, no, I'm past bothering about all that. I'm a creature of the night, so I have to live with those things. Now, get your clothes on and bring a candle. You probably can't see in the dark as well as I can.'

Her voice was light, flirting, but her eyes were serious. There's a strange quality to vampire eyes.

'Very well, but I'm bringing my knife.'

'Don't you trust me?' Her smile showed teeth.

'Genevieve, just now, you and Vargr Breughel are the only people in this place that I do trust.'

He pulled on his trousers and a jacket, and found a pair of slippers which wouldn't make too much noise on the naked stone floors. He relit his candle, and Genevieve tugged at his sleeve.

'Where are we going?'

'We're following my nose.'

'I don't smell anything.'

'Neither do I. That was a figure of speech. I can feel things, you know. It comes with what I am. There's a great disturbance in this place. When we came here, it was clear, empty, but something came along with us and has taken up residence. Something old, something evil…'

'The twenty-seventh wagon.'

Genevieve stopped and looked at him, puzzled.

'Remember, we could never get straight the number of wagons in the caravan,' he explained. 'There were supposed to be twenty-six, but whenever we weren't looking, there seemed to be twenty-seven. If what you're talking about came with us, perhaps it came in that wagon.'

'That could be so. I should have thought of that at the time. I assumed you were just being artistically inept.'

'Thank you very much. It takes a lot of ineptitude to stage a major play, let me tell you. If it weren't for Breughel, I'd be ploughed under with work. It's not all writing and play-acting. There are finances and accommodation arrangements, and you have to feed all these people. There's probably more organization involved than in a military campaign.'

They had ventured into a part of the fortress Detlef didn't recognize. It was partially in ruins, and the cool night air blew through gaps in the walls. Moonlight flooded in. Oswald's men had not been here, and there had been no attempt to clean the place up or to make it safe. Detlef realized how little of the structure he had seen, had been given access to.

'It's near,' Genevieve said, precisely as a gust of wind snuffed his candle. 'Very near.'

He put the warm stub in his pocket and relied on the moon. He couldn't feel, see or smell anything out of the ordinary.

'What precisely are we looking for?'

'It could be anything. But it's big, it's disturbed and it's not friendly.'

'I'm really glad you told me that.'

She looked good at night, with her long, moonlit hair and floorlength white dress. As dead people go, she was a lot prettier than Rudi Wegener. For a moment, he wondered whether he hadn't been lured to this isolated spot for something more intriguing than a simple exercise in corridor-prowling. His blood ran faster. He had never been bled by a vampire, but he had read the erotic poems of Vladislav Dvorjetski, Tsarina Kattarin's lover, and understood from them that the experience was quite something.

He put his hands on her waist, and drew close to her, smelling her hair. Then, they heard the chanting.

Genevieve turned her head and put a finger to her mouth, shushing him. She stepped from his half-embrace, and pushed her hair back from her face. Detlef couldn't tell whether she was baring her teeth consciously or unconsciously. They looked longer and sharper in the moonlight.

The chanting was only just audible, but it had a horrid quality to it. If this were a religious rite, it would be dedicated to one of the gods whose altars Detlef habitually shunned. If this were some magical incantation, it was the work of an outlaw wizard conjuring up something utterly vile.

Slowly, quietly, they crept down the corridor, passing through alternating patches of light and dark. There were doors in the walls, and one – about twenty feet up ahead – was ajar. The chanting came from beyond that door, Detlef was certain. It grew louder as they approached, and he could make out the low pipe music being played under the vocal. Something about the tune turned his stomach. Something that made him fear he had seen his last sunset.

They pressed close to the wall, and edged nearer.

There were lights beyond the door. And people, moving in a confined space.

Detlef had his silver knife out.

They came to the door, and peered through. The slit only afforded a very limited view of what was taking place inside the chamber beyond, but that was enough to make Detlef feel sick again.

In a circle of black candles lay a small figure. A child or a dwarf. It was impossible to tell, because he had been flayed.

His exposed musculature glistened red in the candle-light. Shadows danced around him, cast by unseen participants in this grisly scene.

'Menesh,' whispered Genevieve.

Detlef saw that the red thing in the circle had but one arm. As he gazed at the writhing snakes of the dwarf's intestines, he came to realize that Menesh was still, somehow, alive. He would have vomited then, but there was nothing left in his stomach to come up. Bones stood out white amid the bloody jelly of the remaining flesh.

Genevieve was straining forward, tensing to leap into the room. Detlef held her back by the shoulders. They would have no chance against as many murderers as he thought joined in the chant. She turned, and took his wrists. He felt again the strength of the vampire, and saw red anger flare and die in her eyes. Then, she too realized they couldn't afford to barge in and get killed. She nodded her thanks.

Then they heard the clatter of boots. People were coming down the corridor, and they were caught between the two factions.

Lanterns came out of the dark. Halberds scraped the stone ceiling. Six men-at-arms marched, and Kraly stood at their head. He looked disapproving as he saw Detlef and Genevieve. For once, Detlef couldn't bring himself to be annoyed by the man's presence. Just now, he looked like the Imperial cavalry turning up in the last act to relieve the castle.

The chanting had risen now to a weird ululation that resounded throughout the passageway. Menesh was screaming in time with the music, and the shadows clustered around him.

'What are you doing here?' snapped Kraly.

'Never mind that,' said Detlef, having to shout now to be heard over the chant. 'There's murder being done in this room.'

'So I gather.' He pushed his helmet back, and hooked his thumbs into the pockets of his doublet.

'Kraly, let's end this thing now.'

The steward considered a moment or two. 'Very well.'

Detlef stood back, and let the first pair of Kraly's bully boys crash through the door, knocking it off its hinges. The heavy wood fell with a gust that extinguished the black candles. The chanting and the music shut off suddenly, and there were cries in the dark. Some of the voices were human. Detlef rushed into the room. As he stepped through the portal, the candle he was holding went out and he found himself in total darkness. He had the feeling of being in a vast, exposed plain under a starless, moonless night sky. He stepped in something soft and wet, and heard a groan that told him what it was. Then, he was buffeted this way and that by heavy bodies. There were screams, and the noise of weapons clashing. He was lifted bodily from the ground and thrown across the room. He collided with someone, and went down, his arm twisted under him. There was a wrenching at his shoulder, and he prayed the bone wasn't broken. Kraly was barking orders. Someone stepped briefly on his chest, and he tried to stand up, clutching his agonized shoulder.

Then the lights came in.

Genevieve, a lantern in either hand, stood in the doorway. The chamber was small, and had a dead dwarf in it. Otherwise, Detlef, Kraly and the men-at-arms were alone. In the dark, one of the crown prince's men had been stabbed in the thigh by a comrade, and was bleeding messily as he applied a tourniquet. Genevieve went to his aid, and he cringed away from her as she tied the wound properly. The bleeding stopped and the man seemed somewhat surprised that the vampire let him be.

'Well done, Kraly. Oswald will be proud of you, I'm sure.' Detlef pushed his shoulder back into place, gritting his teeth through the pain.

The steward wasn't rattled by his failure. He was on his knees, examining the dwarf. Detlef was upset to notice the footprint in the new-made corpse's stomach, and thought better of looking at his own slipper.

'The skin's gone, this time. And the kidneys. And the eyes, of course. And... um... the regenerative organs.'

Kraly blushed at having to mention such indecent matters in the presence of a lady.

'He was alive when we came in, Kraly,' said Detlef. 'We probably trampled him to death.'

'He wouldn't have lived.'

'Obviously not, but he might have told us something before he went. We've not done well here.'

Kraly stood up, wiping the dust from his knee-britches. He pulled out a kerchief and tried to get the blood off his hands. He rubbed away at his fingers long after they were clean.

'There must be another way out,' said Genevieve. 'I was at the door. No one came through it after you all pushed your way in.'

They all looked around the room. It was bare stone, with traces of graffiti in a language or languages Detlef didn't recognize as the only adornment. Kraly gave an order, and his men began prodding with their halberds. Finally, when they tried the ceiling, a stone receded above a blade, and a whole section of the wall swung inwards. Beyond lay a hidden passage, its floor thick with the dust of centuries. The cobwebs had recently been parted.

'You first, Kraly,' said Detlef.

The steward, a single-shot pistol in his hand, led the way. Detlef and Genevieve followed, along with four of the halberdiers. They had to leave their halberds behind because the secret passage was too low for the weapons. They all had to stoop.

'This would be a fine escape route for a dwarf,' said Kraly.

'Menesh was the victim, not the murderer,' mentioned Detlef.

'I wasn't thinking of Menesh.'

There was blood in the dust.

'We must have wounded him.'

'Either that or he got covered in the stuff while skinning Menesh.'

'Possibly.'

The passage wound down a spiral staircase, into the heart of Drachenfels. They found a skeleton in centuries-old armour, the skull exploded from within. Detlef shuddered. This place had more horrors than the Northern Wastes. Sigmar himself would think twice at exploring its nether regions.

There were eyeholes in the walls now. Detlef guessed they would peer through the eyes of portraits in the chambers. Either Drachenfels had had a fine sense of irony in his deployment of melodramatic devices, or – more likely – he had invented the clichés later taken up by addlewits out to chill the spines of their audiences. The way things were going, he expected a contested will, devious heirs, corpses concealed in suits of armour and a last-act unmasking of the kindly old steward as a mad killer.

Then they came to a door, and were back in the familiar part of the fortress. This was where the company were billeted.

'Surely that can't be,' Detlef said. 'We descended to the place where Menesh was killed, and now we've come down again, back to where we started.'

'This place is like that,' said Genevieve. 'It's all down, whichever way you go.'

The door swung back, sealing the secret passage. It looked like any other section of the wall.

'Kraly, weren't you supposed to have someone on guard in this corridor? Someone who might have noticed a murderer covered from head to foot in blood creep out of the wall?'

The steward's face was frozen. 'I had to redeploy my forces to search the castle. That's why you're still alive.'

Detlef had to admit he had a point. 'We're alive, yes, but how do we know everyone in these rooms hasn't been slaughtered in their beds? Only, with our luck, they'd have spared Lilli Nissen.'

'Our quarry was in too much haste to do harm to anyone. Look, he left us a spoor to read.'

There was blood on the carpet. It petered out after a few feet. Outside a door. There was a red smear on the knob.

'I believe we have our killer,' said Kraly, grimly satisfied.

'Don't you think that's just a bit too convenient?' asked Detlef. 'Besides, there was more than one person chanting.'

'That's as may be. We'll round up the confederates later. But first let's take our man. Or whatever he is…'

The door was locked. Kraly discharged his gun at the lock. Others opened up and down the passage, and heads peeked out. Detlef would have to ask later what Kosinski was doing in Lilli Nissen's suite. Kraly kicked the door, and it splintered as it slammed back.

Vargr Breughel had jumped out of bed. Kraly looked at him, and gasped. Detlef pushed through, and felt as if he had been punched in the stomach.

His friend and adviser looked up at him through eyes in his chest and hands.

But it was the look in the eyes in his face that struck through to Detlef.

Breughel, the monster, was crying.

II

THERE IS NO pleasure like rising with the sun and finding yourself in the forests of the Empire, thought Karl-Franz I as he made water in the bushes. He listened to the birdsong, naming each individual species in his head as he distinguished it from the rest of the chatter of the morning chorus. It was a fine spring morning, and the sun was already high, streaming through the tall trees. There would be deer along their route today, the Emperor was sure. It was years since he had hunted deer.

In the camp, there were the groans and complaints of those stirred too early from their slumbers. Karl-Franz was amused to find which of his distinguished travelling companions awoke irritable in the wilds, which were nursing heads befuddled by last night's food and drink, and which sprang to their horses enlivened by the call of the birds and the fresh feel of dew underfoot. Herbal tea was being brewed in huge iron pots, and a light breakfast prepared.

Some of the worthies chose to sleep in carriages as well appointed and upholstered as any bed-chamber in any palace, but Karl-Franz wanted only the feel of a blanket

between himself and the ground. The empress disagreed, and
had opted to stay at home with one of her persistent illnesses,
but Luitpold, their twelve-year-old son and heir, was revelling
in the freedom of the forests. There were still men-at-arms
watching out for the Imperial family at every moment – Karl-
Franz couldn't even wander into the woods to empty his
bladder without a sword-bearing shadow following him –
but there was open air about them. The Emperor felt free of
the burdens of state, felt a respite from the stifling procedures
of running the country, of resisting the incursions of evil, of
defying the dark.

The elector of Middenland, who had been protesting very
loudly ever since he learned precisely who Oswald had
engaged to stage his play for him, was rubbing his aching
back, and moaning softly to the red-haired page who always
seemed to be with him. The grand theogonist of the cult of
Sigmar, a frail old man for such a robust deity, had not shown
a hair of his head outside his coach since they left Altdorf,
and his snoring was a source of some amusement. Karl-Franz
observed the other electors and their attendants as they shook
the sleep from their heads, and took tea. He was learning
more of these men and women upon whom the Empire
rested on this trip than he had in years of courtly meetings
and grand balls.

Aside from Oswald, who rode as if born on a horse and
could bring down a pheasant with a single crossbow bolt, the
only elector who seemed entirely comfortable on this journey
was the elder of the Halfling Moot, who spent most of his
time eating or laughing. The young Baron Johann von
Mecklenberg, elector of the Sudenland, was a skilled woods-
man, Karl-Franz knew, having spent half his life wandering in
search of a lost brother and only recently returned to his
estates. Johann gave the impression that he had seen things
which made pleasure trips like this petty by comparison. He
wore his scars like medals, and didn't talk much. The lady
mayoress and chancellor of the University of Nuln, Countess
Emmanuelle von Leibewitz, rumoured to be the most eligible
spinster in the Empire, was not winning any friends with her
whining about the tedious details of the hundreds of masques
and parties she had thrown. Karl-Franz was both amused and

appalled at the realization that the countess was cooing over Luitpold not in any motherly sense but because she regarded the future Emperor as an ideal marriage prospect despite the obvious disparities of age and temperament between them.

The Emperor took a steaming mug of tea from his attendant, and downed a gulp of the hot, sweet beverage. Middenheim was asking how much longer they would be on the road, and Oswald was making a rough guess. Young Luitpold crashed out of the undergrowth, his jerkin soiled and his hair untidy, pushing Resnais of Marienburg aside, and bore a still-twitching rabbit to the fire. His arrow had taken it in the haunches. Karl-Franz noted that his son took his prize to Oswald for approval. The crown prince deftly snapped the dying animal's neck.

'Excellent, highness,' said the elector of Ostland. 'This was well shot.'

Luitpold looked around, grinning, as Oswald tousled his already wild hair. Resnais fastidiously brushed his clothes. Oswald waved to Karl-Franz.

'Your son will feed the Empire, my friend.'

'I hope so. If it needs feeding.'

Talabecland crawled out of his vast tent, bleary-eyed and unshaven. He looked at the bleeding rabbit in Oswald's hand and moaned.

Oswald and Luitpold laughed. Karl-Franz joined them. This was what the life of the Emperor should always be. Good friends and good hunting.

'Here.' Oswald dipped his hand into the rabbit's wounds, and drew red lines on Luitpold's cheeks. 'Now, future Emperor, you have been blooded.'

Luitpold ran to Karl-Franz, and saluted his father. The Emperor returned the salute.

'Well, my hero son, perhaps you should wash yourself off and have some tea. We may rule the greatest country in the Known World, but we have an empress who rules us, and she would want you well fed and warmed out here. Husbands have been skewered through the eye with tent pegs for less.'

Luitpold took his mug.

'Ah, father, but surely the Emperor Hajalmar was assassinated for being appallingly ill-suited to the throne, rather than for his short-comings as a family man. I seem to recall from my lessons that he died childless, and so could hardly be accused of neglecting the welfare of his heirs, unless you count his failure to produce any as a lack of fatherly spirit.'

'Well learned, my son. Now clean your face and have your tea before I abdicate in favour of your little sister and cut you out of the succession.'

Everybody laughed, and Karl-Franz recognized the deep-throated genuine laughter he could sometimes elicit rather than the weak chuckles that came from people who believed an Emperor's joke was automatically funny and that there would be a penalty of death for anyone who thought differently. There was a neighing as the horses were roused in their makeshift pens by the ostlers.

'Father,' asked Luitpold, 'who were the monks who came here last night?'

Karl-Franz was taken aback.

'Monks? I know of no monks. Have you any idea what the lad means, Oswald?'

The elector shook his head, a blank look on his face. Perhaps too blank, as if something were being concealed.

'Last night, when all were asleep save the guards, I was awakened.'

Luitpold told his story. 'I was worried about Fortunato's hoof. His shoe has been working loose, and I thought I heard him whinnying. I got up and went to the pens, and Fortunato was fast asleep. I must have dreamed his cry. But when I returned to my tent, I saw men standing at the edge of the clearing. At first, I supposed them to be the guards, but then I noticed they were dressed in long robes and hoods, like the monks of Ulric...'

The high priest of the cult of Ulric shrugged, and scratched his belly. Talabecland and Middenheim were attentive. Luitpold, enjoying their regard, continued.

'They were standing still, but their faces glowed a little, as if lit by lanterns. I would have called out to them to explain their business, but I didn't want to wake everyone. I was suddenly very sleepy, so I returned to my tent. I assumed you would know what they were about.'

Oswald looked thoughtful.

'Do you suppose my son could have witnessed some apparition? My late father was prone to seeing spirits. The knack could have skipped a generation.'

'I've heard of no such spectral cadre,' said Oswald. 'There are many stories about the hauntings in these woods. My friend Rudi Wegener, whom you will meet at Castle Drachenfels, knows and has told me of dozens of local legends. But these monks do not mean anything to me.'

The Baron von Mecklenberg snorted. 'Then you are less well learned on your own legend than you should be, Ostland. The monks of Drachenfels are widely remembered by necromancers and spirit-chasers.'

Karl-Franz imagined Oswald was discomforted by his fellow elector's knowledge.

The baron poured the last of his tea hissing into the fire, and continued, 'Drachenfels killed many in his time, and was enchanter enough to make his sway over his victims last beyond their death. Their spirits clung to him, became his slaves. Some even became his followers. They were supposed to be seen in habits like monks. Even after their master's death, they are rumoured to cling together, to form an order in the world of ghosts. We travel to the fortress of Drachenfels, and evidently the Great Enchanter's victims ride with us.'

III

LAST NIGHT, AT precisely the worst point, an assistant stage manager had told Detlef 'things will look better in the morning' and lost two front teeth.

This morning, when, as expected, things looked even worse than they had been, Detlef vaguely regretted his temper. He had fallen into a swoon just before dawn, and woke up now with a pain in his skinned knuckles. His head ached worse than it had ever done the morning after a drunken orgy, and his mouth felt as if it had been filled with quick-drying slime.

The servant who brought him his breakfast on a tray had left it at his bedside and not dared to disturb him. He took a mouthful of cold tea, swished it around to clean the scum off his teeth, and spat back into the cup. The bacon and bread were cold and greasy. He took a bite and forced himself to get it down.

It all came flooding back horribly.

His best friend was a strangely altered monstrosity, and Henrik Kraly claimed he was also the madman who had murdered Rudi Wegener and Menesh the dwarf.

He hadn't bothered to undress last night. Now he did, and found fresh clothes laid out for him. He pulled them on, trying to will the fog out of his head. He rubbed his stubbled chin, and decided to put off shaving until his hands were steady enough to hold the razor.

Detlef found most of the company gathered in the main hall, peering at a notice posted on the door, signed by Henrik Kraly.

It was an announcement that the murderer had been caught and that things would now proceed normally. Vargr Breughel was not mentioned, and no one had yet noticed he wasn't with them.

'I bet it's that bastard Kosinski,' said a small voice.

'No, it's not,' said Kosinski, hitting someone.

'Where's the vampire?' asked Justus the Trickster.

'It wasn't her,' said Detlef. 'Kraly's taken Breughel–'

There were general gasps of disbelief.

'And it wasn't him either. At least, it's not been proved to my satisfaction. Where *is* Genevieve?'

No one knew.

Detlef found her in her room, dead in her bed. She wasn't breathing, but he felt a slow heartbeat. There was no waking her.

Even in his current state of disturbance, he took the time to look around. There were books on her dressing table, written in an arcane form of Bretonnian Detlef could just recognize but not follow. Genevieve's diaries? They would make interesting reading. A scarf had been hung over the mirror.

It must be strange to lose familiarity with your own face, Detlef supposed.

Otherwise, the room was like any other woman's. Trunks of clothes, a few pamphlets, keys and coins on the nightstand, an icon-sized portrait of a couple dressed in the styles of seven centuries ago. There was a copy of the *Drachenfels* script on a chair, with annotations in a tiny hand. He would have to ask her about them. Was she studying her own part? Lilli Nissen's part, rather. When she didn't wake up after a minute or two, Detlef left her to the sleep of the undying.

He found Reinhardt Jessner, and told him to take the cast through their lines while he saw to Breughel. The young actor understood immediately, and corralled the company efficiently.

There were Kraly-signed notices up all over the fortress, issuing orders and failing to explain the situation. He must have been up all night putting his signature to them.

Detlef found them in the stables, which had been converted into a makeshift jail-cum-interrogation room. He was drawn to the place by the noise of the thumps.

They'd cleared out one of the stalls, and chained Breughel up naked like an animal in it. Kraly sat on a stool, asking questions, while an inky clerk with a quill taller than his hat scratched down a transcript of the conversation. Detlef wondered how he transliterated the screams.

One of Kraly's halberdiers was naked to the waist, his torso flushed and sweaty. He had armoured gauntlets on, and had been working Breughel over.

The prisoner's human face was bloodied. The rest of him leaked a yellowish fluid.

Even if Breughel had had any answers, he wouldn't have been able to give them, Detlef thought.

'What are you doing here, Kraly? You idiot!'

'Getting a confession. The crown prince will want things sorted out before he gets here.'

'I think if you hit me a couple of times with those gloves on, I'd confess too. Surely, even a cretin like you knows why torture is out of fashion. Unless, of course, you get your amusement this way.'

Kraly stood up. He had Breughel's yellow ichor on his boots. He was freshly barbered and wore an immaculate white cravat. He didn't look as if he had spent the night crawling about secret passageways and leaping to conclusions.

'There are details known only to the murderer. Those are what we are after.'

'And what if he's not the murderer?'

Kraly's lips curled up on one side. 'I think that's unlikely given the evidence, don't you?'

'Evidence! The killer just stuck his bloody hand on a door to point you at a convenient scapegoat, and you've done just what he wanted. A nine-year old wouldn't be taken in by that old trick!'

The torturer took a good shot at Breughel's stomach, disturbing the forest of unclassifiable fronds that grew there. Several of the eyes in his chest had been put out. Another of Kraly's men was heating up a brazier and sticking blacksmithing tools into it. Torture was evidently not a lost art in Ostland. Detlef wondered how Good Prince Oswald would react to all this.

'I was not referring to the bloody door, Mr Sierck. I was referring to... this monstrous abortion, this creature of Chaos...'

Mouths around Breughel's waist snapped open, long tongues darting out. The torturer cried out.

'That stings.' Blue weals rose on his arm.

'You'll be dead in three days,' said Breughel, his voice remarkably unaffected.

The torturer started back, raising his hand to strike. Then panic filled his eyes. He grabbed his arm, as if to squeeze out the infection.

'You can't possibly know that, Breughel,' Detlef said. 'You've never stung anyone before.'

Breughel laughed, liquid rattling in his throat. 'That's true.'

The torturer looked relieved, and cuffed Breughel viciously. Blood flew. The floor of the stall was slippery with various bodily fluids. The place smelled badly. The clerk scribbled down a precis of the incident for posterity.

'Kraly, can I talk to my friend?'

The steward shrugged.

'Alone?'

He nodded his head, got up, and strolled out of the stall. His torturer went with him, rubbing his itching rash. The scribe also withdrew, muttering about judicial procedures.

'Can I get you anything?' Detlef asked.

'Some water would be nice.'

Detlef used a dipper in a bucket that stood nearby, and raised the water to his friend's lips. He found it strange being so close to such a twisted creature, but he swallowed his distaste. Breughel coughed as he slurped, and the water trickled out of his wounded mouth. But his throat worked, and he got some down. He hung there, exhausted, in his chains, and looked expectantly at Detlef.

'Go on,' he said, 'ask me...'

'Ask you what?'

'If I gutted Rudi and took his eyes. And did the same for Menesh.'

Detlef hesitated. 'All right, I'll ask you.'

Breughel's eyes leaked again. He looked betrayed. 'You have to say it out loud. It hurts more that way. The hurting is the most important part of it.'

Detlef gulped. '*Did* you kill them? Rudi and Menesh?'

Breughel painfully formed a toothless smile. 'Is that what you think?'

'Oh, come on now, Vargr! This is me, Detlef Sierck, not some total stranger! We've worked together for... how many years now? You stuck by me all through *The History of Sigmar*, you think I'm going to desert you just because you're a...'

He groped for the word.

Breughel gave it to him. 'A mutant. That's what they're... what *we're* called, these days. Yes, I'm a creature of Chaos. Look at me...'

Breughel pulsated, strange organs emerging from his torso.

'It's a strange disease. I don't know if I'm dying of it, or being reborn. I wish I were a writer like you, then maybe I could describe what it's like.'

'Does it hurt?'

'Some of the time. At others, it's... quite pleasant, actually. I don't have to feel pain if I don't want to. Otherwise, I'd have given Kraly a nice little confession. Unfortunately, I can't protect myself through ignorance, you see. These tentacles in my belly can see what's uppermost in a man's mind. I know the details of the murders Kraly wants to beat and burn out of me. Just as I know how you really feel about what I've become...'

Detlef cringed inwardly, and blurted an apology.

'Don't be sorry. I'm disgusted at what I've become. I've always been disgusted at what I was. It's nothing new. I don't blame you at all. You're the only one who ever gave me a chance. I'm going to die soon, and I'd like you to know how grateful I've been for your friendship.'

'Vargr, I won't let Kraly kill you.'

'No, you won't. I have the choice whether I live or die. I can stop my heart, tear it apart with the teeth I have inside my chest. And I intend to do it.'

'But Oswald is a fair man. He won't see you hanged for murders you didn't commit.'

Breughel's cilia writhed and changed colour.

'No, but what about seeing me hanged for the murders I will commit? Even seeing me hanged for what I am. I'm changing–'

'That's– obvious.'

'Not just in my body. My mind is changing, too. I have impulses. The warpstone warps minds as well as bodies. I've been misremembering things, having strange ideas, strange desires. I'm altering severely. I could go to the Wastes and lose myself in the hordes of Chaos, join with all the other monsters. But I'd not be me any more. I'm losing Vargr Breughel, and I don't think I want to leave behind what I'm about to become.'

Breughel gritted his teeth, and strained against his chains. There was a great grinding inside his chest. His cilia deepened in colour and stuck out like fat sausages.

Kraly and his men came rushing back. 'What's the beast doing?' asked the steward.

Detlef turned and hit him in the gut, hurting his knuckles more. Kraly bent double, swearing and coughing. Detlef wanted to hit the man again, but there was too much else going on for him to bother.

Breughel's torso swelled up, and he snapped his chains out of the wall. Smiling, he advanced on Kraly. The steward screamed as the monster came for him. Breughel rattled his chains and, smiling, slapped his tormentor's face. He continued to expand, rents appearing in his skin. Eyes stood out like boils. He drew a great breath, inflating his lungs. Then, he burst.

Detlef stood back to avoid the splatter. The torturer fell over, putting a hand into the brazier of hot coals to steady himself. He screamed as his hand was roasted through. Breughel fell apart with a great sighing.

As he died, Vargr Breughel said, 'Good luck with the play.'

IV

WHEN, THREE DAYS later, the Imperial party arrived, things were as nearly back to normal as they ever could be. Detlef had supervised the burial of Vargr Breughel, and informed Henrik Kraly that it would be in his own best interests to keep out of his way. Kraly put up notices announcing that Breughel had been the murderer, and muttered to his men that each day which passed without a fresh atrocity proved him right. If the dwarf had confederates, the steward did not spend too much of his time seeking them out. Privately, he expressed the opinion that the voices they had heard in the room where Menesh was murdered were those of the daemons Breughel was summoning with his unholy ritual.

Murderer or not, Breughel was much missed by the company. Detlef called a halt to rehearsals for an entire morning so that everyone could attend the assistant director's funeral. Detlef had him buried on the mountainside, outside the fortress walls. Justus the Trickster, a cleric after all, read the lesson, and Detlef gave a brief eulogy. The only conspicuously absent face was that of Lilli Nissen, and she hadn't even been much in evidence at rehearsals recently. Breughel had more friends than he knew. When Oswald came, Detlef vowed, there would be a reckoning with Kraly, whom he considered his friend's murderer.

The play was set in its final form now. Detlef went through a complete day of rehearsal without adding, deleting or changing any lines, and an enormous cheer went up from the company. He took out his much-scribbled script and pondered a moment before pronouncing the text whole and finished. Then he delivered a fifty-minute lecture on the finer points of the actual production, browbeating, upbraiding, cajoling and pampering those who deserved it and enthusing his followers with the spirit of the piece. Watching from the audience – with a stand-in taking his role – Detlef thought the only dead spot was Lilli, and there was really nothing to be done about that. At least, she still looked incredible, teeth in or out, and her blankness could just barely be interpreted as undead detachment, even if that interpretation went against the grain of the play and the expectations of anyone who had met the real Genevieve Dieudonné. He could not speak for his own performance. That had been one of Breughel's functions, to keep him alert as an actor while he might be overly concerned with other details of the production. He hoped his friend would not be overly critical from the afterlife, and sought to curb the excesses Breughel had continually pointed out to him.

When runners appeared early in the morning to announce the imminent arrival of the Emperor and the electors, Detlef was confident enough to cancel the day's work and leave the company to their own devices. They would perform all the better for the rest and relaxation. And he knew they would appreciate the opportunity to gawk at rich and famous people. More than one young actress or musician vanished to their chambers to dig out their most fetching, and/or revealing, costumes in the hope of attracting a wealthy patron among the Emperor's entourage.

The Emperor Karl-Franz rode into Castle Drachenfels at the head of his caravan, Oswald – Grand Prince Oswald now – a little behind him, and his son Luitpold doing his best to keep abreast. The Emperor waved, and the assembled cast cheered him. The rest of the caravan creaked and lumbered through the castle gates and the courtyard became a chaos of ostlers and coachmen and servants. The dignified personages spilled out of their carriages and were led to the luxurious apartments that had been prepared for them in the wing of the fortress opposite the actors' quarters. Detlef heard Illona Horvathy commenting enviously on Countess Emmanuelle von Liebewitz's ridiculously bejewelled travelling clothes. He recognized the elector of Middenland, who avoided his gaze and hurried off, grey-faced, to find the privies. Some people don't travel well. Kraly turned out and got to Oswald first. He delivered a concise report, and Detlef saw the elector's face grow serious.

Oswald came over to Detlef, leaving Kraly to liaise with the new influx of guardsmen.

'This has been a bad business.'

'Yes, highness, and made the worse for your servant.'

Oswald was grave. 'So I gather.'

'Vargr Breughel was innocent of any crime.'

'Yet he was an altered.'

'That is, in itself, not illegal.'

'For now, maybe. There are moves in the college. However, I assure you this will not end here. Steps will be taken. You will be heard.'

Young Luitpold ran up to Oswald and tugged at his coat, excitedly. Then, he became aware of Detlef, and turned from a normal boy trussed up in a silly soldier suit to a miniature aristocrat with poise and bearing.

'Detlef Sierck, permit me to introduce Luitpold of the House of the Second Wilhelm.'

The boy bowed, his hand fluttering before his face. Detlef returned the bow.

'I am honoured, highness.'

His duty done, Luitpold returned his attention to Oswald. 'Show me where you slew the monster, Oswald. And where your tutor was killed by Ueli the dwarf, and where the gargoyles came out of the walls...'

Oswald laughed, but without much humour. 'That can wait until Detlef's play. You'll find it all out then.'

The future Emperor dashed off, one silk stocking slipping to bunch at his ankle. Oswald looked more the proud parent

than Karl-Franz, Detlef thought. Then, the grand prince
turned serious again, as if suddenly aware of the place he had
returned to.

'We didn't come in through the courtyard, you know,' he
said. 'I only saw this afterwards, in the sunlight. We came in
through the cliff gates, which lie beyond that arm of the
fortress.'

He pointed. By day, Drachenfels was just an ordinary
mountain fastness. Only at night did the dread creep back.

'That's where I saw Sieur Jehan, my oldest friend, with his
throat pulled out, bleeding his last.'

'We have all lost friends, highness.'

Oswald stared at Detlef, as if seeing him for the first time.
'Forgive me. So, this place has claimed more victims.
Sometimes, I think we should have had it pulled down and
scattered the stones, then seeded the site with salt and silver.'

'But then you wouldn't have been able to stage this pageant.'

'Maybe not.'

Detlef could not help but notice that Oswald seemed more
disturbed by the death of Sieur Jehan, twenty-five years ago,
than by those of Rudi Wegener and Menesh the dwarf within
the last week. The aristocrat had grown a tougher skin since
his first visit to this place. The boy hero of Detlef's play was
buried within the skilled politician, the dignified statesman.

A sprightly man in early middle age approached them. He
had doffed his ceremonial coat, and Detlef took a moment to
recognize him in a plain black travelling suit.

'Detlef, here is Luitpold's father.'

Emperor Karl-Franz of the House of the Second Wilhelm
held out a hand. Detlef didn't know whether to shake it or
kiss it, and opted to do both. To his surprise, he found himself immediately liking the man.

'We've heard much of your work, Sierck. I trust you'll not
disappoint us tomorrow night.'

'I shall try not to, majesty.'

'That's all we can ask for. Oswald, come, let's eat. I'm starv-
ing.'

Karl-Franz and Oswald left, arm in arm.

So these, Detlef thought, are the giants, the true gods whose
whims alter the courses of our lives, whose faults slaughter

thousands and whose virtues endure for ever. Like the fortress of Drachenfels, they don't seem so much in the daylight.

Genevieve appeared, hidden behind her strange dark glasses, and flew to Oswald.

For a moment, Detlef wondered if what he was feeling was jealousy.

V

WHILE OSWALD entertained Karl-Franz and the electors in one wing of the fortress, and Detlef oversaw his dress rehearsal in the other, Anton Veidt was preparing to leave Drachenfels. He took his weapons from their hidden places in his room, and cleaned them. He wrapped a coil of rope around his skinny middle. He packed provisions enough for three days in the mountains. And he allowed himself a cigar, keeping the smoke down, controlling the spasms in his chest.

He was not a stupid man. Erzbet dead. Rudi dead. Menesh dead. He could follow the trend. The vampire lady and the grand prince might be foolish enough to stay and invite their fates, but Veidt was getting out now.

Twenty-five years ago, it had been the same. Conradin dead. Heinroth dead. Sieur Jehan dead. Ueli the dwarf dead. Stellan the Warlock dead. Others whose names he couldn't even remember dead. And Veidt alone in the dark, waiting for death.

Sometimes, he wondered if he really had died in the passageways of this castle, and whether the remainder of his life was just a dream, or a nightmare? As his black crab ate more, he felt himself being tugged back to those hours in the dark with the poison creeping into him.

He would wake up at night, certain that the mattress beneath him was the stone floor of Castle Drachenfels.

Could it be only minutes since Oswald and the others had left him to die here? Could he have imagined the whole course of his life in these few moments of unconsciousness? In the dark, the events of twenty-five years seemed a dream. How could he have ever believed such a hazy, marginal existence was real?

These sick thoughts were a symptom of the dangers of this place. He should never have returned. There weren't enough gold crowns in the Empire to hire a man to commit suicide.

He chose his time well, while Oswald was busy with his feast and Detlef his performance. There would be guards about, but they weren't expecting anyone to attempt an escape. He should have no problem. And if he did come up against some itchy halberdier, he had his dart gun and his short sword.

Actually, he had no reason to believe he couldn't just tell Oswald he was leaving and walk away from Drachenfels in the open. But he did not intend to chance the grand prince's whims. Oswald could as easily have him imprisoned as let him free and there was no telling how important Veidt really was to his pageant.

In his old clothes, his hunting clothes, he left his room and crept down to the courtyard. It was well lit and he could see too many men-at-arms. Kraly himself was supervising the watch, fanatically devoting himself to the security of the Imperial party in an attempt to justify his earlier actions. The great doors were closed, so Veidt would have to scale the walls to escape. The risk was too great.

He would have to leave the castle the way they had come in all those years ago, through the gates at the clifftop. He had rope and his grip was as good as ever. He could descend the mountains, get away into Bretonnia. Oswald would never reach for him there and there were felons enough to keep his belly full. He could grow old with Bretonnian wenches and Bretonnian wine, and maybe burst his heart through excess before the crab killed him.

Weeks ago, when they had arrived at the fortress, he had retraced the steps of their original expedition, searching for the spot where he had lain unconscious while Oswald was killing Drachenfels. He had not been able to find it. One stretch of corridor looked much like another. Now, he paced the route again, reversing their path, pushing for the outside. He passed the great hall, where the play-actors were recreating the death of Drachenfels, then worked his way srelowly through the passage where Rudi had been caught in the wooden jaws of the trap. Beyond lay the place of his ordeal, the poison feast chamber, the gargoyle stones, the enchanted door that had killed Stellan, and the outer wall.

His pains had receded in the last few days. Comfortable accommodations and real food will do that to you. He had been lulled by the luxuries, and wilfully ignored the dangers. But now fat old Rudi was gone, and one-armed Menesh, and poor, mad Erzbet. Buried without their eyes. Like him, they should have died here a quarter century ago, but had clung on beyond their time. Veidt intended to cling just a little longer, with just a little more tenacity.

He wandered for hours, longer than he should have, resting for a time in shadowed corners. It was late now. The dress rehearsal would be over, the feast quietening down. This part of the fortress was deserted – shunned, even – and no one stood between Veidt and the safety of the night outside. Rudi had been found here. And the room where Menesh had been skinned was only a few turns of the corridor away.

He was feeling the crab now, feeling it shift inside him. His heart hung like a stone in his chest, and his joints pained him. He was certain he was bleeding inside his clothes. He had to stifle coughing fits lest his noise attract the guards. Or even less welcome presences.

Veidt's feet dragged, as if he were wading through heavy sludge. And he remembered the gargoyle poison seeping through his veins, turning his flesh to the semblance of stone. Perhaps the sickness had just lain dormant in him all these years, awaiting his return to Drachenfels to strike again?

Wet trickled down his face. He touched his hand to the graze, and found it bleeding. The wound made by the gargoyle's horn had opened again.

He stumbled, trying to force himself forwards, and fell headlong. His skull rang as it struck the flagstones. In his convulsive grip, his pistol discharged. He heard rather than felt the dart whizz along the floor under him and bury its tip in his thigh. Then, the pain came. He rolled over, and shuffled back until there was a wall behind him. The shaft was bent, but the head was embedded deep in his muscle. He made a fist around the dart and pulled, but it slipped through his fingers and he was holding nothing. He couldn't get a strong enough hold on the shaft to get it out of his leg.

Tired, he let sleep come…

…then he was awake, alert, the ache in his leg cutting through the fuzziness of his senses.

There were people in the passage with him. His old comrades. There was Erzbet, hanging back, long hair over her face. And Rudi, his loose skin flapping on his skeleton. And Menesh leaking as he held in his guts with a raw hand. There were others. Sieur Jehan with his open neck, Heinroth with his bones on the outside and skin on the inside, a cloud of hanging flesh particles in the rough shape of Stellan the Warlock. And the man in the mask, the man who was not quite Drachenfels, but who would do for the moment, the man who wanted Veidt's eyes.

He realized he had found the spot at last.

VI

AT THE EMPEROR'S feast, Genevieve felt she had been seated with the children. While Oswald and Karl-Franz were at the head table, surrounded by the other electors, Genevieve was considered a suitable adornment to the secondary table, which was lorded over by Luitpold, the Emperor's son. The heir quizzed her excitedly about Drachenfels, but was disappointed to learn she had been unconscious during Oswald's hand-to-hand combat with the Great Enchanter. Genevieve was stuck next to Baroness Marlene's spotty daughter Clothilde, whose entire world was boundaried by her wardrobe and her dance card. Clothilde, who was almost eighteen, insisted on treating her like a very young child in order to assert her own adulthood. With some amusement, Genevieve realized that the girl had no idea who, and particularly how old, she was.

She ate sparingly, and drank nothing. Sometimes, she would glut herself simply for the taste, but she didn't need meat and bread for sustenance and often too much ordinary fare would make her feel constipated and out-of-sorts. She could barely remember eating for the need of it.

Matthias, adviser to the grand theogonist of the cult of Sigmar, nervously asked her if she danced, and she answered rather too emphatically in the negative. He didn't look up from his plate for the rest of the meal.

She kept glancing at the head table, and observing them. Oswald was quiet, sitting back and looking satisfied. The Countess Emmanuelle was endeavouring to outshine everyone in the room, and Clothilde had already rhapsodized about her twenty-foot train with its embroidered tracing of the Imperial family tree and the intertwining line of von Liebewitz, her necklace of three hundred matched sapphires, and her plunging cloth-of-gold bodice. Genevieve assumed the countess's tight clothes were padded. No real woman could fill out that much whalebone and silk.

When the dress rehearsal was over, the feast was joined by a select few invited from the company. Detlef entered, with Lilli Nissen uncomfortably on his arm, and the actress was presented to the court. Some of the electors had the decency to blush, and others the indecency to drool in public. Genevieve was amused to see the look of utter hatred that passed between Lilli and the Countess Emmanuelle. Their gowns were a match for tastelessness and discomfort. Lilli could not compete with the house of von Liebewitz with regards to expense, although she wore enough jewellery to drown a witch, but she could certainly expose more pink skin through cut-away panels and mesh leggings. The countess and the actress kissed each other's cheeks without quite touching lips to skin, and complimented themselves on their youthful appearance, venom dripping from every syllable.

And I'm supposed to be the bloodsucker, Genevieve thought.

'You know,' Genevieve said to Clothilde, who was always forgetting that she was only almost eighteen, 'I must be the only woman in this room who never has to lie about my age.'

The girl giggled, nervously. Genevieve realized she was showing her teeth, and closed her lips demurely.

'I know how old you are,' said Luitpold. 'It's in the ballad of Oswald and Genevieve. You're six hundred and thirty-eight.'

Clothilde choked on her watered wine, quite spoiling her dress.

'That was twenty-five years ago, highness,' Genevieve said.

'Ah, then you must be…'

Luitpold stuck his tongue into his cheek and worked it out in his head. '…six hundred and sixty-three.'

'That's correct, highness.' She raised her glass in salute, but not to her lips.

The meal was over, and the company stood up. Clothilde got as far away as possible, and Genevieve felt a little sorry for the girl. She reminded her of her sister, Cirielle.

Luitpold was attentive now. 'Let's go and see Daddy. He can't stand Middenheim and Talabheim. He'll want to be rescued.'

The future Emperor escorted her to the knot of highly-placed toadies gathered around Karl-Franz. Lilli was doing her best to attract the attention of a tough-looking young man Genevieve believed to be the elector of Sudenland, and not doing terribly well. Countess Emmanuelle was fluttering her eyelashes at Detlef. In the South Lands, Genevieve had seen great black cats being civil to each other over the carcasses of deer and then tearing red flaps from their rivals' glossy hides. Now, she could almost see the claws sliding from their sheaths as the countess and Lilli purred around each other.

Genevieve did feel like a child in this company. Their inter-relationships were so complicated, and the things she could see on the surface of their minds ran so violently counter to the things they said. Still, it was no worse than the court of the First Family of Parravon had been. And she felt better about Karl-Franz than almost any other man of power she had ever met.

Hubermann's musicians were discreetly admitted, and there was dancing. This was not the joyous abandon there had been at the party for poor Rudi, but a courtly ritual that had changed only slightly since it was taught to her as a girl of Luitpold's age. It had nothing to do with enjoyment, and everything to do with ceremony and the reassertion of each dancer's place in the rigid order of the world. In the absence of his wife, Karl-Franz led the dance with the Countess Emmanuelle, looking considerably happier than she as he peered into her cleavage.

Oswald pleaded exhaustion after the journey, and sat at his table. Lilli forced herself on Sudenland, who trampled her feet deliberately and obstinately stayed out of step. Detlef petitioned Genevieve, but she had promised the first pavane to another.

Luitpold was tall for his age, and so they danced well together – the youngest and the oldest in the room. She touched his mind, and sensed his excitement at the occasion. He was looking forward to the play, and to more hunting with his uncle Oswald. In the distance of his life was the Empire and the crown, but he was ignoring them for the moment. She found herself clinging to this ordinary boy in fine clothes, feeling in him a hope for a future she would inevitably have to live to see.

Detlef prised her away from the heir to the Empire, and she realized he was insistent partly because he wished to be with her and partly because he suspected her intentions with regards to Luitpold. Young blood could be so enticing.

They danced together for the rest of the evening. At some point, Oswald slipped away. Genevieve felt his absence less keenly than she felt Detlef's presence, and they continued in each other's arms.

Inevitably, the feast had left her aroused, but unsatisfied. Now, she was thirsty. And here was Detlef, hot blood coursing through his veins.

That night, in Genevieve's chamber, Detlef gave of himself to her. She undid his jerkin and pulled it open, then loosened the drawstrings of his shirt. His hands were in her hair, and his kisses upon her brow. Delicately, with her sharp teeth, she opened a fold in Detlef's neck, just grazing the major artery, and savoured on her tongue the blood of genius. In his blood was everything he was. As she lapped the welling red, she learned of his past, his future, his secrets, his fears, his ambitions. Then, she fastened upon him like a leech as he responded to her caresses, and gulped greedily, smearing her mouth. The blood was warm and salty in the back of her throat as she took it down.

She forgot Oswald von Konigswald, and clung to Detlef Sierck.

VII

CONSTANT DRACHENFELS stared at his masked face in the mirror, peering into his own malevolent eyes, relishing the powers he felt rising within him. He flexed his hands, feeling the strength soaked into the bones with seas of blood. He passed his pointed tongue over long teeth. Inside his armour, his body was drenched with sweat from his recent exertions. He was so close to the attainment of his purpose. He needed water, to replenish his fluids. A jug and a goblet stood by the mirror. He pushed his mask off his face...

...and Laszlo Lowenstein poured himself a drink.

'Great, Laz. You were terrific!' That fool Jessner thumped him on the back. 'You chilled my blood.'

'Thank you.'

Soon, Lowenstein would have to be polite no more, would bow to no man, neither emperor nor director. He looked at the mask in his hand, and saw his real face.

When Jessner had gone, he worked away at the make-up around his eyes, peeling it off. He renewed the subtle paints he had applied over the discoloration of his face. Tomorrow, he would have no need of deceptions and could show himself as he really was. The changes were mainly under the skin, but soon the new bones would poke through. Soon, he would truly fill the armour of the Great Enchanter. Soon...

Long after everyone had left the dressing rooms, Lowenstein departed. He made his way to the part of the fortress where his patron awaited him. There was more to be carved, and Lowenstein was growing ever more skilled at the task.

The man in the mask stood over a corpse, arms casually folded, unattended by any of his ghosts.

'The bones,' said his patron. 'This time, we need the bones.'

Lowenstein's knives worked quickly. He filleted Anton Veidt expertly, carving away the flesh, and soon had the skeleton unclothed. In the red meat there were stringy lumps of a black stuff he had never seen before, but it parted under the knife like ordinary meat.

'Don't forget the eyes.'

Two scoops, and the job was done. Lowenstein imagined his patron smiling behind his mask.

'A fine job, Lowenstein. We have it all, nearly. The heart, the flesh, the skin, the vitals, the bones. From the vampire lady, we shall need the blood...'

'And from the grand prince? From the murderer of the Enchanter?'

The man in the mask paused. 'From him, Lowenstein... from him, we shall take *everything*.'

ACT FIVE

I

AN HOUR TO curtain-up. There was no feeling in the world like it. Each sensation was amplified a thousandfold. The itches of his love-bites, covered now by the high collar of his Prince Oswald costume, excited him. The air in the dressing rooms was electrically charged. He had sat in his chair, applying his make-up, calming himself, thinking himself into the role. Twenty-five years ago, Prince Oswald had won his greatest victory in the great hall of Castle Drachenfels. Tonight, the battle would be refought, but the triumph would be Detlef Sierck's.

He was the young Oswald, working up his courage before daring to challenge the Great Enchanter.

He felt his freshly-shaved chin, and played with his moustaches. A bottle of wine stood unopened on the table. Good luck notes were sorted in order of importance. There was even a modest message of well-wishing from the elector of Middenland, who must be praying for Detlef to trip over his sword on his first entrance and split his tights in the love scenes. He glanced over his shoulder, at a hunched shape he'd glimpsed in the mirror. A hunched shape where there should be none.

It was a cloak, carelessly flung. He picked it up, folded it, and put it away. Vargr Breughel's small chair was empty.

'For you, my friend,' Detlef vowed. 'Not for the Emperor, not for Oswald. For you.'

Detlef tried to feel that Breughel was present, but it was useless. There was nothing.

He felt nervous, but good. He knew the six-hour performance was going to be an enormous drain on his resources. He had worried that Genevieve had sapped his energies too much. On the contrary, since her kisses he had felt doubly alive, as if her strength were shared with him. He felt able to bear the weight of his role. He had the reserves to perform lengthy soliloquies, to take part in strenuous and spectacular fight scenes, to clash with the powerful stage presence of Laszlo Lowenstein.

He could even overcome his distaste and make love to Lilli Nissen.

He left his room, and went among his cast. Illona Horvathy was being sick in a bucket. 'It's all right,' she choked between heaves. 'I'm always like this. It's a good sign. Honest.'

Reinhardt Jessner was taking a few practice swings with his sword.

'Careful,' said Detlef, 'don't bend it.'

The actor bowed as best he could in his padded jacket with its false stomach. He saluted his director. 'You are right, my prince. Know well that I, Rudi Wegener, king of the bandits, will serve you faithfully. To the death.'

Since Rudi's death, Jessner had been throwing himself into his role almost as much as Lowenstein, as if trying to bring the old man back to life through the power of impersonation.

Gesualdo was pumping pig's blood into the bladder in his armpit, whistling as he did so, in defiance of an old superstition. He gave Detlef the thumbs up.

'Nay problem, chief.'

'Where's Lilli?' Detlef asked Justus.

'No one's seen her all day. She should be in her dressing room.'

'Any idea whether the elector of Sudenland came through...?'

The trickster priest laughed. 'Evidently not, Detlef.'

'Good. Maybe the frustration will build up in her. We might see a performance from the monster yet.'

Justus, a gargoyle below his neck, lashed his tail. 'We've come a long way since Mundsen Keep, eh?'

'That we have. Good luck.'

'Break a leg.'

A piercing scream rang out. Detlef looked at Justus, who looked back in astonishment. There was another scream. It came from Lilli's dressing room.

'Ulric in heaven, what plagues us now?'

Lilli's dresser exploded from the room, blood on her hands, screeching insanely.

'Oh gods, she's killed the bitch!'

Justus held the bowed and bent woman, calming her. Detlef pushed into the dressing room.

Lilli stood in the middle of the room, in her Genevieve dress, a stripe of blood running from her face down her bosom to the floor. She had made fists in the air and was screaming at the top of her considerable voice.

An admirer had sent her a present.

Detlef tried to get through to the hysterical actress. When that failed, he took great delight in slapping her face. She lashed out at him, going for the throat, and he had to get a wrestler's hold on her.

'I knew I should never have come here. If it weren't for Oswald, I'd never have worked with you again, you lowest of the loathsome, you vermin-tongued piece of swine-shit, you leech-spawn!'

She collapsed, sobbing, on a divan, and refused to be comforted. Detlef turned to the mess on the floor, and immediately understood what had happened.

It had been like a jack-in-the-box. Once opened, it had flung its contents up at Lilli Nissen. And its contents were only too recognizable. There was a face in there. The eyeless face of Anton Veidt.

'I won't do it! I shan't do it! You can't make me! I'm leaving this accursed place this hour, this instant!'

Lilli shouted at her dresser, and the poor woman freed herself from Justus. She began packing the actress's things into an open trunk.

'Lilli, the show starts in an hour. You can't leave!'

'Just watch me, worm dung! I'm not staying here to be murdered and abused!'

'But Lilli…'

Word was spreading through the company of this latest calamity. There were crowds at Lilli's dressing-room door, peering in at the star in disarray and the gory garbage strewn across everything. Lowenstein appeared, his costume complete but for the mask, and observed dispassionately. Detlef looked to the other actor, knowing that his career would be ruined too if Lilli betrayed them all.

Lilli sat, arms crossed, watching her dresser pack, barking orders at the crying woman. She scraped at the blood on her face, and wiped away her half-applied make-up. She pulled out her fangs one by one and threw them at the floor.

'All of you,' she snapped. 'Out! I'm changing! I'm leaving!'

Her giant slave prodded Detlef in the chest, and he got the impression he ought to get out of the room.

In the narrow passage between the dressing rooms and the stage, he slumped against the wall. It was all going to be ruined! And Lilli Nissen was deserting him again. He'd never be able to get backing for another production. He would be lucky to get a job carrying spears in a provincial production of some tenth-rate tragedy. His friends would desert him faster than oarsmen escaping from a sinking galleass. It would take all he had to stay out of Mundsen Keep. He saw the Known World falling apart around him, and wondered if he might not do best just to sign up with some forlorn-hope voyage of discovery to the Northern Wastes and have done with it.

'Somebody left it for her,' Justus told him. 'It was wrapped like a gift, a gown or something. And there was a coat of arms on the note.'

'Great. Someone wants this play taken off before curtain-up.'

'Here.' The cleric gave him a bent and bloodied piece of stiff paper. There was an unreadable scrawl of a message, and the smudged impression of a seal. Detlef recognized it, a stylized facemask.

'Drachenfels!'

The Great Enchanter must still have supporters out there, desperate to protect their master's reputation by putting a stop to this recreation of his downfall. Lowenstein stood aside calmly, awaiting orders from his director. Justus, Jessner, Illona Horvathy, Gesualdo and the others were all quiet, intent upon him. He could stop it here, and get out of it with the minimum of dignity. Or he could proceed with the play, simply ignoring the absence of the leading lady. Or...

Detlef tore the paper up, and swore to Sigmar, to Verena, to all the gods, to the Emperor, to the grand prince, to Vargr Breughel and to himself, that *Drachenfels* would go on, bitch Lilli or no.

The crowds parted, and someone came through, her lovely face shining.

'Genevieve,' he said. 'Just the person I wanted to see...'

II

EMPEROR KARL-FRANZ I sat in his box at the rear of the great hall, raised above his subjects, with Luitpold to one side and Oswald at the other. An attendant held out a tray of sweet-meats, which Luitpold had been gluttonously helping himself to.

The red curtain hung in front of the raised stage, sporting tragic and comic masks picked out in gold. He glanced over his programme, gathering from the order of the names listed when each player would make his entrance. *Drachenfels* boasted a prologue, five acts, and an *envoi*, with six intervals, including one for a buffet supper. It should run about six hours.

Karl-Franz shifted in his comfortable seat, and wondered whether Luitpold could sit still for the whole thing. It would be a great tribute to Detlef Sierck if the boy could manage it. Of course, Luitpold was eager to learn what his Uncle Oswald had done as a youth.

Oswald himself sat cool and quiet, refusing to be drawn on what he knew of the drama. 'The story is ordinary,' he had said. 'It's the *presentation* which counts.'

The curtain's rise was a good ten minutes late by Karl-Franz's antique timepiece. He had expected no less. In his Empire, nothing ever started on time.

Countess Emmanuelle was wearing another astonishing creation this evening. It took the off-the-shoulder concept to such an extent that it might almost be classed as off-the-entire-body. The Grand Theogonist was already asleep, but he had his adviser Matthias beside him to prod him if he snored too loudly. As usual, Baron Johann von Mecklenberg looked uncomfortable with a roof over him, but he was wearing his court clothes better as time passed. Talabheim and Middenheim were conferring together. Plotting, probably. The halfling was drunk. Middenland had heard there would be dancing girls wearing very little, and was salivating in his corner, his programme quivering over his padded codpiece. Princes, counts, electors, high priests, barons, burgermeisters, dukes and an emperor. This must be the most distinguished audience in history. Detlef Sierck should be proud of it.

A strange thought came to Karl-Franz. If anything were to happen tonight – if a keg of lighted gunpowder were hurled into the audience, for instance – then a country would fall. The empress could never reign in his stead, and all the other logical successors were here. Like every man to occupy his position since the time of Sigmar, two-and-a-half millennia ago, Karl-Franz was conscious of the precariousness of his seat. Without him, without these men, the Empire would be a writhing collection of warring cities and provinces within three months. It would be like Tilea, but stretching the continent from Bretonnia to Kislev.

'When's it going to start, father?'

'Soon. Even emperors must wait upon art, Luitpold.'

'Well, when I'm emperor, I won't.'

Karl-Franz was amused. 'You have to grow up, prove yourself and be elected first.'

'Oh, that…'

The house lights dimmed, and the chatter died down. A spot struck the curtains, and they split, allowing a man in knee-britches and a wig to emerge. There was a smattering of applause.

'Felix Hubermann,' said Oswald, 'the conductor.'

The musicians in their pit raised their instruments. Hubermann bowed, but didn't produce his baton.

'Your Majesty, my lords, ladies and gentlemen,' he said in a high, mellifluous voice. 'I have an announcement to make.'

There was a ripple of murmuring. Hubermann waited for it to die down before continuing.

'Owing to a sudden indisposition, the role of Genevieve Dieudonné will not be taken at this performance by Miss Lilli Nissen…'

There were audible moans of disappointment from several electors who ought to have known better. Middenland spluttered with indignation. Baron Johann and Countess Emmanuelle, for different reasons, sighed with relief. Karl-Franz looked at Oswald, who shrugged blankly.

'Instead, the role of Genevieve Dieudonné will be taken by, er, by Miss Genevieve Dieudonné.'

There was general amazement. Even Oswald was taken aback.

'Your majesty, my lords, ladies and gentlemen, thank you.' Hubermann raised his baton, and the orchestra struck up the *Drachenfels* overture.

The first three basso chords, keyed to the syllables of the Great Enchanter's name, chilled Karl-Franz's spine. The strings came in, and the curtains parted on a rocky promontory in the Grey Mountains. The chorus came forward, and began:

'Listen, my masters, and listen well,
For I have a tale of horrors to tell,
Of heroes and daemons and blood and death
And the vilest monster e'er to draw breath…'

III

AFTER THE APPARITION-in-the-Palace scene, Lowenstein didn't have much to do until the fifth and last act. He had to show his masked face a few times, giving orders to the forces of evil, and he had personally to rip apart Heinroth the Vengeful in Act Three. But it was Detlef's show until the final battle, when he would return to the stage to end it all.

He had the dressing room to himself. Everyone else was watching the play from the wings. Which was a good thing, considering what he had to do.

The material was laid out for him. The bones, the skin, the heart and so on.

A cheer went up from the stage as Detlef-as-Oswald skewered an orc. He heard the dialogue continuing, and the clumping of boots as Detlef strode around the stage, demonstrating his swagger. Lowenstein gathered the vampire wasn't doing badly.

This was the moment his patron had been schooling him for. He read the words from the paper he had been given, not recognizing the syllables, but understanding the meaning.

Lowenstein no longer had the dressing room to himself.

Blue fire burned around the material, as it filled out with the invisible force. Veidt's skeleton, clothed in Rudi's fat and Menesh's skin, sat up. Erzbet's heart began to beat, hungry for Genevieve's blood. The thing had the outline of a man, but was not the man himself.

The eyes were in a box on Lowenstein's dressing table. There were seven of them. One of Rudi's had been squashed beyond use in the struggle. His patron had told him it wouldn't matter. He opened the box, and saw the eyes expressionless and veined in their clear jelly, like a clump of outsized frogspawn.

Lowenstein plucked a blue eye, one of Veidt's, from the sticky mass, and swallowed it whole.

A section of his forehead peeled away.

He took a handful of eyes and, fighting disgust, stuffed them into his mouth. He got them down.

The composite creature watched from its eyesockets.

Pain racked through Lowenstein's body as the changes came upon him fully. Only three more to go. He popped one into his mouth and gulped it back. It stuck halfway, and he had to swallow another to keep it down. Spines sprouted from his knees, and the knobbles of his vertebrae broke the skin.

His bones were expanding. He was in agony. There was one eye left. A brown one. Erzbet's.

As he ate it, the creature embraced him, taking him into its open chest, folding its ribs about him.

The dying and dead sights of Erzbet, Rudi, Menesh and Veidt played back to him.

...himself, masked, bent over a corpse in the Temple of Morr.

...himself, masked, at a table, surrounded by ghosts.

...himself, masked, wielding a red knife in a circle of candle-light.

...himself, masked, crouched in a passageway, pulling bones free from a human ruin.

Fire burned throughout his body, and he completed the ritual, shrieking. It was a wonder no one heard him. But there were wonders enough to go around.

Veidt's bones sank into him like logs thrown into a swamp. Rudi's fat plumped out his gaunt frame. Menesh's skin settled on his own, mottling it. And Erzbet's heart beat next to his own, like a polyp nestling its mother.

He was Laszlo Lowenstein no longer.

Reaching for his mask, he was Constant Drachenfels.

And he was looking forward eagerly to the fifth act.

IV

ON THE STAGE, she felt as if she were floating. Unsupported, she tried to find her way through the play without making a fool of herself. Some of the time, she could remember the lines Detlef had written for her. Some of the time, she remembered what she had actually said. Most of the other actors were good enough to work round her. The scenes with Detlef played marvellously, because she still had the flush of his blood in her. She could read the lines of his play from the surface of his mind, and she could see where she was straying from the text.

Her first scene found her behind the bar in the Crescent Moon, surrounded by crowds, waiting for Oswald to walk into her life. The crowds were extras, hubbubbing softly without words, and from her position she could see Detlef waiting in the wings, his Oswald helmet under his arm, and the faces of the audience out in the darkness.

Unlike the living actors, she could see clearly beyond the footlights. She saw the Emperor, attentive, and the real Oswald a little behind him, watching with approval. And yet, she was also seeing the real tavern, smelling again its

distinctive smell of people and drink and blood. Individual
extras – who would rush off and make themselves over as
courtiers, bandits, villagers, monsters, orcs, gargoyles or forest peasants for later scenes – reminded her of the
individual patrons she had known then. Through his play,
Detlef was bringing it all back.

One of the things about longevity – Genevieve didn't like
to think of it as *immortality*; too many vampires she had
known were dead – was that you got to try everything. In
nearly seven centuries now, she had been a child of court, a
whore, a queen, a soldier, a musician, a physician, a priestess,
an agitator, a gambler, a landowner, a penniless derelict, a
herbalist, an outlaw, a bodyguard, a pit fighter, a student, a
smuggler, a trapper, an alchemist and a slave. She had loved,
hated, killed but never had children – the Dark Kiss came too
early – saved lives, travelled, studied, upheld the law, broken
the law, prospered, been ruined, sinned, been virtuous, tortured, shown mercy, ruled, been subjugated, known true
happiness and suffered. But she had never yet acted upon the
stage. Still less taken her own part in a recreation of her own
adventures.

The story progressed, as Detlef-as-Oswald gathered together
his band of adventurers and set out on the road to Castle
Drachenfels. Again, as on her recent journey along the same
road, Genevieve found herself remembering too much. The
faces of her dead companions were superimposed on the
faces of the actors representing them. And she could never
forget the images of their deaths. As Reinhardt Jessner blustered and slapped his padded thigh, she saw Rudi Wegener's
skin draped over his bones. As the youth she had bled conferred with Detlef, she remembered Conradin's chewed
bones in the ogre's lair. And as the actor playing Veidt sneered
through clouds of cigar smoke, she saw the bounty hunter's
face on Lilli Nissen's dressing room floor.

Lilli would be half-way down the mountain now, speeding
back to Altdorf and civilization. And the creature who frightened her, who murdered Veidt and the others, would be close
by, perhaps coming after her next. Or Oswald.

The play advanced act by act, and the heroes braved peril
after peril. Detlef had imagined a jauntiness in their progress

Genevieve couldn't remember. There were heroic speeches, and a passionate love scene. All Genevieve could recollect of the first trip were long days – painful for her under the sun – on a horse, and desperate, fearful nights around a fire. When Heinroth was found turned inside-out, the script had her make a vow over his corpse to continue the quest. In fact, she had considered backing out and going home. She played it down the middle, her old fears suddenly reborn, and Detlef improvised a response finer than anything he'd written for the scene. The blanket of pig entrails representing Heinroth looked more real, more shocking, to her than the actual corpse had done.

Illona Horvathy had some difficulty working around the changes in the script, and was nervous in her scenes with Genevieve. But Erzbet had always been afraid of her and the actress's uncertainty worked for the character. Watching Illona's athletic dances – she was more skilled than Erzbet had been – Genevieve worried she would take some knocks in the fight scene in the last act, and that the drama would come to a premature conclusion.

In the love scene, Genevieve, still floating with the wonder of it all, opened the wounds on Detlef's neck. She heard gasps from the audience as blood trickled over his collar. The ballads lied about this. It had never happened, at least not this way. Although – twenty-five years later – she realized how much she had desired it, Oswald had never really responded to her, had kept his blood to himself despite his formal offers. He had once given her his wrist, as a man feeds a dog, and she had needed the blood too much to refuse. That still rankled. She wondered how Oswald would react to the perpetuation of the old story, the old lie. How he was feeling now as he sat next to the Emperor, watching a vampire feed on his surrogate?

The hours flew by. In the play, and without, the forces of darkness gathered.

V

FOR DETLEF, THE evening was a triumph. Genevieve was an inspiration. During the comparatively few scenes when the character of Oswald was off-stage, he watched his new leading lady. If she were to apply herself, she could be a greater star than Lilli Nissen. What other actress could really live for ever?

Admittedly, she was drawing on deep personal feeling in the role, and the sheer excitement of the event was getting to her, but she was also a fast study. After a few moments of hesitation in the early scenes, she was growing in confidence and now effortlessly dominated her scenes. There were established, professional actors out there struggling to keep up with her. And the audience was responding. Perhaps the theatre was ready for a vampire star? And he could feel her inside him, whispering in his head, drawing things out of him. Their love scene was the most incredible thing he had ever played on the stage.

Otherwise, the performance was working perfectly, each part falling into place exactly as planned. Detlef keenly missed Vargr Breughel's comments from the wings, but felt by now he could supply them himself. 'Less,' he heard his friend say during one speech; 'more' in another.

The other players gave him what he needed of them, and more. The trick effects functioned on cue, and elicited the proper reactions.

Even Kosinski, drafted in for his bulk in the wordless role of a limping comic ogre, got his laugh and was childishly delighted, begging Detlef to let him come on again whenever a scene could accommodate him. 'Don't you see,' he repeated, 'in the mountain inn, I could be a bouncer... in the forest, a wolf-trapper...'

Detlef had a man stationed near the privies, and after each interval he would report back with what he had heard. The audience – probably the toughest in the Empire, as well as the most influential – was in love with the play. Old men were in love with Genevieve, the character and the actress. Reluctantly, his spy repeated Clothilde of Averheim's gushing enthusiasm for Detlef-as-Oswald, which took in the timbre of his voice, the cut of his moustaches and the curve of his calves. Impulsively, he kissed the man.

Detlef sweated through ten shirts, and consumed three gallons of lemon water. Illona Horvathy shone on stage, and continued to be a total invalid in the wings, clutching her bucket and occasionally throwing up quietly in it. One of the bandit extras was slashed across the arm by Jessner in the duel, and had to be doctored in the dressing room. Felix Hubermann worked like a man possessed, wringing melodies from his musicians that no human ear had ever before apprehended. During the magic scenes, the music became unearthly, almost horrifying.

Detlef Sierck knew this was the night for which he would be remembered.

VI

Then, the last act came.

Genevieve and Detlef were alone on stage, supposed to be at the door of the very chamber in which the play was being performed, the great hall of Castle Drachenfels. Gesualdo, as Menesh, joined them, a miner's pick in his fake right arm. His real arm was strapped beside him, but by squeezing a bulb in his hand, he could control the fake to give it the semblance of life. The musicians were silent, save for a lone flute suggesting the unnatural winds flowing through the haunted castle. Genevieve could have sworn that no one in the audience had exhaled for five minutes. The actors looked at each other, and pushed the door. The scenery descended around them, and the stage seemed to vanish. Genevieve was truly back in...

...a throne-room for a king of darkness. The rest of the fortress had been ill-lit and dilapidated, but this was spotless and illumined by jewelled chandeliers. The furniture was ostentatiously luxurious. Gold gleamed from every edge. And silver. Genevieve shuddered to be near so much of the stuff. There were fine paintings on the wall. Rudi would have wept to see so much plunder in one place. A clock

237

chimed, counting unnatural hours as its single hand circled an unfamiliar dial. In a cage, a harpy preened herself, wiping the remains of her last meal from her feathered breasts.

Detlef and Genevieve trod warily on the thick carpets as they circled the stage.

'He's here,' said Detlef-as-Oswald.

'Yes, I feel it too.'

Gesualdo-as-Menesh kept to the walls, stabbing at tapestries. *One wall was a floor-to-ceiling window, set with stained glass. From here, the Great Enchanter could gaze down from his mountain at the Reikswald. He could see as far as Altdorf, and trace the glittering thread of the River Reik through the forests. In the stained glass, there was a giant image of Khorne, the Blood-God, sitting upon his pile of human bones.*

With a chill, Genevieve realized that Drachenfels didn't so much worship Khorne as look down upon him as an amateur in the cause of evil. Chaos was so undisciplined… Drachenfels had never been without purpose. There were other gods, other shrines. Khaine, Lord of Murder, was honoured in a modest ossuary. And Nurgle, Master of Pestilence and Decay, was celebrated by an odiferous pile of mangled remains. From this stared the head of Sieur Jehan, its eyes pecked out.

Detlef-as-Oswald started to see his tutor so abused, and a laugh resounded through the throne-room, a laugh carried and amplified by Hubermann's orchestra.

Six hundred years ago, Genevieve had heard that laugh. Amid the crowds of Parravon, when the First Family's assassin was borne aloft by daemons and his insides fell upon the citizenry. In that laughter, Genevieve heard the screams of the damned and the dying, the ripples of rivers of blood, the cracking of a million spines, the fall of a dozen cities, the pleas of murdered infants, the bleating of slaughtered animals.

And twenty-five years ago, Genevieve had heard that laugh. Here, in this great hall.

He loomed up, enormous, from his chair. He had been there all the time, but Detlef had cunningly placed him so his appearance would be an unforgettable shock. There were screams from the audience.

'I am Drachenfels,' Lowenstein said mildly, the deathly laugh still in his voice. 'I bid you welcome to my house.

Come in health, go safely, and leave behind some of the happiness you bring…'

Gesualdo-as-Menesh flew at the Great Enchanter, miner's pick raised. With a terrible languor, moving as might a man of molten bronze, Lowenstein-as-Drachenfels stretched out and slapped him aside. Gesualdo-as-Menesh struck a hanging and fell squealing in a heap. Blood was spurting from him. The harpy was excited, and flapped her wings against the bars of her cage, smelling the blood.

Drachenfels was holding the dwarf's arm in his hand. It had come off as easily as a cooked chicken's wing. The enchanter inclined his head to look at his souvenir, giggled, and cast it away from him. It writhed across the floor as if alive, trailing blood behind it, and was still.

Genevieve looked at Detlef, and saw doubt in the actor's face. Gesualdo was screaming far more than he had in rehearsal, and the blood effect was working far better. The dwarf rolled in a carpet, trying to press his stump to the ground.

Lowenstein had torn off his left arm. Gesualdo's real right arm erupted from his back, displacing the fake, as he tried to stop the flow of blood. Then, with a death rattle, he fell still.

Lowenstein…

…Drachenfels opened a window in the air, and the stink of burning flesh filled the throne-room. Genevieve peered through the window, and saw a man twisting in eternal torment, daemons rending his flesh, lashworms eating through his face, rats gnawing at his limbs. He called out her name, and reached for her, reached through the window. Blood fell like rain onto the carpet.

It was her father! Her six-centuries-dead father!

'I have them all, you know,' Drachenfels said. 'All my old souls, all kept like that. It prevents me from getting lonely here in my humble palace.'

He shut the window on the damned creature Genevieve had loved. She raised her sword against him.

He looked from one to the other, and laughed again. Spirits were gathering about him, evil spirits, servant spirits. They funnelled around him like a tornado.

'So you have come to kill the monster? A prince of nothing, descendant of a family too cowardly to take an empire for themselves? And a poor dead thing without the sense to lie down in her grave and rot? In whose name do you *dare* such an endeavour?'

Astonishingly, Detlef got his line out. 'In the name of Sigmar Heldenhammer!'

The words sounded weak, echoing slightly, but gave Drachenfels pause. Something was working behind his mask, a rage building up inside him. His spirits swarmed like midges.

He threw out his hand in Genevieve's direction, and the tide of daemons engulfed her, hurling her back against the wall, smothering her, weighing her down, sweeping over her face.

Oswald came forward, and his sword clashed on the enchanter's mailed arm. Drachenfels turned to look down on him.

She felt herself dragged down, the insubstantial creatures surging up over her. She couldn't breathe. She could barely move her limbs. She was cold, her teeth chattering. And she was tired, tired as she shouldn't be until dawn. She felt bathed in stinging sunlight, wrapped in bands of silver, smothered in a sea of garlic. Somewhere, the hawthorn was being sharpened for her heart. Her mind fogged, she tasted dust in her throat...

VII

LIKE THE REST of the audience, the emperor was amazed and appalled. The death of the dwarf had broken the illusion of the play. Something was badly wrong. The actor playing Drachenfels was mad, or worse. His hand went to the hilt of his ceremonial sword. He turned to his friend…

And felt a knifepoint at his throat.

'Watch the play to its finish, Karl-Franz,' Oswald said, his tone conversational. 'The end is soon.'

Luitpold jumped from his seat at the grand prince.

With grace, Oswald stuck out his hand. Karl-Franz's heart leaped as the knife flashed, but the grand prince simply rapped Luitpold's chin with the hilt. Stunned, the boy fell back onto his chair, his eyes turning up into his head.

Karl-Franz drew a breath, but the knife was back next to his Adam's apple before he could let it out.

Oswald smiled.

The audience were torn between the play on the stage, and the drama in the Imperial box. Most of them were on their feet. The Countess Emmanuelle fell into a dead faint. Hubermann, the conductor, had fallen to his knees, and was

praying fervently. Baron Johann and several others had their
swords out, and Matthias levelled a single-shot hand gun.

'Watch the play to its finish,' Oswald said again, prodding
his weapon into Karl-Franz's flesh.

The Emperor felt his own blood soaking into his ruff. No
one in the audience made a move.

'Watch the play,' said Oswald.

The audience sat down, settling uneasily. They laid down
their weapons. The Emperor felt his own sword being
unsheathed, and heard it clatter against the wall as it was
thrown away.

Never had the Empire seen such treachery.

Oswald turned Karl-Franz's head. The Emperor looked at
the figure of the Great Enchanter, who was swelling on the
stage, becoming the giant the original Constant Drachenfels
must have been.

The laughter of an evil god filled the great hall.

VIII

His own laughter echoed off the walls.

He could barely remember his life as Laszlo Lowenstein. Since eating the eyes, so many other memories crowded his mind. Thousands of years of experience, of learning, of sensation, throbbed like wounds inside his skull. *In the time of the rivers of ice, before the toad men came from the stars, he was battering a smaller creature with a sharp rock, tearing at the still-warm flesh.* With each remembered fall of the icy flint, his mind convulsed, drowning in blood. Finally, something small and insignificant was squashed into dirt. *His stubby, stiff fingers plucked the eyes from the dead thing, and he ate well through the winter.* He felt alive again, and filled his lungs with air flavoured gorgeously by the fear that filled the great hall.

Laszlo Lowenstein was dead.

But Constant Drachenfels lived. Or would live, as soon as his body was warmed by the blood of the vampire slut.

Drachenfels looked from Oswald on the stage, quivering with fear as he had once done, to Oswald in the audience, smiling with resolve as he held his knife to the Emperor's throat.

And Drachenfels remembered…

*The harpy squawked in her cage. The vampire lay in a dead
faint. The dwarf bled slowly, fingers clamped over his stump. And
the boy with the sword looked up at him, tears coursing down his
face, maddened by the dread.*

*Drachenfels raised his hand to strike the prince down, to pulp his
head with a single blow and be done with it. The vampire, he
would amuse himself with later. She might last for as much as a
night in his arms before she was broken, used up and done with.
Thus perished all those who defied the dark.*

*The prince fell to his knees, sobbing, his sword thrown away and
forgotten. And the Great Enchanter stayed his hand. An idea
formed. He would have to renew himself soon, anyway. This could
be used. This boy could be put to good advantage. And an empire
could be won.*

*Drachenfels picked Oswald up, and stroked him as he might a
kitten. He began to propose his bargain.*

'My prince, I have power over life and death. Your life and
death, and my life and death.'

*Oswald wiped his face, and tried to bring his sobbing under con-
trol. He could have been a five-year-old bawling for his mother.*

'You do not have to die here in this fortress, far from your
home. If you wish it, you do not have to die at all...'

'How...' he blubbered, swallowing his sobs, '...how can
this be?'

'You can deliver what I want to me.'

'And what do you want?'

'The Empire.'

*Oswald cried out involuntarily, almost a scream. But he fought
himself, forced himself to look at the Great Enchanter. Under his
mask, Drachenfels smiled. He had the boy.*

'I have lived many lifetimes, my prince. I have outworn
many bodies. I have long since traded in the flesh I was born
with...'

*Unimaginable years earlier, Drachenfels remembered his first
breaths, his first loves, his first kills. His first body. On a vast, empty
plain of ice, he had been abandoned by squat, brutish tribesmen
who would now seem to have more kinship with the apes of Araby
than true men. He had survived. He would live for ever.*

'I am like that girl in many ways. I need to take from others
to continue. But she can merely take a little new blood. Her

kind are short-lived. A few thousand years, and they grow brittle. I can renew myself eternally, taking the stuff of life from those I conquer. You are privileged, boy. I'm going to let you look at my face.'

He took off his mask. Oswald forced himself to look. The prince screamed at the top of his lungs, disturbing the dead and the dying of the fortress, and the Great Enchanter laughed.

'Not so pretty, eh? It's just another lump of rotten meat. It is I, Drachenfels, who am eternal. I who am Constant. Do you recognize your own nose, my prince? The hooked, noble nose of the von Konigswalds. I took it from your ancestor, the loathesomely honourable Schlichter. It's worn through. This whole carcass is nearly at its end. You must understand all this, my prince, because you must understand why I intend to let you kill me.'

The harpy twittered. Oswald was nearly himself now, the complete young prince. Drachenfels had read him right, seen the self-interest in the adventuring, the desperate need to outdo his forebears, the hollowness in his heart. He would do.

'Yes, you shall conquer me, lay me dead in my own dust. And you will be a hero for it. You will grow to great power. Some day, years from now, you will have the Empire in your hands. And you will give it to me...'

Oswald was smiling now, imagining the glory of it. His never-admitted hatred of Karl-Franz, Luitpold's brat of a son, rose to the surface. He would never lick the boots of the House of the Second Wilhelm, as his fathers had done.

'For I shall return from dust. You will find me a way back. You will find me a man with too small a soul, a man steeped in blood. You will be his patron, and I shall enter him. Then, you will deliver to me your friends. I shall take sustenance from them. All who stand with you this day shall die to bring me back.'

An objection fluttered on Oswald's lips, but perished there, unsaid. He looked at Genevieve, prone on the floor, and there was no regret in his heart.

'Then, we shall bend the electors to our purpose. Most will be led by their own interests. The others, we shall kill. The Emperor will die, and his heirs will die. And you will make me emperor in his stead. We shall rule the Empire for an age.

Nothing will stand before us. Bretonnia, Estalia, Tilea, Kislev, the New Territories, the whole world. All shall bow, or be devastated as no land ever has been devastated since the time of Sigmar. Humanity will be our slaves, and all the other races will be slaughtered like cattle. We shall make whorehouses of temples, mausoleums of cities, boneyards of continents, deserts of forests…'

The light was burning inside Oswald now, the light of ambition, of bloodlust, of greed. He would have been this without enchantment, Drachenfels knew. This was Oswald von Konigswald as he was always intended to be.

'Kneel to me, Oswald. Swear loyalty to our plan. Loyalty in blood.'

Oswald knelt, and drew his dagger. He hesitated.

'You could not kill the Great Enchanter without earning a scar or two, could you?'

Oswald nodded his head, and slashed at the palm of his left hand, at his cheek and at his chest. His shirt tore, and a line of red ran across his skin. Drachenfels touched his gloved fingers to Oswald's wounds, and raised the blood to his ragged lips. He tasted, and Oswald was his forever.

He roared his triumph, and whirled about the room, smashing articles he had treasured for millennia.

He took the harpy's cage and crushed it between his great hands, squashing the poor thing inside until it was silent, the bent bars of her prison twisted deep in her flesh. He hurled an oak table through his stained glass window, and heard it shatter on the rocks a thousand feet below, a tinkling patter of multi-coloured shards raining around it.

His enchantment reached throughout his fortress, and his servitors were struck down. Flesh turned to stone, and stone turned to ashes. Daemons were freed, or hurled back to their hells. An entire wing crumbled and fell. And, throughout the world, his expiry was felt by the lesser enchanters.

Finally, when enough had been done, Drachenfels turned again to the trembling Oswald. He snapped the lad's sword between his fingers, and hauled a heavy, two-handed blade down from the wall. It had been dipped in the sacred blood of Sigmar, and plated all over with silver, now worn through in patches.

'This is a weapon fit to kill Constant Drachenfels.'

Oswald could barely lift it. Drachenfels fixed him with his stare, and willed strength into the prince's limbs. The sword came up, and every muscle in Oswald's body trembled with the effort, with the fear and with the excitement. Drachenfels tore open his armour. The stench of his rotting flesh filled the room. The Great Enchanter laughed again.

'Do it, boy! Do it now!'

IX

THIS WASN'T THE finale Detlef had written. Something was badly wrong with Lowenstein. Not to mention Genevieve. And Oswald. And the Emperor. And, in all probability, the world…

Lowenstein-as-Drachenfels, who was acting more like Drachenfels-as-Lowenstein, had departed from the script.

Half the house-lights had come on now, and the company were spilling from the wings towards the auditorium. They kept away from Lowenstein, but their eyes were fixed on him. The audience were in their seats, looking between the monster on the stage and their imperilled Emperor. Grand Prince Oswald, the mask off at last, dared them to try for him. And the actor whose mask was the reality surveyed the chaos he had wrought.

Detlef's prop sword felt very puny indeed in his grip.

Lowenstein stood over Genevieve, who was in her stage swoon. Her eyes opened, and she screamed. He bent down to her, hands like claws.

She rolled away from his grasp, and scrambled to her feet. She stood beside Detlef. They faced the monster together. He felt her in his mind again, felt her fear and her uncertainty, but also her resilience and her courage.

'It's Drachenfels,' she hissed in his ear. 'We've brought him back!'

Lowenstein – *Drachenfels* – laughed again.

Someone in the audience discharged a gun, and a wound opened in the monster's chest. He wiped it shut, still laughing, and threw something small. There was a scream as the gunman went down, writhing in torment. It had been Matthias, the grand theogonist's advisor. Now, he didn't much resemble anything naturally human.

'Does anyone dare defy me?' The great voice said. 'Does anyone dare stand between me and the vampire?'

Detlef was standing between Drachenfels and Genevieve. His immediate impulse was to get out of the way, but the wounds in his neck ached, the wound in his heart kept him where he was. She willed him to go, to leave her to this monster's mercies. But he couldn't.

'Back,' he said, summoning all his acting skills to put the heroic ring into his voice. 'In the name of Sigmar, back!'

'*Sigmar!*' Spittle flew from the mouthslit of the mask. 'He's dead and gone, little man. But I'm here!'

'Then in *my* name, back!'

'Your name? Who are you to defy Constant Drachenfels, the Great Enchanter, the Eternal Champion of Evil, the Darkness Who Would Not Be Defied?'

'Detlef Sierck,' he snapped. 'Genius!'

Drachenfels was still amused. 'A genius, is it? I've eaten of many geniuses. One more will be most refreshing.'

Detlef realized he was going to die before the curtain came down on his play.

He would die before his best work was done. To future generations, he would be a footnote. A minor imitator of Tarradasch who showed promise he never lived to fulfil. A nothing. The Great Enchanter was not just going to take away his life, but was going to make it seem as if he had never been, never walked on a stage, never lifted a quill from its pot. Nobody had ever died as thoroughly as he would die now.

Drachenfels's hand fell on Detlef's left shoulder. The fire of agony coursed through his arm as it popped out of joint. The

Great Enchanter was exerting enough pressure to crush his bones to fragments. Detlef twisted in agony, unable to break the hold, unable to fall away in ruins. By degrees, Drachenfels applied more force to his grip. His putrid grave-breath was in Detlef's face. The actor's entire left side tried to curl up to escape the merciless pain. Drachenfels's fingers burrowed into his flesh like lashworms. A few more moments of this, and Detlef would be glad of the release of death.

Behind the monster's mask, evil eyes glowed.

Then Genevieve jumped.

X

THREE TIMES BEFORE had the killing frenzy fallen upon her. She always regretted it, feeling herself no better than Wietzak or Kattarin or all those other Truly Dead tyrants as she wiped the innocent blood from her face. The faces of her dead sometimes bothered her, as the face of Drachenfels had been tormenting her dreams these last few years. This time, however, there would be no regrets. This was the righteous killing for which she had been made, the killing that would pay back all those whose lives she had sapped. Her muscles corded, her blood took fire, and the red haze came over her vision. She saw through blood-filled eyes.

Detlef hung from Drachenfels's fist, screaming like a man on the rack. Oswald – smiling, treacherous, thrice-damned Oswald – had his knife in Karl-Franz's throat. These things she would not tolerate.

Her teeth pained her as they grew, and her fingers bled as the nails sprouted like talons. Her mouth gaped as the sharp ivory spears split her gums. Her face became a flesh-mask, the thick skin pulled tight, a mirthless grin exposing her knife-like fangs. The primitive part of her brain – the vampire part of her, the legacy of Chandagnac – took over, and she leaped at her enemy, the killing fury building in her like a passion. There was love in it, and hate, and despair, and joy. And there would be death at the end.

Drachenfels was knocked off balance but stayed upright. Detlef was thrown away, landing in a heap.

Genevieve fastened her legs about the monster's midriff, and sank her claws into his padded shoulders. Strips of Lowenstein's stage costume fell away, disclosing the festering meat beneath. Worms crawled through his body, twining around her fingers as she dug through his flesh to get a snapping grip on his bones. She had no distaste for this thing now, just a need to kill.

There was pandemonium in the audience. Oswald was shouting. So was everyone else. People were trying to escape, fighting each other. Others stood calm, waiting for their chance. Several elderly dignitaries were in the throes of heart seizures.

Genevieve pulled a hand from the monster's opened shoulder and tore at Drachenfels's mask. The leather straps parted under her knife-sharp nails and the iron plates buckled. It came free and she hurled it away. There were screams from the audience. She avoided looking him in the face. She retained that much rationality. She wasn't interested in exposing his face anyway. She just needed to get the iron guard away from his neck.

Her mouth opened wide, her jawbone dislocating itself as new rows of teeth slid out of their sheaths, then snapped shut. She bit deep into the monster's neck.

She sucked, but there was no blood. Dirt choked her throat, but she still sucked. The foulest, most rancid, most rotten taste she had ever known filled her mouth and soaked through to her stomach. The taste burned like acid, and her body tried in vain to reject it. She felt herself withering as the bane spread.

Still, she sucked.

The scream began as Lowenstein's last gasp, then grew in sound and fury. Her eardrums coursed with pain. Her skeleton shook inside her body. She felt mighty blows on her ribs. The scream was like a hurricane, blasting all in its path.

A stale trickle flowed into her mouth. It was more disgusting than the dry flesh.

She bit away the mouthful she had been working on, and spat it out, then sunk her teeth in again, higher this time. The Great Enchanter's ear came away, and she swallowed it. She scraped a patch of grey meat away from the side of his skull, exposing the cranial seams. Clear yellow fluid seeped through between the bony plates. She extended her tongue to lick it up.

A hand covered her face, and pushed her back. Her neck strained, near to snapping point. She bit through the thick glove, but couldn't lodge her teeth in his palm. Another hand gripped her waist. Her legs unwound from Drachenfels.

The killing frenzy ebbed, and she felt her vampire teeth receding. Convulsing, she vomited the ear she had eaten, and it stuck to the hand over her mouth.

She felt death touching her again. Chandagnac was waiting for her, and all the others she had outlived in her time.

Drachenfels tore her clothes, baring her veins. Her blood, the blood she had renewed so many times, would make him whole again.

By her death, she would resurrect him.

XI

DETLEF WAS STILL alive. Half of his body was numb with shock, and the other half crawling with pain. But he was still alive.

Drachenfels's scream filled the hall, pounding like nails into everyone's heads. Stones were shaken loose from the walls by the noise, and fell on members of the audience. Every pane of glass in every window shattered at once. Old people died and young people were driven mad.

Detlef got to his knees, and crawled away.

Genevieve had sacrificed herself for him. He would live, at least for the moment, and she would die in his stead.

He could not allow that.

On his feet, stumbling, he knocked over a section of scenery. The person who had been hiding behind it – Kosinski – fled. Ropes fell around Detlef, and weights from above. Flats collapsed, buckling upon each other. A lantern fell, and a ring of burning oil spread from it.

He had lost his sword. He needed a weapon.

Leaning against the wall was a sledge-hammer. Kosinski had hefted it when the scenery was being put together. It should have been packed away. It was dangerous where it was. Someone could easily trip over it on their way backstage. Detlef had fired people for less.

This time, if he lived, he would treble Kosinski's salary and cast the brute in romantic leads if he wanted it...

Detlef picked up the hammer. His wrists hurt with the weight of it, and his wounded shoulder flared with pain.

It was just an ordinary hammer.

But it was no ordinary strength which flooded from it into Detlef's body.

As he raised the hammer to strike, Detlef imagined a slight glow about it, as if gold were mixed with the lead.

'In the name of Sigmar!' he swore.

His pains vanished, and his blow connected.

XII

DRACHENFELS TOOK THE full force of the swing in the small of
his back. He held Genevieve to him, unwilling to give up the
blood that would revivify him.

Detlef Sierck swung round with his blow, and faced the
Great Enchanter.

Drachenfels saw the shining hammer in his hands, and
knew a moment of fear. He didn't dare say the name that
came to him.

*Long ago, he stood at the head of his defeated goblin horde, hum-
bled by the wild-eyed, blonde-bearded giant who held his hammer
high in victory. His magics deserted him, and his body rotted as the
hammer blows connected. It had taken a thousand years to claw his
way back to full life.*

The light that shone in Detlef's eyes was not the light of
genius, it was the light of Sigmar.

*The human tribes of the north-east and all the hordes of the
dwarfs had rallied to that hammer. For the first time, Drachenfels
had been bested in battle. Sigmar Heldenhammer had stood over
him, his boot on the Great Enchanter's face, and ground him into
the mud.*

Genevieve struggled free of him, and darted away. Another blow fell, on the exposed plates of his skull.

Deep inside Constant Drachenfels, Laszlo Lowenstein floundered in death. And Erzbet, Rudi, Menesh and Anton Veidt. And the others, the many thousand others.

Detlef jabbed with the hammer, using it like a staff, and Drachenfels felt his nose cave inwards.

Erzbet's heart burst, flooding bile into his chest. Rudi's fat turned liquid and gushed down into the cavity of his stomach. Menesh's skin split and sloughed off him in swathes. Veidt's bones cracked. Drachenfels was betrayed by his kills.

Waiting in the wings, Drachenfels saw the monk-robed figures. That semi-human ape tribesman would be there, and the thousands upon thousands who had followed him into death.

Detlef, paint streaming from his face, berserker foam in his mouth, swung his hammer.

Lowenstein's thin body stood alone in the ruin that would have been the Great Enchanter. Drachenfels cried out again, feebly this time.

'Sigmar,' he bleated, 'have mercy…'

The hammerblows landed. The skull cracked open like an egg. Drachenfels collapsed, and the blows continued to come.

It had been cold on the plains, and he had been left behind to die, too sickly to be supported by the tribe. The other man, the first kill, had chanced by and he had fought to take the life from him. He had won, but now… fifteen thousand years later… he knew he had lost after all. He had only held off death for a few moments in the span of eternity.

For the last time, the life went out of him.

XIII

KARL-FRANZ WAS bleeding badly now. Oswald's hand wasn't steady, and the blade was biting deep. It was only luck that had kept him from severing the artery, or poking through to the windpipe.

The spectacle on the stage was not what anyone had expected. The Emperor felt Oswald's body shake as Detlef Sierck demolished the actor playing Drachenfels.

The traitor's plans had gone awry.

'Oswald von Konigswald!' shouted Detlef, bloody hammer held aloft.

The auditorium grew quiet. There was the crackle of flames, but all the crying and shouting stopped.

'Oswald, come here!'

Karl-Franz could hear the elector whimpering. The knife shook in the groove it had carved in his neck.

'Stay where you are or the Emperor dies!' Oswald's voice was weak now, too high, too slurred.

Detlef seemed to shrink a little, as if coming to his senses. He looked at the hammer and at the dead thing on the stage. He laid the weapon down. Genevieve Dieudonné stood beside him, her arm about him when he was ready to sag and drop.

'Kill Karl-Franz and you'll be dead before he hits the floor, von Konigswald,' said Baron Johann von Mecklenberg, his sword raised. The elector of Sudenland was not alone. A forest of swordpoints glittered.

Oswald was looking around desperately for a way out, for an escape route. The back of the box was guarded. The sweetmeat man stood there, in a wrestler's stance. He was one of the Imperial bodyguards.

'Know this, Karl-Franz,' Oswald whispered to him, 'I hate you, and all your works. For years, I've had to swallow my disgust in your presence. If nothing else, I shall end the House of the Second Wilhelm tonight.'

Sssssssssssnick!

Oswald pushed Karl-Franz away, waving his bloodied knife in the air, and vaulted over the side of the box.

XIV

GRAND PRINCE OSWALD hit the floor in a crouch and ran down the side of the great hall. A high priest of Ulric stood in his way, but the man was old and was knocked down easily. As he fled, Oswald upturned the chairs the audience had been sitting in, hindering his would-be pursuers.

Baron Johann and his confederates stood before the main entrance, waiting for their quarry.

Oswald backed away from them and made a dash for the stage. Genevieve saw him coming and staggered into his way. She was weakened from her attack on Drachenfels and nauseous from the after-effects of his poison flesh. But she was still stronger than an ordinary man.

She made a fist and struck Oswald in the face, mashing his aristocratic nose. She licked the blood off her knuckles. It was just blood, nothing special.

Detlef stood by, and watched. An audience, for once. Whatever had possessed him – and Genevieve had a fairly good idea about that – during his fight with the Great Enchanter had gone now, leaving him puzzled, drained and vulnerable.

Enraged, Oswald hurled himself at her. She sidestepped, and he fell.

He stood up, his boot slipping in the pool Drachenfels had left of himself. He swore, the knife darted out, and Genevieve's arm stung.

More silver.

He stabbed at her, and missed. He flung the knife, and missed.

Fangs exposed, she lunged for him. He dodged away.

With a clean motion, he drew his sword, and brought the point to rest against her breast.

It was silvered too. A simple thrust and her heart would be pierced.

Oswald smiled sweetly at her. 'We must all die, my pretty Genevieve, must we not?'

XV

A SWORD ARCED up from the auditorium, spinning end over end. Detlef stuck out his hand and snatched the hilt from the air, getting a good grip.

'Use it well, play-actor!' shouted Baron Johann.

Detlef lashed out and struck Oswald's blade away from Genevieve's heart. Genevieve stepped away.

The grand prince turned, spat a tooth at him, and assumed the duelling stance.

'Hah!'

His sword swiped, slashed Detlef across the chest, and returned to its place.

Oswald smiled nastily through the blood. Having demonstrated his skill, he would now take Detlef apart piece by piece for his own amusement. He had lost an empire, but he could still kill the fool dressed as his younger self.

Detlef hacked, but Oswald parried. Oswald struck out, but Detlef backed away.

Then they fell at each other with deadly seriousness.

Detlef fought the weariness in his bones, and summoned extra reserves of strength. Oswald wielded his sword with desperation, knowing his life depended upon this victory. But also he had had a courtly education, the private tuition of Valancourt of Nuln, the best blades. All Detlef knew was how to make a mock battle look good for an audience.

Oswald danced around him, slicing his clothes, scratching his face. Tiring of the game, the grand prince came to kill him…

And found Detlef's swordpoint lodged between his ribs.

Detlef thrust forward, and Oswald lurched off his feet, sliding the full length of the sword until the hilt rested against his chest.

The grand prince spat blood, and died.

ENVOI

AFTER THE PREMIERE of *Drachenfels*, everyone needed lots of bed-rest. They all had scars.

The Emperor survived, but spoke in a whisper for a few months. Luitpold suffered nothing worse than a swollen jaw and a severe headache and complained of missing the end of the play. Genevieve fed herself from volunteers and recovered within a day or two. Detlef collapsed moments after the grand prince's death, and had to be nursed back to health with hot broth and herbal infusions. His shoulder was always stiff after that, but he never let it be a handicap.

Baron Johann von Mecklenberg, elector of Sudenland, took over, and saw to the burial of Oswald von Konigswald in an unmarked grave in the mountains. Before leaving it, he spat onto the earth and cursed the grand prince's memory. The remains of the Drachenfels thing he cut apart and threw into the valley for the wolves. What there was wasn't much like anything that had ever lived.

He imagined he saw a group of cowled figures watching him as he disposed of the monster, but when the business was done with they were gone. The wolves died, but few were sorry of that. The grand theogonist of Sigmar, in mourning for his Matthias, and the high priest of Ulric forgot their differences for an afternoon and jointly held a ceremony of thanks for the deliverance of the Empire. It was not well attended, but everyone considered their duty to the gods done.

Detlef's company milled around, loading up their equipment on their wagons. Felix Hubermann and Guglielmo Pentangeli took over the running of the troupe while Detlef was indisposed and was collecting a pile of invitations to stage *Drachenfels* in Altdorf, with its original ending intact. The conductor held off the many managements, knowing that Detlef would have to rewrite the story in accordance with the known facts. The nature of the conspiracy between the Great Enchanter and the grand prince of Ostland would never be known, but whatever Detlef chose to write would be the accepted version.

The elector of Middenland sent a note of apology to Detlef's bedside, and promised to settle any outstanding debts accrued during the production of *Drachenfels*, providing he were given a token percentage of the profits of any eventual staging of the work. Hubermann translated Detlef's reply into a polite 'no', and refinanced the company by asking the actors and musicians to invest their own money. Somehow, he found some old gold and silver artefacts of elven manufacture in a trunk and used them for capital. Guglielmo drafted the business agreements that founded the Altdorf Joint Stock Theatre, and cheerfully signed the running of the company over to Detlef Sierck.

The electorals conferred briefly, one seat around the table conspicuously unfilled, and requested that the Emperor nominate a new elector of Ostland. The princedom was due to pass to a cousin of Oswald's, but the electoral vote, it was decided, should be disposed of elsewhere. The Emperor's first suggestion, that the Imperial family be granted a vote in the college, was turned down. And, in the end, the vote went with the kingdom after all. Maximilian von Konigswald had been a good man, and all the others of his line before him. But the whole family were stripped of power thanks to the treachery of a single son of the house. The Emperor's choice of successor was approved. The new electors of Ostland would in future be the von Tassenincks.

Finally, it was decided that the fortress of Drachenfels should be destroyed, and alchemists were brought in to place explosive charges throughout the structure. Baron Johann watched from the opposite mountain, conscious again of the hooded phantoms in the periphery of his vision, and the whole place exploded most satisfactorily, raining down enough stone into a nearby valley to keep the villagers of three communities supplied with blocks for household repair for generations to come.

Henrik Kraly was arrested and charged with murder. Despite Detlef's deposition, he was acquitted on the grounds that Vargr Breughel had more or less killed himself and was probably a dangerous mutant anyway. However, without a salary from the House of von Konigswald, the former steward ran up a huge legal bill he was unable to settle, and spent the rest of his life as an inmate in Mundsen Keep. His dearest ambition, to become a trusty, was never fulfilled.

Lilli Nissen was briefly married to a successful pit fighter until an accident in the ring cut short his career. Her much-vaunted Marienburg production of *The Romance of Fair Matilda* was a costly failure, and she retired from the stage soon after being offered her first 'mother' role. After several more marriages, and a well-publicized affair with a cousin of Tsar Radii Bokha, she retired completely from public life and drove to despair a succession of collaborators engaged to help her with her never-to-be-completed memoirs.

Peter Kosinski became a popular jester in a double act with Justus the Trickster.

Kerreth the cobbler became official dress designer to the Countess Emmanuelle von Liebewitz, and was a great favourite with the ladies of Nuln.

Szaradat became a grave robber, and was torn apart by daemons while looting a tomb that happened to be under a particularly severe curse.

Innkeeper Bauman was persuaded by Corin the halfling to re-enter the Black Bat in the Street of a Hundred Taverns' dicing tourney, and the inn's team swept the event three years in succession.

Reinhardt Jessner and Illona Horvathy were married; they named their twins Rudi and Erzbet.

Clothilde of Averheim discovered a herbalist who successfully treated her skin condition, and she became the most celebrated beauty in this corner of the Empire.

Clementine Clausewitz left the Sisterhood of Shallya and married an apothecary. Wietzak the vampire returned to Karak Varn and was destroyed by a secret society dedicated to the memory of the Tsarevich Pavel.

Lady Melissa d'Acques grew bored with the Convent of Eternal Night and Solace and travelled widely, it was rumoured, in Lustria and the New World in the company of a series of foster parents.

Sergei Bukharin lost an eye in a bawdy house brawl on the Altdorf waterfront and later succumbed to untreated syphilis.

Elder Honorio continued to offer refuge to world-weary vampires, and opened a sister refuge for werewolves and other shape-shifters.

Governor Gerd van Zandt was indicted on charges of corruption, and sent to command a penal colony in the Wasteland.

Seymour Nebenzahl converted to the worship of a new-discovered demi-god of frosts and ice, and became the most influential soothsayer in Norsca.

No one ever asked what happened to Lazslo Lowenstein.

Detlef Sierck recovered and rewrote *Drachenfels* as *The Tragedy of Oswald*. He took the title role in the first run at the Temple of Drama in Altdorf, but Genevieve Dieudonné could not be persuaded to repeat her one and only venture as an actress. The play ran for some years, and Detlef followed it up with *The Treachery of Oswald*, which told the end of the story, and in which he surprised everyone by casting Reinhardt Jessner as 'Detlef Sierck' and himself taking the twin roles of Laszlo Lowenstein and Drachenfels. Then, he produced a succession of mature masterpieces. With the profits of the Oswald plays, he bought a theatre which, by common consent of the company, he renamed the Vargr Breughel Memorial Playhouse. *The History of Sigmar* was rewritten and staged to some critical acclaim, although it never equalled the popularity of Detlef's later works. Even the critics who hated him personally came to acknowledge him as at least the equal of Jacopo Tarradasch. Although no one ever called him devout, he made substantial donations to the cult of Sigmar and built a shrine to the hammer in his town house. He spent some years with Genevieve, and discovered many new sensations with her. His sonnet cycle *To My Unchanging Lady* is widely held by scholars to be his best work. They were finally parted by the years, when Detlef was in his fifties, and Genevieve still seemed sixteen, but she remained the love of his life.

Genevieve lived for ever. Detlef did not, but his plays did.

GENEVIEVE UNDEAD

A novel by Jack Yeovil (aka Kim Newman)

HE HAD A name once, but hadn't heard it spoken in years.
Sometimes, it was hard to remember what it had been. Even he
thought of himself as the Trapdoor Daemon. When they dared
speak of him, that was what the company of the Vargr Breughel
called their ghost.

He had been haunting this building for years enough to
know its secret by-ways. After springing the catch of the hidden
trapdoor, he eased himself into Box Seven, first dangling by
strong tentacles, then dropping the last inches to the familiar
carpet. Tonight was the premiere of The Strange History of Dr
Zhiekhill and Mr Chaida, originally by the Kislevite dramatist
VI Tiodorov, now adapted by the Vargr Breughel's genius-in-res-
idence, Detlef Sierck. The Trapdoor Daemon knew Tiodorov's
hoary melodrama from earlier translations, and wondered how
Detlef would bring life back to it. He'd taken an interest in
rehearsals, particularly in the progress of his protégé Eva
Savinien, but had deliberately refrained from seeing the piece
all through until tonight. When the curtain came down on the
fifth act, the ghost would decide whether to give the play his
blessing or his curse.

He was recognized as the permanent and non-paying
licensee of Box Seven, and he was invoked whenever a production went well or ill. The success of A Farce of the Fog was laid
to his approval of the comedy, and the disastrous series of accidents that plagued the never-premiered revival of Manfred von
Diehl's Strange Flower were also set at his door. Some had

glimpsed him, and a good many more fancied they had. A theatre was not a proper theatre without a ghost. And there were always old stage-hands and character actors eager to pass on stories to frighten the little chorines and apprentices who passed through the Vargr Breughel Memorial Playhouse.

Even Detlef Sierck, actor-manager of the Vargr Breughel company, occasionally spoke with affection of him, and continued the custom of previous managements by having an offering placed in Box Seven on the first night of any production. Actually, for the ghost things were much improved since Detlef took over the house. When the theatre had been the Beloved of Shallya and specialised in underpatronised but uplifting religious dramas, the offerings had been of incense and a live kid. Now, reflecting an earthier, more popular approach, the offering took the form of a large trencher of meats and vegetables prepared by the skilled company chef, with a couple of bottles of Bretonnian wine thrown in. The Trapdoor Daemon wondered if Detlef instinctively understood his needs were far more those of a physical being than a disembodied spirit.

Eating was difficult without hands, but the years had forced him to become used to his ruff of muscular appendages, and he was able to work the morsels up from the trencher towards the sucking, beaked hole of his mouth with something approaching dexterity. He had uncorked the first bottle with a quick constriction, and took frequent swigs at a vintage that must have been laid down around the year of his birth. He brushed away that thought – his former life seemed less real now than the fictions which paraded before him every evening – and settled his bulk into the nest of broken chairs and cushions adapted to his shape, awaiting the curtain. He sensed the excitement of the first night crowd and, from the darkness of Box Seven, saw the glitter of jewels and silks down below. A Detlef Sierck premiere was an occasion in Altdorf for the court to come out and parade.

The Trapdoor Daemon understood the emperor himself was not present – since his experience at the fortress of Drachenfels, Karl-Franz disliked the theatre in general and Detlef Sierck's theatre in particular – but that the Prince Luitpold was occupying the Imperial box. Many of the finest and foremost of the Empire would be in the house, as intent on being seen as on seeing the play. The critics were in their corner, quills bristling and inkpots ready. Wealthy merchants packed the stalls, looking up at the assembled courtiers and aristocrats in the circle who, in their turn, looked to the imperial connections in the private boxes.

A dignified explosion of clapping greeted the orchestra as Felix Hubermann, the conductor, lead his musicians in the Imperial national anthem, 'Hail to the House of the Second Wilhelm.' The ghost resisted the impulse to flap his appendages together in a schlumphing approximation of applause. In the Imperial Box, the future emperor appeared and graciously accepted the admiration of his future subjects.

Prince Luitpold was a handsome boy on the point of becoming a handsome young man. His companion for the evening was handsome too, although the Trapdoor Daemon knew she was not young. Genevieve Dieudonné, dressed far more simply than the brocaded and lace-swathed Luitpold, appeared to be a girl of some sixteen summers, but it was well-known that Detlef Sierck's mistress was actually in her six hundred and sixty-eighth year.

A heroine of the Empire and something of an embarrassment, she didn't look entirely comfortable in the Imperial presence, and tried to keep in the shadows while the prince waved to the crowd. Across the auditorium, the ghost caught the sharp glint of red in her eyes, and wondered if her nightsight could pierce the darkness that sweated like squid's ink from his pores. If the vampire girl saw him, she didn't betray anything. She was probably too nervous of her position to pay any attention to him. Heroine or not, a vampire's position in human society is precarious. Too many remembered the centuries Kislev suffered under Tsarina Kattarin.

Also in the prince's party was Mornan Tybalt, grey-faced and self-made Keeper of the Imperial counting house, and Graf Rudiger von Unheimlich, hard-hearted and forceful patron of the League of Karl-Franz, a to-the-death defender of aristocratic privilege. They were known to hate each other with a poisonous fervour, the upstart Tybalt having the temerity to believe that ability and intellect were more important qualifications for high office than breeding, lineage and a title, while the pure-blooded huntsman von Unheimlich maintained that all Tybalt's policies had brought to the Empire was riot and upheaval. The Trapdoor Daemon fancied that neither the Chancellor nor the Graf would have much attention for the play, each fuming at the imperially-ordained need not to attempt physical violence upon the other in the course of the evening.

The house settled, and the prince took his chair. It was time for the drama. The ghost adjusted his position, and fixed his attention on the opening curtains. Beyond the red velvet was darkness. Hubermann held a flute to his lips, and played a strange, high melody. Then the limelights flared, and the audience was transported to another century, another country.

The action of *Dr Zhiekhill and Mr Chaida* was set in pre-Kattarin Kislev, and concerned a humble cleric of Shallya who, under the influence of a magic potion, transforms into another person entirely, a prodigy of evil. In the first scene, Zhiekhill was debating good and evil with his philosopher brother, as the darkness gathered outside the temple, seeping in between the stately columns.

It was easy to see what attracted Detlef Sierck, as adaptor and actor, to the Tiodorov story. The dual role was a challenge beyond anything the performer had done before. And the subject was an obvious development of the macabre vein that had been creeping lately into the playwright's work. Even the comedy of *A Farce of the Fog* had found room for a throat-slitting imp and much talk of the hypocrisy of supposedly good men. Critics traced Detlef's dark obsessions back to the famously interrupted premiere of his great work *Drachenfels*, during which the actor had faced and bested not a stage monster but the Great Enchanter himself, Constant Drachenfels. Detlef had tackled that experience face-on in *The Treachery of Oswald*, in which he had taken the role of the possessed Laszlo Lowenstein, and now he was returning to the hurt inside him, nagging again at the themes of duality, treachery and the existence of a monstrous world underneath the ordinary.

His brother gone, Zhiekhill was locked up in his chapel, fussing with the bubbling liquids that combined to make his potion. Detlef, intent on delaying the expected, was playing the scene with a comic touch, as if Zhiekhill weren't quite aware what he was doing. In his recent works, Detlef's view of evil was changing, as if he were coming to believe it was not an external thing, like Drachenfels usurping the body of Lowenstein, but a canker that came from within, like the treachery forming in the heart of Oswald, or the murderous, lecherous, spiteful Chaida straining to escape from the confines of the pious, devout, kindly Zhiekhill.

On the stage, the potion was ready. Detlef-as-Zhiekhill drained it, and Hubermann's eerie tune began again as the influence of the magic took hold. Dr Zhiekhill and Mr Chaida forced the Trapdoor Daemon to consider things he would rather forget. As Chaida first appeared, with Detlef performing marvels of stage magic and facial contortion to suggest the violent transformation, he remembered his own former shape, and the Tzeentch-born changes that slowly overcame him. When, at the point Detlef-as-Chaida was strangling Zhiekhill's brother, the monster was pulled back inside the cleric and Zhiekhill, chastened and shaking, stood revealed before the philosopher, the ghost was slapped by the realization that this would never happen to him. Zhiekhill and Chaida might be in an eternal struggle, neither ever gaining complete control, but he was forever and for good or ill the Trapdoor Daemon. He would never revert to his old self.

Then the drama caught him again, and he was tugged from his own thoughts, gripped by the way Detlef retold the tale. In Tiodorov, the two sides of the protagonist were reflected by the two women associated with them, Zhiekhill with his virtuous wife and Chaida with a brazen slut of the streets. Detlef had taken this tired cliche and replaced the stick figures with human beings. Sonja Zhiekhill, played by Illona Horvathy, was a restless, passionate woman, bored enough with her husband to take a young cossack as a lover and attracted, despite herself, to the twisted and dangerous Mr Chaida. While Nita, the harlot, was played by Eva Savinien as a lost child, willing to endure the brutal treatment of Chaida because the monster at least paid her some attention.

The murder scene drew gasps from the auditorium, and the ghost knew Detlef would, in order to increase the clamour for tickets, spread around a rumour that ladies fainted by the dozen. While Detlef's Chaida might be a triumph of the stage, the most chilling depiction of pure evil he had ever seen, there was no doubt that the revelation of the play was Eva Savinien's tragic Nita. In A Farce of the Fog, Eva had taken and transformed the dullest of parts – the faithful maidservant – and this was her first chance to graduate to anything like a leading role. Eva's glowing performance made the ghost's chest swell wet with pride, for she was currently his special interest. Noticing her when she first came to the company, he had exerted his influence to help her along. Eva's triumph was also his. Her Nita quite outshone Illona Horvathy's higher-billed heroine, and the Trapdoor Daemon wondered whether there was anything of Genevieve Dieudonné in Detlef's writing of the part.

The scene was the low dive behind the temple of Shallya, where Chaida makes his lodging, and Chaida was trying to get rid of Nita. Earlier, he had arranged an assignation here with Sonja, believing his seduction of the wife he still believes virtuous will signify an utter triumph over the Zhiekhill half of his soul. The argument that led to murder was over the pettiest of things, a pair of shoes without which Nita refuses to go out into the snow-thick streets of Kislev. Gradually, a little fire came into Nita's complaints and, for the first time, she tried to stand up to her brutish protector. Finally, almost as an afterthought, Chaida struck the girl down with a mailed glove, landing a blow of such force that a splash of blood erupted from her skull like juice from a crushed orange.

Stage blood flew.

Then came the climax, as the young cossack, played by the athletic and dynamic Reinhardt Jessner, having tracked Chaida down from his earlier crimes, bursts into the fiend's lodgings, accompanied by Zhiekhill's wife and brother, and puts an end to the monster during a swordfight.

The Trapdoor Daemon had seen Detlef and Reinhardt duel before, at the climax of *The Treachery of Oswald*, but this was a far more impressive display. The combat went so far beyond performance he was sure some real enmity must exist between them. Offstage, Reinhardt was married to Illona Horvathy, to whom Detlef had made love in the company's last three productions. Also, Reinhardt was being hailed as the new matinee idol of the playhouse. His attractions for the young women of Altdorf were growing even as those of his genius employer diminished somewhat, although diminishing was certainly not what Detlef's stomach was doing with passing years of good food and better wine.

Detlef and Reinhardt fought in the persons of Chaida and the cossack, hacking away at each other until their faces were criss-crossed with bloody lines, and the stage set was a shambles. Slashing a curtain exposed the hastily-stuffed-away corpse of Nita, and Sonja Zhiekhill fainted in her brother-in-law's arms. Not a breath was let out in the auditorium. In Tiodorov's original, Chaida was defeated when Zhiekhill at last managed to exert himself and the monster dropped his sword. Skewered by the cossack's blade, Chaida turned back into Zhiekhill in death, declaiming in a dying speech that he had learned his lesson, that mortals should not tamper with the affairs of the gods. Detlef had changed it around completely. At the point when the transformation began, the cossack made his death thrust, and Chaida parried it, striking with his killing glove and crushing the young hero's throat.

There was a shocked reaction in the house to this reversal of expectations. It had been Zhiekhill who had killed his wife's lover, not Chaida. This wasn't the story of the division between good and evil in a man's soul, but of an evil that drives out even the good. Throughout the third act, the ghost realized, Detlef had been blurring the differentiation between Zhiekhill and Chaida. Now, at the end, they were indistinguishable. He didn't need the potion any more.

In a cruel final touch, Zhiekhill gave his bloody sword to his wife, of whose corruption he approves, and encouraged her to taste further the delights of evil by killing Zhiekhill's brother. Sonja, needing no potion to unloose the monster inside her, complied. With corpses all around, Zhiekhill then took his wife to Chaida's bed, and the curtain fell.

For a long moment, there was a stunned silence from the audience.

The ghost wondered how they would react. Looking across the dark, he saw again the red points of Genevieve's eyes, and wondered what emotion was hidden in them. *Dr Zhiekhill and Mr Chaida* was hard to like, but it was undoubtedly Detlef Sierck's dark masterpiece. No one who saw it would ever forget it, no matter how much they might wish to.

The applause began, and grew to a deafening storm. The Trapdoor Daemon joined his clamour with the rest.

THE FUTURE EMPEROR had been impressed with the play. Genevieve knew that would please Detlef. Elsewhere at the party, there was heated debate about the merits of *The Strange History of Dr Zhiekhill and Mr Chaida*. Mornan Tybalt, the thin-nosed Chancellor, quietly expressed extreme disapproval, while

Graf Rudiger had apparently yawned throughout and glumly didn't see what all the fuss was about. Two critics were on the point of blows, one proclaiming the piece an immortal masterpiece, the other reaching into the stable for his metaphors.

Guglielmo Pentangeli, Detlef's business manager and former cell-mate, was happy, predicting that whatever a person might think of *Dr Zhiekhill and Mr Chaida*, it would be impossible to venture out in society in the next year without having formed an opinion. And to form an opinion, it would be necessary to procure a ticket.

Genevieve felt watched, as she had all evening, but no one talked to her about the play. That was to be expected. She was in a peculiar position, connected with Detlef and yet not with his work. Some might think it impolite to express an opinion to her or to solicit her own. She felt strange anyway, distanced from the play she'd seen, not quite able to connect it with the man whose bed she shared – if rarely using it at the same time he did – or else able to understand too well the sparks in Detlef that made him at once Dr Zhiekhill and Mr Chaida. Recently, Detlef had been darkening inside.

In the reception room of the Vargr Breughel, invited guests were drinking and picking at the buffet. Felix was conducting a quartet in a suite of pieces from the play, and Guglielmo was doing his best to be courteous to von Unheimlich, who was describing at length an error in Reinhardt's cossack swordsmanship. A courtier Genevieve had met – whom she had once bled in a private suite at the Crescent Moon tavern – complimented her on her dress, and she smiled back at him, able to remember his name but not his precise title. Even after nearly seven hundred years in and out of the courts of the Known World, she was confused by etiquette.

The players were still backstage, taking off make-up and costumes. Detlef would also be running through his notes to the other actors. For him, every performance was a dress rehearsal for an ideal, perfect rendition of the drama that might, by some miracle, eventually transpire, but which never actually came to pass. He said that as soon as he stopped being disappointed in his work, he'd give up, not because he would have attained perfection but because he would have lost his mind.

The eating and drinking reminded Genevieve of her own need. Tonight, when the party was over, she'd tap Detlef. That would be the best way jointly to savour his triumph, to lick away the tiny scabs under his beardline and to sample his blood, still peppered with the excitement of the performance. She hoped he didn't drink to excess. Too much wine in the blood gave her a headache.

'Genevieve,' said Prince Luitpold, 'your teeth...'

She felt them, sharp against her lower lip, and bowed her head. The enamel shrank and her fangs slid back into their gumsheaths.

'Sorry,' she said.

'Don't be,' the prince said, almost laughing. 'It's not your fault, it's your nature.'

Genevieve realized Mornan Tybalt, who had no love for her, was watching closely, as if he expected her to tear out the throat of the heir to the Imperial crown and put her face into a gusher of royal blood.

She had tasted royal blood and it was no different from a goatherd's.

Since the fall of Arch-Lector Mikael Hasselstein, Mornan Tybalt had been the emperor's closest advisor, and he was jealous of the position, afraid of anyone – no matter how insignificant or unlikely – who might win favour with the House of the Second Wilhelm. Genevieve understood the ambitious Chancellor was not a well-liked man, especially with those whose hero was Graf Rudiger, the old guard of the aristocracy, the electors and the barons. Genevieve took people as she found them, but had been involved enough with the great and the good not to want to pick sides in any factional conflicts of the Imperial court.

'Here's our genius,' the prince said.

Detlef made an entrance, transformed from the ragged monster of the play into an affable dandy, dressed as magnificently as the company costumier could manage, his embroidered doublet confining his stomach in a flattering manner. He bowed low to the prince and kissed the boy's ring. Luitpold had the decency to be embarrassed, and Tybalt looked as if he expected another assassination attempt. Of course, the reason Detlef and Genevieve were allowed such intimacy with the imperial presence was that, at Castle Drachenfels, they had thwarted such an attempt. If it were not for the play-actor and the bloodsucker, the Empire would now be ruled by a puppet of the Great Enchanter, and there would be a new Dark Age for all the races of the world. A Darker Age, rather.

The prince complemented Detlef on the play, and the actor-playwright brushed aside the praise with extravagant modesty, simultaneously appearing humble, yet conveying how pleased he was to have his patron bestow approval.

The other actors were arriving. Reinhardt, a bandage around his head where Detlef had struck too hard in the final fight, was flanked by his wife Illona and the ingenue. Several artistically-inclined gallants crowded around Eva, and Genevieve detected a slight moue of jealousy from Illona. Prince Luitpold himself had asked if an introduction could be contrived to the young actress. Eva Savinien would have to be watched.

'Ulric, but that was a show,' Reinhardt said, as open as usual, rubbing his wound. 'The Trapdoor Daemon should be delighted.'

Genevieve laughed at his joke. The Trapdoor Daemon was a popular superstition in the Vargr Breughel.

Detlef was given wine, and held his own court.

'Gené, my love,' he said, kissing her cheek. 'You look wonderful.'

She shivered a little in his embrace, unconvinced by his warmth. He was always playing a part. It was his nature.

'It was a feast of horrors, Detlef,' the prince said. 'I was never so frightened in my life. Well, maybe once...'

Detlef, briefly serious, acknowledged the comment.

Genevieve suppressed another shiver, and realized it had passed around the room. She could see momentarily haunted faces in the cheerful company. Detlef, Luitpold, Reinhardt, Illona, Felix. Those who'd been at the performance in Castle Drachenfels would always be apart from the rest of the world. Everyone had been changed. And Detlef most of all. They all felt unseen eyes gazing down on them.

'We have had too many horrors in Altdorf,' Tybalt commented, a mutilated hand stroking his chin. 'The business five years ago with Drachenfels. Konrad the Hero's little skirmish with our green-skinned friends. The Beast murders. The riots stirred up by the revolutionist Kloszowski. Now, this business with the warhawk...'

Several citizens had been slaughtered recently by a falconer who set a hunting bird on them. Captain Harald Kleindeinst, reputedly the hardest guardsman in the city, had vowed to bring the murderer to justice, but the killer was still at liberty, striking down those who took his fancy.

'It seems,' the chancellor continued, 'we are knee-deep in blood and cruelty. Why did you feel the need to add to our burden of nightmares?'

Detlef was silent for a moment. Tybalt had asked a question many must have pondered during the evening. Genevieve didn't care for the man, but she admitted that, just this once, he might even have a point.

'Well, Sierck,' Tybalt insisted, pressing his argument beyond politeness. 'Why dwell on terrors?'

The look came into Detlef's eyes that Genevieve had learned to recognize. The dark look that came whenever he remembered the fortress of Drachenfels. The Chaida look that eclipsed his Zhiekhill face.

'Chancellor,' he said. 'What makes you think I have a choice?'

THE LEGEND OF SIGMAR
by Graham McNeill

When a mighty horde of orcs threatened his lands, Sigmar united the tribes of men to stand against them at Black Fire Pass. In defeating the great necromancer Nagash, he saved mankind, securing the future of the Empire and taking his first steps on the road to godhood.

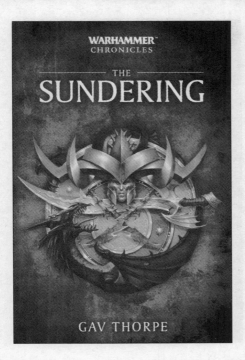

THE SUNDERING
by Gav Thorpe

Malekith, betrayer and usurper, architect of the great war that will forever divide the race of elves. Alith Anar, wrathful avenger whose spirit will forever haunt the traitorous druchii. Caledor, reluctant leader, the one elf who can hold back the darkness and restore peace to Ulthuan.

THE RISE OF NAGASH
by Mike Lee

Nagash is the first necromancer and the supreme lord of undeath. When the priest-kings of Nehekhara stood united against him, he broke their armies and sacked their cities. He raised the largest army of the dead the world has ever known and became an immortal dark god.

Find this title, and many others, on **blacklibrary.com**

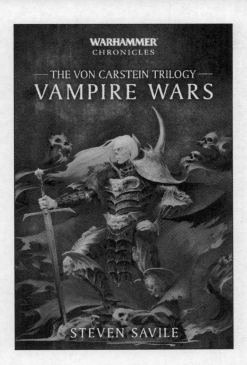

VAMPIRE WARS
by Steven Savile

Charting the vampire family's rise to power and their century-spanning wars with the Empire, this omnibus edition collects all three of Steven Savile's classic von Carstein novels – *Inheritance*, *Dominion* and *Retribution* – into one gore-drenched volume.